Maria Louise Pool

Roweny in Boston

Maria Louise Pool

Roweny in Boston

ISBN/EAN: 9783337022877

Printed in Europe, USA, Canada, Australia, Japan

Cover: Foto ©Andreas Hilbeck / pixelio.de

More available books at **www.hansebooks.com**

ROWENY IN BOSTON

A Novel

BY

MARIA LOUISE POOL
AUTHOR OF "DALLY" ETC.

NEW YORK
HARPER & BROTHERS, FRANKLIN SQUARE
1892

CONTENTS.

ROWENY IN BOSTON.

I.

MARTHA S. TRYING "TO GIT A FIT."

"WHICH one of them Tuttle girls is it that is so sut on goin' to Borston?"

"I should think you'd know 'thout bein' told. It's the one that wears that soft felt hat with scarcely no trimmin' on it to meet'n'."

The relation between wearing a scantily decorated soft felt hat and being "sut on goin' to Borston" seemed very clear and close to this speaker, however obscure it might appear to the ordinary human being. Mrs. Warner's two daughters always wore very stiff hats with large quantities of cheap flowers on them, and they had never announced any intention of visiting Boston. Perhaps, therefore, their mother had her reasons for coming to her present conclusion.

"I want to know!" exclaimed Martha Hancock.

"Then it's Roweny. Wal, she never was like your girls, Mis' Warner. Of course Hiram Tuttle can't give her a cent to go with. And then the temptations there. I hope she won't come to no bad end."

Mrs. Warner drew in her lips and shook her head. She remarked that she had been greatly blessed in her children, but that there was a mighty sight in bringing up. She didn't believe, if she did say it herself, that either of her girls would ever git a notion that they must go where their parents never'd been. Of course no one could tell what would happen, but she did think that wouldn't happen.

Miss Hancock shook her own head in sympathy. She was forty-four years old, and had never married. She always said, when rallied on this fact, that she had never been inclined to matrimony. She saw enough of it in the lives of her married friends. The apparent acidity of this speech was attributed to the fact that no one, so far as was known in the neighborhood, had ever desired to marry Miss Hancock.

The people in this village were not given to belief in those words of Thackeray's that any woman may wed any man, if she makes up her mind to it. On the contrary, they were sure that all the old maids in the world were so from dire necessity.

Miss Hancock was commonly called " Marthy

S.," to distinguish her from another Martha with the same surname who lived in the same district. When Marthy S. mentioned her vocation, she said she "dressmaked" for such as wanted her. She would usually add that, though she made no pretensions to being stylish, she did think she could put a touch on to a garment that could be equalled by few.

This was true, although in a different sense from what she meant it. Her patrons, or her victims, always presented the same trussed appearance across the chest, and always suffered from the same sense of restraint in the elbows. Naturally, those who had never had any other dress-maker, and these were many in this locality, believed that to be trussed, and to be confined at the elbows, was the condition of woman when she was " dressed up "—it was one of the inevitable misfortunes of being born feminine instead of masculine.

Marthy S. took in *The Fashion Delineator* and she did not think it necessary to go anywhere to see what "folks were wearing." She frequently made up patterns. She said she wouldn't give in to anybody in the matter of making up patterns.

Sometimes she was asked if she had ever been in Boston. She always replied: " No, but she had been in Providence."

It seemed to her that the fact of her having seen the capital of Rhode Island would in a way establish her as a traveller, and would atone for her not being familiar with Boston. Her Uncle George had taken her to a restaurant in Providence and they had each had an oyster stew. She often mentioned this stew as being one of the most delicious dishes she had ever tasted.

I do not know why it is, but the person who comes from the real country to a city always orders an oyster stew at the eating-house where he stops, and he feels a certain sense of exhilarating dissipation when he eats it, and when he pours in some of the table-sauce he has a sense that he is a cosmopolitan. He thinks he would give a great deal if he could take all his meals at a restaurant. He reads with awe and enjoyment those curious names of wines on the other side of the bill of fare. But he is a Son of Temperance.

Mrs. Warner was "running the machine" while Marthy S. cut and basted. At intervals there were pauses while one of Mrs. Warner's daughters would be "fitted." This fitting was sometimes very tedious, and the person undergoing it would at last get very squirmy. It was not agreeable to have Miss Hancock standing by you with her mouth full of pins, pulling you here and pulling you there. She confessed that she did not, at such times, think anything about the sufferings of her patient. She only thought of "gittin' a fit."

The youngest of Mrs. Warner's daughters was about sixteen. She was pale and thin and nervous-looking. She was considered to have grown too fast. It was she who was now beneath Miss Hancock's hands. At first she was very calm and patient. She was acting upon a firm resolve she had made, and privately communicated to her sister, that "she wouldn't git into no tantrums this time."

But after a while she became fascinated by the way Marthy S. put pins into her mouth. The child watched with ever-increasing horror. It seemed to her that no human mouth could hold so many pins, and still they went in and disappeared behind those thin lips.

Why did not the points of some of them protrude through the dress-maker's cheeks? How large was that mouth inwardly, anyway? Viewed from the outside, it was small, and nipped in at the corners.

Eunice began to grow faint from standing. Objects were vague before her. She suddenly grasped Marthy S. around the waist, leaned upon her, and cried out, brokenly:

"Oh, you'll swaller um! you'll swaller um!"

Miss Hancock made a gurgling, rattling noise,

and hastily ejected a great many pins into the palm of her hand. She had almost swallowed them in her sudden alarm lest Eunice would faint. She put the child down on a lounge while the mother brought out the camphor.

"You'd made anybody swaller a rhinoceros, yelling like that," cried Miss Hancock, in uncontrollable anger, when she saw a tinge of color coming to the girl's face.

Eunice sobbed. She turned her eyes to her mother.

"She'd got in twenty-nine, mother," she said, "and I knew if she put in the thirtieth I couldn't bear it, 'n' she did," with another sob, "she put it in."

"It's none of our business if she puts in a bushel of pins," said the mother, soothingly.

"But I tell you I can't endure to see her do it," cried Eunice, hysterically, pushing aside the camphor-bottle and spilling some of the liquid in her eyes. "Rowena Tuttle says that pins don't hurt dress-makers, even when they do swaller um. And she didn't think they'd hurt Miss Hancock, anyway."

"Did she say that? Did Roweny Tuttle say that?" indignantly asked Marthy S.

But why should it make one angry to be thought able to take pins safely into the internal economy? Particularly, why should one whose calling is that of a dress-maker be annoyed by any such cause?

Poor Eunice was trying to clear her eyes of the camphor; she was using her mother's apron for that purpose, and she did not see the warning looks which her parent directed to her. She went on with entire recklessness:

"Yes, Rowena said so, 'n' when I said I didn't believe that pins was good fur anybody, she said your stomach must be lined with um, and when a person had a brass inside, a few pins more or less wouldn't make no dif'runce."

"How silly you do talk, Eunice!" said Mrs. Warner. "She don't mean nothin', Marthy. She's kinder high-strickey, she is."

Eunice was laughing and crying, and could not say whether she meant anything or not. The waist of her new blue cashmere was pinned about her, and her arms were bare. She huddled a shawl on her shoulders.

"You're dretful foolish to talk so," whispered her mother. "You see Marthy's jest 's mad 's she can be."

But Eunice did not seem to repent.

The dress-maker had turned to the table where she had been "cutting out." She lifted the long shears which lay there and viciously snapped them in the air. One felt sure, from her action and from the expression of her face, that if

Rowena Tuttle had been between those blades in reality, as she was in Miss Hancock's imagination, Rowena Tuttle would have been cut in twain.

Marthy presently bethought herself that she was a professor. She walked about the room with the shears uplifted in her hand.

"I never could endure that girl, anyway," she said, in a high voice, "'n I sha'n't like her any better now, you may be sure, Mis' Warner. What is one of Hiram Tuttle's girls, I sh'd like to know, more'n other folks? And she er stickin' up her nose at everybody!"

"She don't stick up her nose."

These words came very decidedly from the lounge where Eunice sat. "She's jest brighter than some people, that's all."

"Eunice!"

Mrs. Warner spoke severely.

"Let her go right on, Mis' Warner; let her go right on," said Marthy S., red with excitement.

"Well, she is brighter," persisted Eunice.

Possibly the girl was taking her revenge for the uncomfortable way in which Miss Hancock had pinched and pushed her while trying to get a fit.

Mrs. Warner now informed her daughter that whether she was faint or not, if she spoke another word in the next ten minutes she should leave the room.

This threat had its effect. There was entire silence on the part of Eunice. Her mother again told Miss Hancock that "it was only them children's silly talk, 'n' she didn't think Marthy ought to take it so serious."

It is so very easy to be calmly cheerful over an annoyance which affects some one else. It may be that Mrs. Warner's cheerfulness irritated the dress-maker. At any rate this latter person repeated that dreadful motion with her shears, and she remarked in a shrill voice that "Mis' Warner hadn't been told she had a brass inside."

"Law!" responded the other, comfortably, "I almost wish I had got one; then mebbe fried cakes 'n' pickles wouldn't be so apt to hurt me."

She went on to say for the third time, with great seriousness, that she did think that Marthy was making a great deal too much of a few thoughtless words that "didn't really mean nothin'."

After a few more minutes had passed the dress-maker resumed her work. Eunice was unpinned and allowed to put on her old gray wool gown. She was sulky and did not attempt to speak, even when the time prescribed for silence had passed.

Miss Hancock's scissors hissed through the

blue cashmere and the cambric with dangerous swiftness. Mrs. Warner's sewing-machine whirred on with pauseless industry. The winter sunlight came in at the small-paned windows and fell brightly on the gay braided rugs on the yellow floor. The cat placed herself in the middle of the sunshine, curled her tail about her front paws and blinked and purred.

Eunice sat for some time by one of the windows and stared out on the narrow road, which made a turn here, and went off straight up a long hill. At the turn was a guide-board, and on the board the words "To Boston—29 miles;" there was also a hand with the stump of an index finger pointing up that hill. That direction might have said 290 miles to Boston, and the idea of distance would not have been any greater to the child looking at it. People around here were not in the habit of going to Boston. Nothing called them there. The nearest railroad station was eleven miles away. It was true that there were people over in the "middle village" who often went to the city. But this hamlet was in effect almost as remote as if it had been a great deal farther away from any large town.

Up at "the Corners" there was a boat-shop where they built boats, and from which, about once a week all the year round, a man drove to Boston with two boats. The smaller was set into the larger, they were fastened on two pairs of wheels very far apart, and drawn by one horse. The driver started in the morning. The next day he returned, sitting on a folded horse blanket near the front wheels.

Eunice often thought this man must know the world thoroughly. She envied him. Now as she sat with her forehead pressed against the glass she heard the rattling of wheels coming down the long hill. She knew instantly that it was the rattle of the boat-cart on its way home. There was no snow, the road was hard and almost white; everything passing over it resounded.

"There's Reuben Little comin' home," said Mrs. Warner, as she stopped her machine and drew out a long seam from it. "It must be mighty tedious drivin' so fur in the winter-time."

"I guess Reub keeps liquor enough down to make the time pass tollable well," responded Marthy S. "I should think his wife 'd hate to have him go to Borston so, where he c'n git liquor so easy."

The dress-maker threaded her needle before she added that wives had to put up with a good many things that they'd have dif'runt if they could.

Mrs. Warner said "that was so" with more fervor than she would have employed if she had

not wished to propitiate Marthy S. for the treat-
ment she had received at the hands of Eunice.

Meantime the four wheels had clattered down
the incline, turned with dangerous shortness
round the corner, and had very unexpectedly
stopped a little beyond the house.

Mr. Little apparently did not wish to take the
trouble to leave his position among blankets and
old buffalo robes.   He made a beckoning movement with his whip towards Eunice, who immediately dashed out of the side door and ran up
to him.

The man finally disinterred a brown paper
package from somewhere near his feet. He held
it out to Eunice.

"Roweny had me git that framed in Borston,"
he said, "'n' she told me to give it to you when
I come by. They said where they put on the
frame that it was ruther good for a emmytoor.
Mebby you know what a emmytoor is.   I
don't. I told um my niece done it. I let um
know she could do lots better 'n' that. Clk!
Git up!"

He swung the whip around, the horse started,
the wheels began to rattle.

Eunice dashed back into the house again.
Her mother and Miss Hancock had been watching her with that keen curiosity which seems in-
separable from a life among such surroundings.

They both hung over Eunice as she tore the wrappings from her parcel.

"I declare!" exclaimed Mrs. Warner, in undisguised delight, "ain't it jest as nat'ral as life? 'N' there's the old butternut, 'n' I do believe it's the roan cow by the brook there. 'N' the chimney—look at the chimney!"

In the speaker's mind it seemed little short of marvellous that a chimney could be made so "life-like."

It was a water-color sketch of the old Warner place. Perhaps it was crude, perhaps it showed great ignorance, but there was something in it that was able to hold the attention for a moment, something which might make one say: "There is life."

To those now gazing at it the sketch seemed phenomenal.

A gray house with a two-story front, and sloping down to one low story over the kitchen. No projection, no "jet" at the eaves, everything bare and rigid. An immense chimney with many chinks in it; a stretch of meadow at the right with a brook running through it, and some cows standing. Not a tree, save one distant butternut and some young willows by the stream; a pale-blue summer sky overhead.

Eunice breathed a long breath of delight. Mrs. Warner was stepping here and there to get new views of the picture. Her face also was radiant.

Marthy S. preserved an unflattering calmness of demeanor. She said she never seen no sky but what was bluer 'n that.

Eunice cast a withering glance at her, but did not think it worth while to speak.

"The grass ain't anywhere nigh green enough," went on the dress-maker, feeling her critical powers expanding with use. "And I never noticed that medder when there wa'n't more crows flyin' over it."

Here she sniffed very decidedly, and said that anybody could make a picture as good as that.

Eunice now lost her ability to keep silent. She looked up at Marthy S.

"You're talkin' like that," she said, with the unutterable scorn of youth, "because Rowena said that about pins. I should be ashamed to be so mean!"

Mrs. Warner was still so pleased with the sketch that she could not rebuke her daughter as she ought to have done.

Miss Hancock again was conscious of the strong necessity of remembering that she was a professor.

"We'll hang it up in the parlor next to the scene," said Mrs. Warner, with pride; "they'll kinder set each other off mighty well."

There was a large chromo in the Warner parlor. It had been there ever since Eunice could remember. It consisted of a pile of mountains at the right, two deep chasms at the left, and in the middle, very far away, were the turrets of a massive castle. There was a red gloom over the whole like the hue on the stage when the red lights have almost died away.

The name of this object was "A Scene in Germany," but it was always deferentially mentioned in the family as "the scene." The possession of it was felt to confer a kind of distinction.

Eunice had a vague feeling that she did not wish her gift to be placed near the scene. The only well-defined objection which she could urge, however, was that if this sketch were hung in the parlor no one could ever see it, for the parlor was always shut up.

Miss Hancock had gone back resolutely to her basting.

The sunlight had suddenly left the kitchen. There was only a brilliant glow in the west, which was reflected vividly on the old house and over the now brown meadow.

A rush of bitter cold air from the north-west came against the doors and windows, making them rattle.

Miss Hancock took her basting to the lightest place; she glanced out, thinking that she should have to borrow an extra shawl when she walked home after supper.

As she looked she saw a figure coming from among a clump of pine-trees, through which the road ran to the west. It was the figure of a young girl walking rapidly.

The dress-maker's aquiline face darkened with irritation as she gazed.

"If that ain't her now," she exclaimed to herself. "I don't see how in time she happens to look so stylish, I declare I don't. She don't dress, nohow, but there's something or other about her."

When the girl came nearer it could be seen that her fur cap was quite worn and shabby, and had been cheap to begin with. Her coarse blanket shawl was like other blanket shawls. Nevertheless, Miss Hancock was perfectly right, though rather indefinite, when she said of this girl that "there was something or other about her."

II.

GOING BY BOAT.

"THERE'S Rowena now," cried Eunice Warner, as a dark object went quickly by the window.

The child started up and carefully put down the sketch she had been holding.

"I guess she's come over to be thanked," remarked Miss Hancock, with some venom.

Eunice had no time to retort, for the porch door opened immediately and Rowena Tuttle entered.

"Take your things right off," said Mrs. Warner, hospitably, "'n' stay to supper. I s'pose Georgiana's had to keep some scholars after school or she'd be here by this time; but 'tain't late neither. It does git dark so quick this season of the year."

Rowena had nodded at the dress-maker and looked at Eunice. She sat down and threw back her heavy shawl.

"No, I can't stop to supper," she answered.

"I was down here to Mrs. Morris's, and so I came to see Georgie a minute."

"She'll soon be to home now," responded Mrs. Warner. "We've ben admirin' the picture, Roweny. We set a lot by it already."

"She's goin' to hang it by the scene," said Eunice, discontentedly. "You know the scene, don't you, Rowena?"

The girl smiled brilliantly.

"Oh, yes."

Then she seemed to restrain a laugh. She knew that the dress-maker was looking at her, and she also knew that, for some reason, there was malevolence in her gaze.

When Rowena spoke she uttered her words in a clear-cut way that sometimes seemed almost incisive in contrast with the slovenly manner in which people chewed their syllables in this village. This was one of the sins which were laid at her door. She was too good and too fine to talk like other folks, "and she nothin' but Hiram Tuttle's daughter." From a child, however, Rowena had taken to correctness of speech as some boys take to mischief as soon as they can compass it. When she spoke, even in the most casual manner, there was a curious thrill in her voice which always made a stranger turn quickly to see who had spoken. She was hardly responsible for this, and if it suggested deeps, or heights, or anything in her nature out of the common, ought she to be blamed?

"It was awful good of you to give me that," said Eunice, with enthusiasm.

"I thought you might like a keepsake when I'm away," was the reply.

"So, you're really goin', be ye?" asked Mrs. Warner, with some awe mingled with reproach in her speech. It could not be right for a girl to leave a good home where she might have a chance to sew straw part of the year and do slop work when straw was dull.

It must be remembered that this was the one of Mr. Tuttle's daughters who was "sut on goin' to Borston."

"Yes, I am really going. I must have a chance, Mrs. Warner; I feel that I must."

As she spoke, the girl rose and walked to the window. She turned there and looked back at the woman who was preparing to make griddle-cakes for supper.

As she moved across the floor one saw that it is not clothes that make a person "stylish," though clothes are not to be despised as aids. A woman is born stylish just as she may be born with blue eyes. The attribute may not be immediately perceptible, but it is ready to appear at the proper time, if it be her birthright, as the second teeth come at the appropriate period.

Rowena's rusty dress hung on her "with an air;" the shawl slipped off her shoulders now as she stood there as shawls never slip from shoulders undowered with that mysterious, elusive gift which Marthy S. could recognize, but could not achieve.

"I suppose you think I am very wicked, Mrs. Warner," said Rowena. "I know your girls never would think of leaving home—unless they were married."

"I'm terrible afraid you'll git into temptation, Roweny," said Mrs. Warner, stirring her cake batter rapidly. "Somehow it don't seem right."

"Temptation?" cried Rowena. "I shall be hard at work; I shall have one little room and get my own meals. I shall live like a slave compared with the way I live now."

"Then why do you go?" wonderingly questioned her hostess. "But I s'pose you expect to make a lot of money. Now for a picture like that you give Eunice I shouldn't wonder if you'd git as much as a dollar, or a dollar 'n' a quarter, shouldn't you?"

"It's more likely I shouldn't get a cent," replied Rowena. "But I've got to make money, somehow. It's all father can do to let me have what I've been earning this last year."

"I should think," remarked Miss Hancock, now folding her work with remarkably quick motions, " I should think that a good principled girl 'd stay to home, if she had a home. Women that go gallivantin' round hither and yon ain't thought much of by folks that keep where they should. 'Tain't gen'rally liked here that you should leave your father 'n' mother 'n' brother 'n' sisters, Roweny. I speak as a friend. It seems my duty to say what is gen'rally thought."

Rowena looked for an instant in silence at the dress-maker; a scarlet flush rose to her face as she did so.

" I wonder why it is that when folks speak as a friend they are always so horribly disagreeable," she said.

" The truth ain't always pleasant, Roweny," responded Marthy S., feeling an inspiring sense of having performed a duty.

She had intended for a long time to tell this girl what folks thought. She now felt better natured. She advanced from the window and inquired if Rowena had a pattern of that skirt, or did she git it out of *The Delineator*. She was told that she had no pattern, and it did not come out of *The Delineator*.

" It ain't just right; there's too much of a fall to the back, but still—" began the dress-maker.

Here the porch door again opened, and a short, thick-set girl came in impetuously and rushed across the room at Rowena, exclaiming:

"I was 'most sure that was you I saw through the winder. Now you've got to stay to supper, 'n' Eunice 'n' I'll walk home with you."

This was Georgiana Warner, who taught school in the north district. She brought in a great whiff of fresh, keen air with her. She laid violent hands on Rowena, and carried off that person's "things" into the bedroom, Mrs. Warner looking on admiringly the while. Everything Georgie did was admirable in her mother's eyes. What other girl of her age had earned a "chamber set?" Who but Georgie could have combined a herring-bone pattern with something else as indescribable as it was lovely, and have introduced the combination into a bed-quilt?

The three girls clustered round the lamp-stand, leaving space for Marthy S. to continue to baste at one side of it.

"Seems to me you're dreadful sober," at last said Georgie, after the sketch had been volubly commented on.

In truth Rowena felt an odd tightness about her throat as she looked around the familiar room and listened to the familiar voices.

"I don't know when I sh'll be here again," she said, huskily.

"But you ain't goin' 'fore next week," hastily exclaimed Eunice.

"Uncle Reuben goes Monday with the boats.

I'm going with him to save money. I shall be too busy to come here again."

Afterwards Miss Hancock felt constrained to say that Roweny Tuttle "did show some signs of feelin' about leavin' them Warner girls that night. Whatever end Roweny might come to, she certainly did show feelin' that night."

The snow was slow in coming this winter. The roads were still bare and hard on that day when Rowena came out of the door of her home as she heard her uncle Reuben's cart rumbling along the stretch of level ground from the west.

At this moment she almost wished she had never "sut out" in this way.

The cart stopped. Dimly she saw her father and uncle tugging and straining to get her trunk into the smaller boat, which was set down in the larger.

Her mother and two younger sisters were clustered about her.

"Don't go out yet, Roweny, you'll only git chilled 'fore you start," said Mrs. Tuttle, her lips quivering as she spoke. "It'll take um some time to h'ist that trunk in. You might's well se' down. Put your feet right on that stick of wood in the oven 'n' keep um warm. I'll be wrappin' up the soapstone."

Rowena sat down as she was bidden and put

her feet, with "rubbers" over her boots, in the edge of the oven of the cook-stove.

She could not speak. She had never felt so utterly miserable in her life. She hated Boston. She was no longer interested to know how the city looked. She did not know, after all, as she could ever learn to be even the most ordinary art student. It seemed utterly preposterous now that she had ever thought of trying to study art. She could not do it.

She was struggling against a powerful desire to turn and fling herself in her mother's arms and declare that she could not leave her. Her ears heard dully her mother's voice saying:

"You know I've put the plum-cake 'n' the corn' beef 'n' the bread in the right-hand top of your trunk. I wouldn't resk puttin' in no pies nor no preserves, though I did want to, you're so fond of um. Your father's put the lamp kerosene stove in a separate box. Don't forgit to have Reuben leave it where you stop. You'll want it to boil your coffee and eggs, 'n' do whatever you can do. I s'pose you'll have to live mighty close. You know we sh'll send in victuals 'most every week by Reuben.

Mrs. Tuttle kept talking on as if she were afraid to stop. The sound of the commonplace words helped her not to break down entirely.

When she had wrapped up the hot soapstone

in an old newspaper that steamed about the stone,
she came and stood by her daughter's chair.

Rowena pulled off her mitten, put her hand
out, and took her mother's hand in a close clasp.
She could not help sobbing a little as she did so.

"Don't, Roweny," whispered the mother, trembling.

"No, no, I won't. And Boston isn't so far but
I can come back any day."

"Any day. And be dearly welcome."

Now Mrs. Tuttle sobbed. Rowena pressed her
cheek against the rough hand.

"Mother, if you cry I shall feel like killing myself," she said, almost violently.

"Sho, now! How foolish we be!" responded
the mother, immediately swallowing her tears.

One of the girls had gone to the window, and
from that position she now announced that "Father had got a ladder, 'n' they were tryin' to shove
the trunk up on that. But it kep' a-slippin' back."

"I hope I sha'n't keep slipping back," remarked
Rowena, with a hysterical laugh.

Mrs. Tuttle laughed too, even more hysterically. She said she hoped they wouldn't hender
Reuben too long. She was thankful the wind
was in the north-west, and so Roweny wouldn't
have to face it.

The girl rose and walked about the room. She
looked at everything in it as if she should never

be there again.   But she did not dare to look at her mother's face.

"There! The trunk has tumbled in," cried the observer at the window.

"All ashore that's goin' ashore!" shouted Uncle Reuben's jolly voice.

Rowena hurriedly kissed her sisters, held her mother fast a moment, and heard the tremulous words:

"I know you'll keep straight, Roweny. 'N' don't forgit us."

She ran down the path.   Her father held the ladder in place, and she climbed up and stepped over into the boat.   There were a great many blankets and shawls in the bottom of the boat. Mrs. Tuttle came out with the hot soapstone, which was carefully placed at the girl's feet by her father, who had come aboard with her.

He also said: "I'm sure you'll keep straight. P'raps the Tuttles ain't no great for layin' up, but they ain't crooked. Good-bye."

He went down the ladder and then set it carefully against the fence.

All the Tuttles were in the yard. They waved their hands.

Uncle Reuben said "it wa'n't nothin' to go to Borston. Clk! Git up!"

In another moment the cart had gone round a curve. The Tuttles ran into the house. How the wind swept about! How the dust blew over the frozen road!

There was a slight gray film rising in the north and west.

Mr. Tuttle stood a good while by the kitchen stove with his hands in his pockets. He was a thin man with a stoop in his shoulders, a long face, with a great development on his head of the bump that is called benevolence.

He would have been rather "beforehanded" if he had not twice "signed" for friends who were sure they could pay long before the notes were due. But they did not pay, and Mr. Tuttle had to raise the money each time.

His wife had made him pledge himself never to sign again. He was now out of the debts so incurred, but he was no longer a young man.

At last he said that if the wind got into the east he guessed there'd be a tough snow-storm, by the way the sky looked.

He walked out towards the barn. His wife, watching him, thought he was more bent than usual.

"He always did think everything of Roweny," she whispered. Then she hurried about the house-work which had been "left standing." She was glad there was so much to do. She hustled the girls off to school, for it was not yet nine o'clock.

When the boats passed the Warner place all the family came to the door. Rowena stood up and flung out her hand. She saw that Georgie was crying.

Uncle Reuben repeated his remark that "it wa'n't nothin' to go to Borston."

After that Rowena wrapped herself heavily, and gave herself up to her thoughts. They were not quite so dismal, now the wrench of parting was over. She began to see the road-sides and the distant pastures. She thought the different hues of brown were charming. She began to compound in her mind the colors she would use in sketching that far - away hill, where the stunted savins now looked blue-black in the cold air.

All at once she became aware that Uncle Reuben was pulling in his horse and saying, "Whoa!"

An open wagon was driven alongside, and a young man sprang out of it. In some way he managed to get into the boat with two or three agile movements.

"You'd better remember that these horses won't bear much courtin' this weather," said Uncle Reuben, slapping his hands against his chest.

Now he was in the boat with Rowena, the young man apparently had nothing to say. He stammered, and was very red.

"I wanted to say good-bye," he at last began. "I think it was kinder mean not to let me say good-bye."

"I am not hindering you," responded Rowena.

Uncle Reuben chuckled. The young man, whose name was Barrett, felt it was very hard to have old Little sitting there listening. He had a clear vision of Little in the store the next evening telling every particular of this interview, with dreadful embellishments.

Philip Barrett took a good grip of his resolution, and turning his back on the place where the driver sat, he murmured, in a pleading voice,

"I do wish you'd write to me, Roweny."

"I shall be so very busy," was the reply, in the same murmur.

"But think how lonesome I sh'll be! I tell you I can't stan' it, Roweny."

Barrett reached down and seized the thick mittens that contained the girl's hands.

At that moment his horse, left alone, began to walk forward, and its owner was obliged to straighten himself and cry out:

"Whoa! Hold still, can't ye?"

He saw that Rowena was smiling when he turned to her again. He grew more red.

"'Tain't no laughin' matter with me, I c'n tell you," he cried, indignantly. "I jest as lives hang myself if you don't write. Stop, you old brute, you! Little, do git down 'n' stop that hoss!"

"I'm too stiff in the joints to keep climbin' in 'n' out er this rig," was the response.

"Oh, I'll write," hastily said Rowena.

Barrett squeezed the mittens hard for an instant. Then he scrambled down somehow and ran headlong after his horse, which was now trotting along the road.

Mr. Little looked over his shoulder at his passenger. He told her it must be a great thing to be a girl 'n' have beaus; but she did not reply.

Finally the long stretches of country were left behind. There were large villages now. Rowena looked at them eagerly. Then tall buildings, the gilded dome of the State-house, spires, chimneys were in sight. But it was a long time then before they reached the pavements. The film over the sky had increased. Some flakes of snow were falling when the boat-cart turned into Atlantic Avenue, where the load was to be delivered.

Rowena never knew how she got down. She had not known a city was like that. A "thick-settled place" she had expected, but not this rattle and turmoil.

She had a glimpse of ships and the water in the harbor when she rose to her feet in the boat.

There was some joking among the men where

they stopped about the passenger old Little had brought.

She walked with her uncle to a melancholy-looking house on Hudson Street. This was where he took his meals while he was in Boston. He bought so many tickets for three dollars, he explained to her, and he used these tickets for his meals. The woman who kept this house would let Rowena a room. This woman came to the two as they waited in a dark parlor, which was supposed to be heated through a register. This register apparently opened into a boiler wherein cabbage was cooking in some underground regions.

Mrs. Jarvis nodded at Rowena. She asked her if she had ever been in Borston before, and when the girl said "No," she said, "Indeed," and looked at her in pitying surprise.

Mrs. Jarvis was a very spare woman with a narrow forehead, and gray hair rolled up in that fashion sometimes called "pompadour." This roll appeared to increase the length of her face by a great deal more than the height of the roll itself. When Rowena first looked at her she had a bewildered idea that at least a third of Mrs. Jarvis's height consisted of face and hair.

Mr. Little explained that this was the girl who wanted that room. Mrs. Jarvis said "Certainly," and went and said something down a spout which obviously led into the kitchen. This spout, so

Rowena thought, must also act as a conductor of cabbage odor, for even a register going at its full capacity could not bring up so strong a fragrance. Mrs. Jarvis returned to the parlor, but had a preoccupied air, as if waiting to hear from the spout.

She remarked to Rowena that she would find Borston very pleasant. She appeared to be about to say something more when a hollow sound was heard in the spout, and the lady immediately told Rowena that, as the servants were all busy, she herself would show her the room.

Mr. Little, who was somewhat subdued, said he guessed he'd go down and take his grub, and he disappeared in a place even darker than the parlor and hall were, and which Rowena afterwards learned was the stair-way leading to the dining-room and kitchen.

Rowena followed her hostess up four flights, and was then shown into a little room with a very small cylinder stove with no fire in it.

"Shall you require fuel?" asked Mrs. Jarvis.

Rowena felt very miserable and helpless. She said feebly that she would need a fire. She could hardly speak.

"Fuel will be extry," said Mrs. Jarvis, "though some lets their room doors remain open dooring the day, and has heat from the halls."

Rowena had not noticed that there was much

heat in the halls, save what would unavoidably come in the warm cabbage vapor.

It was at last settled that a servant should come immediately and make a fire.

Mrs. Jarvis turned to go, but she came back to ask:

"Shall you require meals?"

"No."

"You will do light house-keeping?"

Rowena did not know just what light house-keeping was, but she said she thought she should do it. Mrs. Jarvis said again that she believed Rowena would find Borston very pleasant. Then she went out into the hall. The girl sat down on the bed, and said aloud that she would go home with Uncle Reuben the next day.

She was very hungry and very cold, and with all her emotions there was mingled a delirious desire to demolish that pompadour roll on the top of Mrs. Jarvis's head.

At last the fire was made, her room was warm, and she had eaten some bread and corned beef from her trunk. There must be something stimulating in corned beef, for Rowena now felt that she could better combat her inclination to retreat.

III.

INVITED TO A SEA–ANTS.

ON the morning after her arrival at that house in Hudson Street, Rowena rose long before it was light. She felt that if she should fail of seeing her Uncle Reuben when he came for his breakfast she should die.

The fire had long since gone out in her stove. It seemed miles away, in an undiscovered and dreadful country, that the supply of kindling and coal probably was kept.

She did not dare to turn on the gas lest something should explode. She knew that there was nothing gas liked so well as exploding. She would get a small kerosene lamp that very day. When kerosene exploded she knew where she was, or thought she did, which was equally comforting.

She dressed herself in the semi-darkness. With a shawl wrapped about her she went out into the narrow, musty hall and leaned over, listening. An Irish servant girl came out of the room opposite and brushed indifferently by her. Rowena wished she dared to ask if she might come down and get some wood and coal, but the girl went clumping along flight after flight, and Rowena could not speak. The house was as mysterious to her as any Radcliffe Castle. Once, when some door was slammed open far down in the abyss, she heard a frightful sound, and did not know that it was the milkman's call. She wondered if she should always be trying not to cry.

Presently there were more steps somewhere in the halls. She heard Mrs. Jarvis's voice asking somebody where "them tickets were," and then inquiring if "the reg'lars had begun to come in yet." She could not hear the replies. She told herself that her Uncle Reuben must be more of a reg'lar than otherwise, since he was there at certain times. The cabbage odor of the day before had become stagnant now, and the active perfume was that of frying liver and bacon, with something that was probably called coffee. Rowena did not care whether she ever ate or not. She had no oil for her little lamp-stove, and no coal. She could not imagine when she should have any breakfast. But she could not swallow food.

She knew that she must go down to the ground floor if she expected to see her uncle. He was part of her home.

"My darling home," she said, in a whisper, and twisted her hands in her shawl.

What if Reuben Little had eaten already and gone?

She started hastily, but she was obliged to go slowly, it was so dark, and she was sure there were rents in the stair carpets. As she went on the smell of bacon became stronger and the sounds of dishes rattling louder. And this was Boston!

At last she finished her cautious descent and stood in the hall into which the street door was opening constantly to admit what she supposed to be the reg'lars. Each deposited a ticket with Mrs. Jarvis, who sat at a small table in the open door-way into the parlor. Nearly all of this lady's patrons were of those who are obliged to be at their work at seven o'clock.

There was the most reduced flame of gas going at the mouth of the one burner which stood out from the wall high up towards the dingy ceiling. This blue flame revealed the fact that every one who came in was covered with snow. Few had umbrellas. There was a hasty stamping of feet, a flinging down of hats, a delivery of tickets, and then a rush down the stairs into the basement.

It seemed to Rowena as she stood there shrinkingly that nearly all of these were girls. Where did they all come from? What were they doing? As they went by her each gave her one swift, cold glance.

Mrs. Jarvis was constantly saying "good-morning" in a dry, impersonal tone. She kept her tickets in piles. She wore a wadded, loose morning-gown. It was so much wadded, and had such a large pattern of palm-leaves on it, together with a hitherto unclassified tropical fruit, that the wearer looked very much as if she had wrapped her bed-comforter about her. The pompadour roll on the top of her head was so exactly as it was the night before that Rowena, gazing tremulously at it, felt almost sure that it must have been taken off and put in a box before its owner retired.

In a lull in the arrivals Mrs. Jarvis leaned back wearily in her chair, and her wandering glance rested upon Rowena. She said "good-morning" again, this time with a slight show of interest. The girl hurriedly advanced.

"Do you know whether my uncle, Mr. Little, has come in yet?" she asked, quickly.

"I don't think so; good-morning, Miss Chute," as a pallid girl in a long, straight "gossamer' deposited her ticket, and then almost ran down the stairs.

"I hope I haven't missed him," said Rowena, in a low, strained voice.

"I presume not; I presume he will soon be here. Did you sleep well, Miss—Miss—"

"Tuttle," said Rowena, feebly.

But Mrs. Jarvis did not hear her. Somebody had come to buy a package of twenty-five tickets for three dollars. This person was a stout young man, with an ulster so long that it draggled about his heels. Rowena had stepped into the parlor and was standing directly behind Mrs. Jarvis, leaning over that lady's chair and watching the door eagerly.

She did not see the young man. But he watched her quite intently. As he put the tickets into his pocket she uttered a cry and rushed out into the hall again.

"Holloa, Roweny!" cried Uncle Reuben, stamping his feet briskly. "Bright 'n' early, ain't ye? Grand snow-storm. Guess Phil Barrett 'll wish you could try his sleigh. If this keeps up I sh'll have to go back on runners. Of course, you ain't got to goin' yet. Come down to breakfast with me. I've got lots of tickets. I ain't in any hurry. How do you like Borston?"

Rowena caught the man's hand and held it fast.

"I hate Boston," she answered, with subdued violence.

"That's 'cause you ain't got to runnin' yet. You'll think dif'runt in a day or two."

Uncle Reuben spoke so comfortably that the girl felt calmed. She went down-stairs with him. By this time the outward flow had set in; but people were constantly filling up the empty places. Rowena did not see a single face; there was for her only a confused nightmare-like medley of human beings, a good deal of heavy, much-chipped white crockery, a lavish provision of food and drink, some talking and laughing, two black-haired Irish girls running back and forth between kitchen and dining-room, bearing plates and cups and saucers.

Mr. Reuben Little felt that he was doing the honors of Boston. He conversed affably with the stout young man opposite, who had taken off his voluminous ulster, and now revealed a large, pale-pink necktie that bulged out a great deal in front, and threatened to retain a number of crumbs of bread and potato and some drops of coffee. It did not have the least effect on the pink necktie that its wearer was constantly trying to thrust back into a more retiring position. Rowena did not know that this person was talking at her, though he never addressed her. But all the other girls at the table knew it, and most of them thought she was a bold piece to allow it. When she walked away they looked at her. The young man hurried up-stairs after her. He opened the front door with his ulster on his arm. Then he lingered. The clouds were breaking away. The sun was beginning to shine.

Reuben Little would not, after all, be delayed

by the storm. He said good-bye to his niece. He wondered why she clung to him so, and what made her so pale; but he concluded it was because she hadn't got to runnin' yet.

Mrs. Jarvis, still at her ticket-table, saw the parting. She told Rowena to come right into the parlor a minute and stand by the register. She spoke as if standing by the register would be very comforting. So Rowena did as she was bidden. She crouched by the iron lattice, and felt that her misery was greater than she could bear.

After a time Mrs. Jarvis beckoned to her. Rowena went to the woman's side and began to look at the pompadour roll, succumbing more and more to the strange fascination it had for her.

"You'll soon be cheerful," said Mrs. Jarvis, feeling her rather dried-up heart going out somewhat towards this girl. "Of course, I'm always busy, but if I have a minute I will try to make Borston agreeable. I think you'll find Borston very pleasant. It is a privilege to live here.

Rowena tried not to groan. She said "thank you," and was moving towards the stairs, thinking she would go up to her cold room and cry the rest of the day.

"Stop a minute, Miss—Miss—"

"Tuttle," again said Rowena, and again her

hostess did not hear her, for she went back to
her table to take two tickets from two girls who
were laughing so that they seemed to fall down
into the lower hall.

" I was going to say," went on Mrs. Jarvis, returning, " that it would probably do you good to
come into the parlor here this evening. We are
going to have a sea-ants."

Rowena looked and felt bewildered. But she
was thankful to know that Mrs. Jarvis meant to
be kind.

" Madame Van Benthuysen will be present,"
said Mrs. Jarvis, with great unction. " Of course
you have heard of Madame Van Benthuysen?"

" No, ma'am," said Rowena, conscious of a de-
praving ignorance.

Mrs. Jarvis looked at her pityingly. The roll
of hair even had a commiserating aspect.

" Madame makes it her home in Borston,"
went on Mrs. Jarvis. " She resides in Harrison
Avenoo. She says the mental atmosphere of
this city is more congenial than the mental atmosphere of any other place. She sometimes
speaks of it as soulful. I do not suppose there
is a human being on the face of the globe as sensitive to mental atmospheres as Madame Van
Benthuysen."

Rowena stood in silence. She was greatly perplexed. She wished, confusedly, that if the air

here were soulful she might have a realizing sense
of it. She had not thought of the air as being
in the least like that. But perhaps it was different in Harrison Avenue.

"I shall be glad to have you present this evening at about eight," resumed Mrs. Jarvis. "We
expect the sea-ants to be peculiarly interesting.
Madame gave me to understand that she was almost sure that her first husband, Major Stanger,
who was killed in the battle of Bull Run, would
be with us."

Mrs. Jarvis made this ghastly announcement
with the utmost satisfaction of manner. Rowena
felt her hair rising. How could she be present?
And yet it seemed ungracious to refuse. She
wished Major Stanger would not appear. It was
possible that an engagement in heaven or hell,
or in some intermediate sphere, would keep him
away. Still, the girl knew she must come expecting to meet the major.

It was only in the vaguest and slightest way
that Rowena had ever heard of Spiritualism, and
she knew nothing of any of the terms used by
its followers.

"Have you ever attended a sea-ants?" inquired
Mrs. Jarvis.

"No, ma'am. I don't know what they are."

"Is it possible? And you don't know whether you could be a medyum or not?"

"Oh, no, no!"

Rowena put out both her hands, as if warding off the thought. She began to make a backward movement towards the door.

"You have that peculiar expression about the eyes that usually indicates great medyumistic powers," went on Mrs. Jarvis, showing a new interest in her lodger. "Have you never had no thoughts of being developed?"

"Oh, no! no!" cried Rowena again, this time more emphatically than before. A wild idea came to her that she would run away if there were danger of being developed.

"You shrink now because you are ignorant," said Mrs. Jarvis. "Ignorance is always cowardly; it is only as you reach forward that you get into the full stream of spiritualistic light. I'm sure madame will be interested in you. Don't fail to come at eight."

Rowena did not know how she could escape the sea-ants. She gave her promise to be present, thinking she might die before night.

When she had climbed half the stairs to her room, she came back and asked if she might take up some fuel. She was shown into a dungeon underneath the house, where there was a quantity of coal and some small bunches of kindling. She was told to come here for fuel, and did not know that she paid for having it carried to her room.

An hour later she was sitting over her little stove, which was now red-hot. She had tidied her room, she had made a list of the things she must immediately buy. She must go out on the street. She wished that she had something besides that heavy, coarse shawl—a jacket, for instance. But she must hoard all her money for her living and her lessons. She looked at a card she held in her hand. "Mr. Allestree, Studio 4, No. — Tremont Street."

In five minutes she was walking up Beach Street, with a small portfolio of her own sketches under her arm. She was very pale, and her heart beat heavily. She had to inquire her way a good many times; and when at last she had mounted the broad and what seemed to her magnificent staircase of that building on Tremont Street, she found that Mr. Allestreè would not come for nearly two hours. It was now not much after eight.

She went back, and sat the two hours in her room. She could not buy tea, or kerosene, or any such vulgar necessity until she had seen Mr. Allestree. It seemed to her that she could hardly breathe until she had seen him. And perhaps he would not take her.

She held herself in her room ten minutes after

the time mentioned by some official she had seen in that place.

She did not know whether to knock or go boldly in. She knocked twice, and then had her hand on the latch, when the door was suddenly flung open from the inside by a lady who held a palette in her left hand, together with a maul-stick, and who had a paint-brush between her lips.

As soon as she released the door she removed the brush from her mouth and said :

"I don't know why you can't come right in."

Rowena stepped in, and the door clanged shut behind her. She felt dazzled. She knew vaguely that there were busts and casts and statues and drapery and pictures, framed and unframed, everywhere about ; but what dazzled her was the woman who had opened the door, and who now stood looking at her with that calm kind of a gaze which one gives to an inanimate object which cannot look back. Rowena knew very well that she was only an object to this person ; she was indignant, but she was drawn all the same.

The woman was dressed in something light gray and soft ; there was a fall of pale, thin silk at one side of her skirt, and some of the same silk was fluffed about her throat, and by some means stood up high, and, in a manner, framed the face, which was radiantly colorless, except for the lips.   It was high-featured and thin and disdainful and questioning.   It had a quantity of light, reddish hair, short and curly on the forehead—hair of the exact hue of the thick eyebrows and eyelashes.   Rowena, who, even in her most embarrassed moments, involuntarily noticed colors, said to herself:

"Her eyes are green, and oh, how red her lips are!"

"I wanted to see Mr. Allestree," said Rowena, at last, making a great effort.

The woman now turned and walked off to an easel at the end of the room.   She had evidently been at work there.   As she walked she said that Mr. Allestree might not be in for an hour; that Rowena might wait if she chose.   Was she one of his pupils?

Rowena shyly followed across the immense room.   She was possessed by a desire to see this woman's work.

"I want to be one of his pupils," she said.

Her voice sounded so young, so clear, and it had so markedly that quality in it which has been mentioned that the other occupant of the room turned again, then deliberately put down her palette and other tools.

"Have you brought some of your sketches in that portfolio?" she asked.

"Yes."

"Show them to me. I've studied everything. Now I'm digging at art. Show me your sketches."

Rowena resented the tone, but she obeyed the command. She was very slow in untying the ribbon which bound her portfolio; her fingers trembled so, and she could not steady them. The other woman watched her intently.

"You have good hands," she remarked, coolly, not caring that the words made Rowena flush hotly. "I like them." Then she suddenly added: "I hope you haven't come here to Allestree just because you can daub placques, and put awful hints of daisies on squares of black satin to hang up in your rooms. Horrible things! That's what most women do, and think it's art. If I can't do some real work, I shall—ah, did you do that?"

IV.

MAJOR STANGER.

ROWENA had at last spread open her portfolio. The first sketch that lay there was the original of the Warner homestead, a copy of which she had given Eunice.

Her companion reached out a long, slim hand with an imperative motion and took the sheet. But she did not say anything, though Rowena stood looking at her with dilated, hoping, and fearing eyes.

Every sketch was taken out and gazed upon slowly and keenly, and in silence.

At last Rowena could bear it no longer. She walked to the easel, where this woman had been at work.

Presently a voice close beside her asked :

" What do you think of it ?"

" I think it is bad," said Rowena.

" And you dare to tell me so ?"

" Why not tell you so, since you asked me ?"

The country girl turned an astonished glance at her interlocutor, who answered it angrily.'

"Mr. Allestree does not say it is bad," she remarked.

" Perhaps it isn't ; I only think it is," responded
Rowena, humbly, " and I am very ignorant."

The other woman's face flushed and paled.
Every movement of hers had a certain graceful,
final decision in it, and was rapid without being
hurried. She took up a brush and drew it across
the landscape in oil, which was almost finished,
on her easel. A broad line of crimson paint was
left on the picture. The action seemed to have
dissipated her anger. She turned with a sin-
gularly sweet smile to the girl who was close
to her.

" I knew it was bad all the time. I'm not a
fool," she said, " but all my friends praised it.
They said I ' must stick to my latest fad,' ' I was
born to be an artist,' and all that rot. You have
told me the truth ; you can't lie. I might better
have stuck to theosophy. What do you think
of theosophy, Miss ——?"

" Tuttle," said Rowena, and as she said that
word a vivid vision of Mrs. Jarvis and her morning-gown and her hair rose before her.

" Miss Tuttle," said her companion, promptly,
" what idea have you formed about theosophy?"

" I don't know what it is," replied the girl,
blushing with shame.

" Nobody knows what it is," was the unexpected rejoinder, "but it is sometimes entertaining to talk as if we knew. A whole lot of us meet here and there and talk and talk. It is great fun at first, but afterwards it gets to be a bore. But one must do something, or what's the use of living in Borston?"

The speaker was standing directly in front of Rowena. She spoke in a voice that was not high or loud, but that could be heard with a peculiar distinctness, each word being like a perfectly formed bit of marble suddenly chipped off and sent out on its mission. It was evidently a habit, long cultivated, that she should speak thus.

Rowena tried to listen understandingly, but she was waiting for the master to come, and she was wishing she dared to ask what this stranger had thought of her sketches. But of course she had not liked them, or she would have told her.

Just then the great door of the studio clanged again. A large man in a fur-coat entered briskly.

"There is Allestree," said the woman, in an undertone to Rowena, who began to tremble pitiably. She gathered her sketches hastily into her arms and hurried out towards the door. Allestree saw her coming, and was sorry for her.

"Another poor devil who thinks she can paint," he said to himself, as he threw off his cap and coat. She stood and waited.

"Well?" he said.

"Will you look at these?"

Rowena now held herself straight and stiff. She was thinking she could go home. Her father and mother would be glad to see her. She could get a school.

The man glanced to where the other woman stood, far away, near her easel.

"Good-morning, Miss Phillipps," he said.

Rowena thought he dreaded to look at her work. Again she said to herself, "I can go home. If I can't get a school, I can do slop work."

Allestree threw himself down in a long chair and put his legs on the foot-rest.

"Give them to me, please," he said.

She laid her armful across his knees. He took up a sheet.

"H'm," he said.

He took up another sheet. Again he said "H'm."

He had so much beard on his face that the girl could not make out one expression more than another, and at last she lowered her eyes and waited in despair.

Finally he turned himself sideways and looked at her.

"Did you want me to give you lessons?"

"Yes—if you think—"

"We'll make a beginning. Come to-morrow at eleven."

He held out her sketches to her. She took them mechanically. It was all she could do not to cry with relief and joy. Since Allestree would teach her there must be some promise in her work.

She did not know how she got to the door. As she was trying to open it Miss Phillipps walked quickly to her.

"Here is your portfolio," she said. With two or three deft movements she fastened the sketches in place.

"Wait one moment outside for me," she said, and opened the door for Rowena, who stepped without, and stood dazed and tremulous. She thought of Uncle Reuben, and hoped she should soon "git to runnin'."

The door swung open again, and Rowena was joined by Miss Phillipps in heavy furs.

"It occurred to me that I could take you home," she said. "My carriage will be here. You seemed so overcome." The two went down the stairs. "You were afraid Allestree would not teach you?"

"Yes."

"He would not if he had not seen you had some talent. It's my opinion that you have a great deal. He took me because—I am Miss Phillipps," with a little laugh. "Here's the carriage. Get in. Where do you live? Hudson Street, driver."

Miss Phillipps sat down beside Rowena, who was almost sure her senses were leaving her. But through the whole time a shrewd good sense had enabled her to guess that her companion was a person who had whims, and who could afford to indulge them.

"I shall see you at the studio," remarked Miss Phillipps.

"But you have spoiled your picture."

"I spoiled that long ago. I shall begin another. How old are you?"

"Almost twenty-two."

"And I'm thirty. I suppose you are very poor?"

"Yes."

"Don't look so proud. I'm not going to offer you alms. Is this your place? What is that sign over the basement window? 'Twenty-five tickets for three dollars '—tickets for what?"

"For meals."

"Oh! Do you have tickets?"

"No. I'm going to do light house-keeping in my room at the top of the house."

"Oh! Cook your own meals? I should like that much better. Perhaps when you know me well you will invite me to lunch? You look as if you never would. Don't let your face show so plainly what you feel. What are you going to do evenings?"

"This evening I am going to a sea-ants in the parlor here," replied Rowena, with some desperation in her manner.

"A sea-ants? Mercy! Can it be there are still Spiritualists? I went through all that long ago."

"I haven't been through it yet," said Rowena.

The driver had been holding the door open for the last few minutes, but Miss Phillipps had put a detaining hand on Rowena's arm as she asked her questions.

"Well, good-bye."

Miss Phillipps smiled and leaned slightly towards the young girl as she said this. Rowena wished that she did not feel such a strong attraction towards this lady when she smiled like that.

She stepped out onto the sidewalk. As she did so, Mrs. Jarvis looked from the parlor window. She was dusting that room that it might be in good order for the evening.

The carriage rolled away through the mud and slush, and Rowena mounted the steps. Her cheeks burned and her eyes sparkled.

Mrs. Jarvis came to the parlor door, which was always open into the hall. There was almost deference in her manner.

"Wasn't that Miss Phillipps?" she inquired.

"Yes."

"I didn't know she was a friend of yours. I've

seen her preside at different meetin's, woman suf-
frage, and so on. She's a great reformer, I expect."

Mrs. Jarvis looked at Rowena as if hoping she
would explain.

"She isn't a friend of mine. I never saw her
before. She was at the studio. I don't know
why she brought me here."

Rowena thought she would be dishonest if
she did not say this.

"She must be very kind," remarked Mrs. Jarvis, beginning to whisk her feather-duster again.

As Rowena climbed the stairs she said to herself that Miss Phillipps did not seem exactly kind
to her. And yet the girl had not resented the
questions, nor the incisive abruptness of them.

By supper-time Rowena told herself she was
"settled," and felt as if she had been occupying
that attic for months. She made tea and boiled
eggs on the top of her kerosene stove. She
dipped a tough-looking substance from a tin can
labelled "Swiss Condensed Milk" into her solitary teacup. She had some baker's rolls and
something she had bought for butter. She had
really begun to "room-keep;" she was doing
light house-keeping.

Even the dexterity and the thrift of a New
England country girl cannot make it cosey or
home-like to get one's meals on the top of a

small oil-lamp stove. There is a certain desolation about a boiled egg that has been hopping up and down in a saucepan over that flame.

Rowena was conscious of the desolation, even in her triumph that Allestree would give her lessons. Besides, her eggs were store - eggs, and had forgotten that they had once been laid by real hens. She wished she had not spent her money for them, but had eaten corned beef from her trunk, as she had done for dinner. But, for some unknown reason, even corned beef, if you have brought it in a trunk, loses the original delicacy of flavor which so endears this dish to the rural inhabitant.

Rowena had "made out her supper," as her mother would have said, and was pensively trying to stir a second wad of condensed milk into a second cup of tea. She was thinking that she had been very remiss in not asking at the very first the price of the painting-lessons. She was also trying not to think about that old house she had left the day before. She was impatient to become hardened. All those girls down-stairs —who were coming and going through the hall —they were hardened, of course. They were not homesick.

She sat long in front of her stove. The door was open, and she could look in upon the bright coals. She did not light her new lamp. All at once she found that she was sobbing and the tears were running down her cheeks.

Somebody knocked at the door. Rowena went and opened it, glad that her room was so dark.

There was a rustling of black silk as Mrs. Jarvis, in her best gown, entered.

" I was afraid you had forgotten the sea-ants," she said. " I'm expecting Madame Van Benthuysen every minute. Most of the friends are here."

Mrs. Jarvis did not say that she had told the friends that her new lodger was a particular friend of " that Miss Phillipps."

Rowena went timidly down the stairs behind her hostess, who had waited for her to make her piteously simple toilet.

At the last step Mrs. Jarvis suddenly was aware that some very nervous fingers were clutching her arm.

" Remember," hurriedly whispered Rowena, " I won't be developed! I wouldn't be a medium for the whole world !"

She shuddered violently. Before any reply could be made the outer door, directly in front of them, was opened, and a young man entered, followed by a tall lady in a gray fur circular. It seemed to Rowena that the ulster of the man was familiar; the way it flopped about the ankles recalled something to her. The next instant she knew that it recalled a pale pink necktie and bread crumbs and coffee drops.

Mrs. Jarvis rushed forward to greet the person in the circular. The two women kissed each other loudly. They talked in a mumbling, rapid way for a moment, while the young man took off his hat in a pointed manner to Rowena, who still kept her place on the lower stair. She could hear the murmur of conversation from the parlor. She had thoughts of flying back up the stairs. The young man appeared to suspect that she had such thoughts, for he moved around behind the two and whispered, with a deprecating look:

"Don't go; you'll find it great fun."

Rowena forgot how very improper it was to speak without an introduction.

"If I do stay," she said, in the same voice, "I won't be a medium."

Then she blushed painfully, and knew she had done very wrong.

The young man flushed up with pleasure because she had answered him. He was going to say something more, when Mrs. Jarvis turned and drew the girl forward, saying:

"This is my young friend, Miss—I didn't quite catch your name, my dear."

"Tuttle," said Rowena.

"Oh yes, Tuttle. You see, she is a sensitive subject, open to influence."

Madame Van Benthuysen was not only tall, but large, and her circular made her almost immense. She had a dark face, with heavy-lidded eyes and thick, black eyebrows.

She took Rowena's hand with one of her own and put the other arm over the girl's shoulders. A great fold of the cloak nearly enveloped the slight figure.

"My dear child, I am truly glad to see you," said madame, in a rolling, unctuous voice, that was indicative of great good nature and enormous self-esteem. "The conditions are lovely to-night. I knew it as we came along in the horse-car; I said to my nephew, 'Ferdinand,' said I, 'I feel that the conditions were never more propitious than to-night.'"

The speaker pronounced propitious as if it were spelled "propishuous," and she uttered the word with such an air that Rowena almost thought that she herself had always been mistaken about that word.

"Were you coming to the sea-ants in the hope of being developed?" inquired madame, still holding the cold, slender hand warmly in her fat fingers.

Rowena, with a great effort, removed her hand. Again the nephew of madame, who was now in

the background, saw that she had the impulse
to run away up those stairs. He moved forward
rather precipitately, and asked if he might be
presented to the young lady. His aunt immediately performed the introduction with effusion.
Then she proceeded to lay aside her circular.
During this process she informed Mrs. Jarvis,
who was assisting her, that the reason her circular wore so well and looked so fresh was because
she never sat down in it. If you sat down in a
circular you ruined the fur and crushed the silk.
Economy was one of the first of virtues with
her. She was never ashamed of economy. The
major had always said she could dress better on
twenty-five dollars than any other woman could
on a hundred.

She was now smoothing the front breadths of
her black satin gown, and adjusting herself generally before the small mirror in the hat-rack.
Rowena was conscious of a sort of shock when
she saw that madame also wore a pompadour
roll—and how black it was, and how it shone!

Involuntarily the girl's hand went up to her
own head ; she feared lest she herself might have
such a roll—it might be the first visible symptom
of development towards mediumistic powers.

"Is Major Stanger coming to-night?"

It was Rowena who asked this question, because an ungovernable curiosity prompted her.

Madame turned from patting her hair. Rowena did not know why the young man broke into a laugh, which he instantly strangled. It was the most natural thing in the world, Rowena thought, for her to make that inquiry. Had not Mrs. Jarvis told her that that gentleman was expected? Rowena still hoped he would not be present.

"It is impossible to tell until I am under control," rather coldly answered madame. And then they all went into the parlor, and the dozen ladies present all shook hands with madame, and the one man who was already there nodded icily at madame's nephew.

They all sat down. Madame was opposite a closed card-table. At first there was a little desultory talk, but very soon there was complete silence. Everybody looked at madame save the stout young man, who looked at Rowena.

Madame continued to smile in a broad, general way, even after her elbows began to twitch and she had shut her eyes.

All at once she crossed her legs in a very pronounced manner. She placed one hand on her hip. She put the other hand to her face and appeared to twirl a mustache.

"Gad," said she, in a husky voice.

Everybody moved a little, in subdued wonder and admiration.

"Gad," said madame again; "seems to me there's a new gal here, ain't there?"

More admiration.

"It's the major," whispered some one.

Mrs. Jarvis held up her finger for silence. Everybody listened breathlessly for more words of wisdom.

Madame asked for a cigar. She said something about a cocktail. She seemed to smoke and to drink. She was evidently now a personating medium.

Rowena was sorry for her. She did not reply when Mrs. Jarvis asked in a very low tone if it wasn't wonderful.

But after a moment Rowena, in that clear voice of hers, asked if it was Major Stanger. On being told that it was, without a doubt, she said it was very lucky that the major had been killed, for he must have been horrid when in the flesh.

She could not guess why such daggers were looked at her. She had forgotten that the major had once been the husband of the medium. She was liable to forget such things, and therefore her remarks were sometimes quite electrifying in their frank simplicity. Ferdinand, who, she now perceived, was sitting very near her, thrust his handkerchief into his mouth and looked at her over it with eyes that almost frightened her.

V.

A BUNCH OF MATERIALIZED PINKS.

MRS. JARVIS'S narrow forehead appeared narrower than ever with that frown upon it. She looked at Rowena with such persistence that the girl's face grew deeply red.

Madame Van Benthuysen continued to smoke an imaginary cigar and to sip an imaginary cocktail. She seemed to find the occupation rather exhilarating. She said something more about a "new gal," and wanted to know where the deuce she came from—referring to Rowena. She said there was nothing so thundering skurse in the world as a pretty gal. If they had any of that article, just trot um out. If he was a judge of anything on the footstool he was a judge of that article.

I find that I do not know whether to use the masculine or feminine pronoun in my present description. When I say "she" I am thinking of the medium, and when I say "he" I am thinking of her "control." I could wish that the pronoun of common gender had been invented; this would include both Major Stanger and his widow, and would relieve a reporter of any embarrassment.

The company began to titter in a delighted manner, and to look at each other. Those who had had the pleasure of the gentleman's acquaintance before the battle of Bull Run explained that they should have known him anywhere. Those who had not previously met him said that it must be the major, for they could almost smell the cocktail, and if it had been an impostor they could not possibly have done that, now, could they?

Ferdinand Foster, the nephew, began to be afraid that his aunt would get drunk; he thought she showed symptoms of ordering another cocktail. He wished he knew what to do. He thought he would ask for a communication. He consulted with Mrs. Jarvis, who, in the bottom of her heart, was beginning to think they had had enough of the gallant soldier. Stanger had now relapsed into a silence that was only broken by an occasional "Gad." This remark was varied by whiffs of tobacco and sips of liquor. Rowena's face showed such unutterable disgust that young Foster was afraid she would leave the room.

Suddenly madame threw away the stump of

the invisible cigar. With her eyes fast closed she rose from her chair and stepped over to where Rowena was sitting. (Let me say here in parenthesis that, in justice to my narrative, I find that I must use the masculine pronoun part of the time.) Madame Van Benthuysen put his arm about Rowena's shoulders.

"Thunderin' pretty gal!" he said.

Rowena started up with a furious motion. At the same instant Ferdinand seized madame's arm and led her back to her chair, in which she sat down heavily.

The other gentleman here rose with some pomposity, and remarked that "the control was perhaps too strong for the medyum. It was sometimes the case that, when the conditions were specially favorable, the control was too powerful for the medyum."

He walked to madame, whose head was hanging down and mouth hanging open. He made a few passes across her forehead. She soon began to twitch again and to gasp. She opened her eyes, looked wildly about, and then resumed her natural expression. She asked if the major had been there.

All this time Rowena was standing, holding the back of her chair.

Before any one could answer madame's question, Ferdinand said impressively that he had been hoping to hear from his grandmother that night. He had come to the sea-ants in that hope.

Madame did not notice his remark. She looked at Rowena and asked if there was no one in the spirit land she would like to have a message from.

Rowena said that she had no one in the spirit land; none of her friends had died.

"No bond of affection in other spheres?" exclaimed madame, who was evidently preparing now for a very different control from the major.

It was plainly felt that it was an unlucky thing that Rowena had no friends who had "passed away." One little woman questioned her closely. Were her uncles and aunts all living? Grandparents on both sides? Cousins? Indeed! How singular! Suddenly Rowena remembered that one of her mother's sisters had died before the girl's birth. This fact she acknowledged under cross-examination.

"I was sure of it!" cried the little woman. She turned towards madame. "A precious aunt of our sister here has gone on into the flower spheres. Cannot we hear from that dear one?"

But Rowena was now inwardly almost frantic. She tried to be calm. She said she did not wish to hear from that aunt. She said she would not hear from her. She had never known her and

was not interested in her. She was very tired.
She thought she might better go to her room.

She walked to the door. They all looked at
her as the girls at the table had looked at her.

Ferdinand was so angry that it was with diffi-
culty he restrained himself from getting up and
kicking over his chair.

His aunt saw his face. She was very fond of
him. She rose hastily and followed the girl, who
was mounting the stairs rapidly.

"My dear," said the rolling, full voice, very
kindly, "do come back for a moment."

Everybody felt how honored that little chit
was. What did it mean?

Rowena came back, very tremulous and very
indignant.

"It is not polite to Mrs. Jarvis," said madame.
"Come." She held out her hand and Rowena
put hers in it. As she did so the woman drew
her nearer and whispered: "There will be a
slight c'lation by-and-by. Sometimes there is
charlotte-russe."

There was such a curious mixture of moth-
erly kindness and ridiculousness in the woman's
words and manner that the lonely girl was touched. She wanted to cry and to laugh.

"There! there!" whispered madame again.
"Did the major try to make love to you?"

"He was dreadful!" hotly cried Rowena.

Madame smiled complacently. " I knew the conditions were very propishuous," she said. "The major was always fond of young ladies. It was his way."

The two entered the room again. Young Foster sprang to see that their chairs were ready for them. Madame Van Benthuysen resumed her place by the card-table.

The gentleman who had made passes over the medium's forehead now again came forward. He said he was under influence. He said he should be obliged to ask madame to give him her hand. He requested that from himself and the medium there be a circle of joined hands formed. He was obeyed. While the circle was forming the gentleman became more and more agitated. He even uttered a smothered war-whoop, and betrayed symptoms of jumping up and down.

Ferdinand confidentially informed Rowena that old Thompson's control was Red Jacket, and that he guessed Red Jacket was coming on the stage, by the appearance of things. The speaker had kept out of the circle because he saw that Miss Tuttle was careful to do so.

It was evident that madame was not over-pleased at the advent of Red Jacket. She looked rather glum, and let her hand lie very loosely indeed in the man's clasp. As she told Mrs. Jarvis later when the c'lation began, " It was always very trying when that old Thompson put himself forward. There were lots of spirits crowding to be heard through her, but they had to go back to their spheres on account of Red Jacket. And Red Jacket was never interesting."

He was not interesting now. As Mrs. Jarvis said, "he hollered a good deal." He also had recurrent inclinations to engage in a war-dance, and was only restrained by the persistent and unyielding power of the circle of hands.

Mrs. Jarvis was always afraid her furniture would suffer at the hands of this control. She had not meant that Mr. Thompson should be present this evening, but he had come. She knew how very ready a hole was to appear in her worn carpet, and how the horse-hair of the chairs was longing to unravel itself. There were reasons connected with the charlotte-russe, too, why she would have preferred that this medium should stay away.

Her face was now very strained and anxious. Red Jacket had just jumped up and down on the poorest place in the carpet. If he did it again she was sure— Here her attention was diverted by the appearance of Madame Van Benthuysen. That lady was plainly going into her second trance. She sank into a chair; the circle was broken; Mr. Thompson gradually disposed of Red Jacket, and seemed to be quite sulky at the necessity for such disposal. Madame began to murmur something about "Flowers of heaven! Beautiful blooms of the spirit land! How beautiful!"

She went on in a low voice which charmed Rowena's ears. The words flowed in an easy tide, not meaning much, but seeming to the girl to mean something extraordinarily lovely.

Rowena sat spellbound, eagerly bending forward in her chair, her eyes on madame's face, which now did not seem so swarthy nor so "fleshly."

After a few minutes Mrs. Jarvis rose and noiselessly made a request of Mr. Foster, who immediately stood up and turned off the gas from all the burners of the chandelier.

Rowena was inexpressibly astonished. At first the room seemed entirely dark, but presently the light from a street lamp dimly relieved the absolute darkness. No one spoke, save that madame went on with her monologue. Rowena was somewhat subdued and somewhat alarmed.

Suddenly the girl was aware of the odor of flowers. The odor made her think of the perfume from the bed of pinks in the front-yard of the old house at home; and of warm summer days when the birds were singing in the apple-trees. She felt a stinging of the eyes and a hurrying of the pulses.

Something cool and soft touched her hands, which lay clasped tightly in her lap. The voice went on. Through the mist in her eyes she dimly saw Foster's figure moving towards the chandelier again. The monotonous voice of madame ceased. There was the crack of a match, and then the glare of the gas again.

All the people looked at each other; then they looked at Rowena, who perceived on her lap a bunch of white carnation pinks.

With an exclamation she raised the flowers to her face. As she did so she saw Foster's eyes upon her, and something in their expression made her think of Philip Barrett. She heard one of the women saying:

"They have been materialized," and she wondered what those words meant. She was still thinking of that bed of pinks at home.

It was not for some time that she understood that these were supposed to be spirit flowers. She was not quite clear whether they had been made by spirit influence out of the air of the room, and had accidentally fallen into her lap, or whether they had dropped there directly from heaven.

She did not like to think they had been procured by Mr. Foster; no one appeared to suspect him in the least, and he, after that first glance, looked so impressively innocent that Rowena gave up all thought, save that of simple gratitude for the blooms themselves.

Then there was the collation, which was brought round on plates by Mrs. Jarvis and one of her friends. There was cake, and bread, and cold ham ; but there were no " charlottes." Mr. Thompson spoke somewhat feelingly of the absence of this delicacy, and Madame Van Benthuysen said that she was always conscious of a great sense of sinking after being under influence, and charlottes removed this sinking more rapidly than anything she had ever tried. Rowena judged from appearances that perhaps ham might in time have an effect on that sensation in madame's internal organization.

Mrs. Jarvis seemed very much worried ; she explained that at the last moment her baker had disappointed her, and she had always found charlottes from every other baker to be rancid. This was a sweeping libel on other bakers, but the company seemed to accept it and tried to hide their disappointment. The little woman said emphatically that nothing in this world " took hurt " so quickly as charlottes. You might get a mess and think they were as good as they could be, and all at once they were taken hurt. She didn't know why 'twas they were so perishable.

Very soon after the collation the company

broke up. The person whom Red Jacket controlled went away in a very glum manner. Perhaps he had reckoned on damaging Mrs. Jarvis's
furniture more seriously, and was disappointed.

Madame Van Benthuysen took a very affec-
tionate farewell of Rowena. The great circular
again partially enwrapped the girl. Its owner
whispered that she was longing to know her
better, and that she should call on her upon the
first spare moment that the spirits gave her. She
spoke as if the spirits worked her very hard.

At last the street door had shut on the last
woman. Mrs. Jarvis looked so weary as she began to set back the chairs that Rowena stopped
to help her.

"I sha'n't have no chance in the morning," said
Mrs. Jarvis; "the reg'lars begin to come so early,
and I can't trust anybody else to take the tickets. I sh'll have to pick up and wash these dishes before I go to bed. I can't ask the servant-
girls to do it. Sometimes I think it don't pay
to try to have a good time. That old Thompson set me all on edge."

Rowena packed up the dishes and hurried
down into the kitchen with them. The water-
bugs scuttled away in battalions as she opened
the door. The small gas-jet revealed their hurrying forms. The country girl had never seen a
water-bug before. If they had not retreated be-

fore she could possibly turn her back, she would have run.

She had never seen any place so desolate as that kitchen was. It was so different from that cosey room where one might live in thrifty comfort in her own home.

The steaming water came out of the faucet onto the pile of dishes in the pan. Mrs. Jarvis, coming down after her labor in the parlor, found that she had very little to do. Her thin, worn face lighted up.

"I declare, you do know how to take hold," she said.

At last the furnace was attended to and the two women slowly mounted the dingy basement stairs. It was after midnight. Rowena went into the parlor for the bunch of pinks she had left there that she might work.

Mrs. Jarvis paused an instant to look at them. She glanced up in the girl's face, but Rowena was bending over the blooms.

"I should think a sight of them if I'd had them," remarked the elder. "'Tain't often the conditions are all right. I do almost think you'd develop first-rate."

Rowena hurriedly said "good-night." But before Mrs. Jarvis could lay herself down to rest, she must pull out the bed-lounge in the back parlor and arrange it that she might repose upon it. By that time the arrival of the earliest reg'lars seemed so near that Mrs. Jarvis again asked herself whether or not it paid to have a sea-ants, particularly if old Thompson were coming.

VI.

A LETTER FROM THE COUNTRY.

"WHAT did you have at the seance last night?" suddenly asked Miss Phillipps, as she paused close to where Rowena sat at work drawing.

"Carnation pinks."

"From where?"

"From heaven."

"Oh yes, I remember. We used to have flowers from heaven at our seances—if the conditions were right—if no frost had touched the conservatories of Paradise. What else?"

"Ham and bread and cake."

"From heaven, also?"

"No; from the butcher's and the baker's, at the corner."

Rowena suddenly laid down her pencil. She looked up at the woman near her.

"Miss Phillipps," she said, earnestly, "truly, where do the flowers come from?"

The girl's face was so earnest and innocent and eager that Miss Phillipps, who resisted very few impulses, felt that she deserved praise for

not yielding to the temptation to kiss that
face.

She said, instead, gravely and distantly, on account of her resistance :

"They are materialized."

Rowena was silent, and resumed her work.

This was her first lesson. She was told to do
what she could, with cardboard and pencils, with
a clay figure of a dog set up before her. Allestree
had told her that, technically, she knew absolutely nothing.

Miss Phillipps had tried to encourage her by
saying that Allestree had never told her even as
much as that. Technique was something that
might be acquired, but one had to be born with
talent. Of course, she would not be obliged to
do anything at all with that clay dog. Allestree did not care what he put people at, at
the first. He watched them to see what was in
them.

The girl flushed and paled as she heard those
words. Miss Phillipps went on with her own
work. She seemed to do exactly what she pleased
in the studio. She had now begun a cluster of
Indian-pipes, growing from a patch of grayish-
green moss, near a small clump of sweet-fern.
She said that any idiot could do flowers, after a
fashion; they would not be flowers, but people
would think they were, particularly if you labelled

them. She doubted if Indian-pipe was a real flower, however. Probably it was a kind of fungus.

There were a dozen or more pupils at work now in the great studio. They were very silent. Allestree, in a blue velvet jacket, was walking slowly behind them, pausing and criticising, then standing in the centre of the room and talking instructively, often using phrases of which Rowena was entirely ignorant. If she had dared she would have thought him verging on the grandiloquent; but he was so big, and had such a beard, that it was appropriate that he should be grandiloquent.

The girl felt very small and helpless and wretched, even though she had been admitted here.

" Elsewhere," Allestree had just said, in his magnificent baritone, "elsewhere they talk about art; in Boston they love it."

Then he walked up and down, his beard gathered in his left hand, his head bent. He had a large diamond on the third finger of the hand that held the beard, and every time Rowena looked up a ray from the diamond seemed to smite her.

He went on talking. He did not examine very particularly the work of his pupils this morning. He stopped oftenest at the side of the latest comer, but he made no remark. As Miss Phillipps had said, Rowena could do very little with that clay dog. She wondered why it had been given her. She drew and erased, and drew and erased, until she felt that there was no hope for her. The hour was nearly over.

Nobody talked, save that Miss Phillipps made one or two remarks concerning the folly of thinking that more than one or two in a century might learn to paint. The principal point, she said, was to find out who these one or two were; when that was discovered, the rest might put away their brushes.

Allestree listened to her with some deference, but he made no reply. Such a theory as that would not be good for the painting-master.

Miss Phillipps suddenly looked at her watch, and then left abruptly, not again speaking to Rowena, who felt unreasonably depressed, and who was very thankful when the lesson was over. One or two of the other pupils smiled at her and nodded, but the majority did not notice her. Why should they?

She passed by Allestree, who was standing with a brush in his hand before a winter landscape. He turned and watched her as she went towards the door.

Something made his face soften. He stepped quickly after her. The thought in his mind was that he should like to make a sketch of her as she walked. What he said was:

"Don't be discouraged. This is only the first lesson."

A flash of sunlight seemed to fall suddenly on the girl's face.

"Oh, thank you!" she said, hurriedly, and went out of the door.

The rest of the week was very dreary indeed, in spite of all she had to encourage her. She would only take one lesson a week at present. She had learned the price of those lessons, and they were very high. She did not see Miss Phillipps: she hardly saw Mrs. Jarvis. She stayed in her room most of the time and did light house-keeping. Sometimes, when she went out for a bit of butter or some rolls, she would walk up to a brighter part of the city and stroll across the Common, thinking it was a very poor make-believe of the country. Once, in a carriage that quickly turned the corner of Park Street, she thought she saw Miss Phillipps with a gentleman beside her, and both were talking animatedly.

The sight made the girl more gloomy than before.

The "reg'lars" seemed to be very faithful at their meals, and Mrs. Jarvis was faithful at her ticket-table in the parlor door-way. Rowena began two or three sketches, trying to obey, in the attempts, some hints Allestree had given. But everything was confused and vague. She wrote a long letter home: in the letter she talked of everything in the country, but of nothing in the city. She would have it ready for her Uncle Reuben, for whose coming she longed pitiably. But the day she expected him there came a blinding snow-storm. Now she did not know when to expect him. She would have sent her letter by mail, but she knew her father only went to the post-office when other business called him to "the Corners." The letter might lie there a long time.

On this day she received an epistle directed with such extreme care, on ruled lines on the envelope, that Rowena stared at it for some time before she opened it. She had never seen Philip Barrett's handwriting before. She was surprised at the warmth of her feeling when she saw his name. But the letter was far from being warm. It had evidently been composed under the influence of a determination to write a letter, let the consequences be what they might. It began, "Respected friend," and it was signed, "Respectfully, P. Barrett." It bore not the slightest internal evidence as to whom it was addressed.

The writer related every particular of a recent snow-storm; gave the depth of the snow on the level, and the height of the highest bank. He spoke in a tone of considerable awe of the fact that corn had risen three cents a bushel within
6

the last week. In this connection he stated that wharf-rats had done a good deal of damage in the corn-houses. It was not known how that kind of rats had come so far inland. The writer had shot one. He was still lame from this act, for his gun was an old one and had never been very good, and had kicked considerably.

All throughout the epistle the author of it never once wrote the pronoun " I," but always referred to himself as " the writer."

At the conclusion the writer hoped that he might receive an early reply.

Rowena smiled, with a quiver in her lip; then she laughed as she had not done since that time, so long ago, when she lived at home.

She wondered how long it had taken Philip to compose this document. She could guess how arduously he had worked at it. And he had not put in it a single item of interest. It was as if he had started with the idea that everything that the recipient might care to know must be scrupulously kept out. And he had adhered to this idea with perfect success. He had not even mentioned his horses and his two setter dogs, and he knew how Rowena liked them.

The average bucolic mind of New England does not consider the art of familiar composition as one that is needful in this life. The average bucolic mind is very stiff in the joints

when contemplating the perpetration of an epistle to a friend. There are instances, generally
among women, where one is able to "reel off a
letter jest as easy;" these instances are looked
upon as remarkable, and the person thus gifted
is not envied, but is thought to have an extreme
liability to shiftlessness. The connection between
shiftlessness and a certain "glibness" with the pen
is obscure, but powerful. Philip Barrett had not
this glibness, and he was not shiftless.

When this young man had finished this article
he read it many times, and copied it until the
words ceased to mean anything to him. He said
to himself that he would rather mow the whole
east meadow than to write another letter. But
he knew he should write another; he knew he
should feel so drawn to Rowena Tuttle that he
could not help it. The perspiration burst from
his forehead as he thought of another attempt
like this one.

It was wonderful, considering the power it required to inspire this man to write, that there
should be no sign of the inspiration in the result. It would have been as appropriate to
send that missive to old Uncle Lenas Torrey as
to Rowena.

Philip's mother furtively watched the progress
of the composition. Her son sat at his father's
old desk at one end of the kitchen. The first

evening he wrote something on a slate. After a great deal of "smooching" a few paragraphs were let to stand over night, and were carefully locked in a drawer.

Mrs. Barrett grew very weary as every evening this writing was continued. One night her boy seemed to be so nervous that she silently steeped some catnip and offered it to him. It was refused. She told Eudory Barnes that "if Philup didn't git his letter done 'fore great while she, for one, should go ravin' distracted."

But there came a day when the last copy was made and the thing was put in the post-office at the Corners. Then there was a reaction. Philip sat as if half alive over the cook-stove the next evening. He was picturing Rowena as getting the letter and reading it in the midst of luxury. He had a nebulous belief that all people in cities lived in luxury. This thought gave him very uneasy feelings concerning Rowena. If she forgot him, it should not be because he did not write to her. Some day he should go to Boston and call upon her. But not yet. He had not got round to it yet. He was resolved to do it, though. Meanwhile he could be thinking about it.

Rowena, sitting by her little stove, and forgetting that her tea was boiling on the lamp, wondered why Philip's unimportant words made her, after she had laughed, feel so much like crying.

She allowed her tea to continue boiling, and wrote to him. And again she said nothing about the city, but asked a score of questions about the country. She wanted to know how the dogs were, the horses, the sleighing, the evening meetings. She hardly knew what she did write, only that she was unusually moved. The home she had left seemed so remote, but so unutterably dear.

She heard the wind and the snow moaning around her window. She tried to drink her tea, but it was bitter. It seemed as if it must be very late in the evening. She looked at her watch, and found it to be half after seven. By this time her father and mother had been sitting a good while by the kitchen stove. Her eldest sister had become sleepy over her "sums" for the next day. The rest had gone up-stairs to bed in the "open chamber," where it was so cold, and where the snow would be sifting in.

Rowena started up and began frantically walking the room and wringing her hands. How was she to bear it? What should she do? Again she thought of the slop work and the straw, and perhaps Georgie Warner would speak to the committee about getting her a school.

"Ain't you at home?" This question was asked impatiently outside her door. When the door was opened, it revealed Mrs. Jarvis standing there. She said she didn't know how many times she had knocked. Then she added, with some awe:

"You've got a caller down in the parlor."

"It's Uncle Reuben! He has come after all!"

Rowena was going to rush by her hostess. But a hand detained her.

"'Tain't your Uncle Reuben. It's a lady. I guess she'll be tired of waiting."

"But I don't know any lady."

"It's that Miss Phillipps." Mrs. Jarvis could hardly have told why she always employed the demonstrative adjective pronoun in mentioning that lady.

In her mind at this moment two emotions were struggling — resentment because she had just been snubbed by that Miss Phillipps, and pride that this woman had chosen to call on one of her lodgers.

Rowena ran down the stairs. By this time she had acquired a useful dexterity in avoiding the holes in the stair carpet. As she went she wished she were not quite so glad of this visit. Her common-sense told her that it was a perilous attraction which she felt. Miss Phillipps fancied to take her up; by-and-by she would set her down. Entirely inexperienced as she was, Rowena had this fear strongly; she could not have told why; perhaps something intangible in the lady's presence itself gave it to her.

The visitor stood beneath the one gas light. The long, close fur cloak and small bonnet, the thick fluff of hair, thin face and vivid eyes, made a picture which Rowena's glance took in eagerly. She liked it. It stirred her pulses. It was new and strange. The lady was not pretty, but she had grace and lovely clothes and *savoir-vivre*, and, above all, she showed her interest in her new acquaintance.

Miss Phillipps stepped forward quickly. She held out both her hands. She wore gloves which fitted as Rowena had never known gloves to fit.

"I'm glad you have come," exclaimed Miss Phillipps. "Five minutes more in this room would have made me insane. Why do they always have the trial of Effie Deans in such a place as this? And that dreadful portrait of a 'Spirit Friend?' Won't you ask me up to your own room? However dreadful it is, it can't be so bad as this. You will have diffused an atmosphere in it. It isn't because the furniture is poor. I hope you don't think I care a rap for that kind of thing. I'm not so low as that. It is—" here the speaker gave a little shudder, "it is the feeling of it—as if it had held so many commonplace people in it, and they had all left their impress. I suppose the walls are covered with invisible portraits of dull folks. You know there's a theory that the walls of houses retain pictures of every scene which has been enacted within them. Some day something will be discovered that will bring out all those impressions. It will be an awful day. I've been looking into that. It is quite bewitching."

As she talked in her careful, rapid way, Miss Phillipps continued to hold Rowena's hands closely. Now she looked at her keenly, curiously.

"You have been crying," she asserted. "What a pale face you have! And what a curious little quiver in the right side of your upper lip. You would cry again, now, if I were not here. Please do take me to your room. If I stay here I shall be very disagreeable; and I feel as if I could be quite the reverse if you will make the conditions right."

Rowena spoke for the first time. She said "Come," and the two went up the stairs.

Miss Phillipps cast a rapid glance about her. She sighed.

"This is better. Any place where you stayed would be better. I'm going to take off my cloak. I told the driver not to come for an hour. Do you mind unfastening this upper clasp? Thanks."

Rowena put the cloak on her bed. Her guest did not seat herself immediately. She stood, slowly removing her gloves.

She looked almost continuously at the girl, and her face grew softer and softer, until Rowena

wondered why she had ever thought it disdainful.

"Will you allow me to kiss you?"

The question was unexpected, but it should
not have been so, as it was in keeping with the
expression of the speaker's countenance.

Rowena smiled and came nearer. The lady's
lips touched hers gently. Then she sat down in
the little rocker close to the bit of a stove, and
Rowena drew up a chair near her. How very
strange it was to the girl. She knew that her
guest had spoken truth when she had just said
she could be very agreeable if the conditions were
right. Evidently they were right. Although Miss
Phillipps sat silent for a few moments, she seemed to radiate satisfaction and enjoyment; when
a person produces such an effect that person is
usually agreeable.

Miss Phillipps's feet were stretched out towards the stove; she leaned far back in her chair,
her hands, which to-day were ringless, hanging at
each side of her. Although she sat in such a
position, she could not look indolent.

Rowena waited for her to speak. At last she
made this remark:

"We are weeding out our Browning Club."

VII.

SOME SALESLADIES.

ROWENA tried to look interested in the fact that a Browning Club was, as her father would have put it, "bein' wed out," like a bed of parsnips. The country girl could not have believed it possible that that great man's name could be mentioned so flippantly, not to say disrespectfully. She did not know how to make any response to such a remark. She did not know that in Boston nothing is so great but one may become familiar with it.

She had once belonged to the book-club which led a struggling and doubtful existence in Middle Village. She had then taken out a volume of poems called *Men and Women.* She had read "One Word More" with ardent eyes and beating heart. She should always remember the author's name.

"They were getting insufferable," went on Miss Phillipps. "Several of them pretended to understand him. I decided to form a new club and drop those creatures."

"Why shouldn't they understand him?" asked Rowena, calmly. "I think he is real easy."

Miss Phillipps suddenly sat upright. She turned a confounded face towards her companion.

"Well, you are delicious!" she said, more slowly than she usually spoke.

Rowena reddened with anger. For some reason she did not find it agreeable to be called delicious.

Miss Phillipps seemed to wish she had some kind of a glass with which to examine the girl. At last she became conscious of what she was doing. She withdrew her eyes. She laughed, noiselessly, but with intense enjoyment. She put out her hand and took Rowena's reluctant, cold fingers.

"Do forgive me!" she said, pleadingly. "But what can I do before one who finds Browning 'real easy?' What have you read of his?"

Rowena told her, stiffly.

Miss Phillipps suddenly became warmly caressing, and the girl's anger melted before that manner.

"I always think of what Jo Gargery said about reading, 'When you do come to a J and a o, how interestin' readin' is!' When you do understand Browning, he is divine. And what should we do here in Borston without him? We can have a go at Psychic Research, Christian Science, and no end of things; you think you can see your way into them, but there's always Browning. No, we couldn't get along here without him. Mr. Herndon said at our last meeting that he didn't think life would be worth living when he was once convinced that he understood 'Sordello.' There would be no object. I don't feel precisely like that, but still—"

Miss Phillipps's gaze came back from what she would have called "the all-where," and rested on Rowena for a moment in silence. Her next remark was so unexpected that the girl felt helpless before it.

"I have the dearest little seal-skin jacket," said she. Then she added, "but it doesn't fit me across the shoulders."   ·

As she spoke her eyes rested on Rowena's shoulders in an interrogative manner. She went on. "How did you get a dress to look like that? It is really chic. That must be a miraculous country from which you came. Who is your dressmaker?"

Rowena laughed.

"Marthy S. is the dress-maker in our deestrict," she answered, with a drawl. "She can cut coats and pantaloons, too. She's bound to git a fit."

The girl laughed again, and then grew suddenly sober, as the picture of the lonely, snow-covered fields, the narrow sleigh-track, the melancholy houses, came vividly to her mind.

As for Miss Phillipps, she felt as if she had an entirely new specimen of humanity before her; and she exulted accordingly. This was not her idea of a country girl at all; and yet she was keen enough to take in, as if it were a delightful odor, the innocence, the utterly unsophisticated nature with which she was now in contact. She also felt that she had discovered Rowena, and she had a pleasing and decided consciousness that, so far as the girl proved interesting, she was in some sense not only the discoverer, but the author, the proprietor.

"Marthy S. not only got a fit, she got more—an air—in this instance," said Miss Phillipps. "She ought to come to Borston. If there is anything Borston needs it is style. She has brains enough. If we can only combine brains and style, we shall have the most delightful result in the world. Now I know a New York woman if I only catch a glimpse of the hem of her gown; there's a something about that hem that tells the whole story. But the chances are that the owner of the gown has never heard of Madame Blavatsky, or if she has, she thinks madame is some kind of a milliner."

Miss Phillipps resumed her lounging position

in the very unadaptable chair furnished by Mrs. Jarvis to her top-story lodgers.

Rowena blushed as she said that she did not employ Marthy S.; she cut and made her own dresses. She found she had kind of a knack, and so she had saved some money that way.

"Oh," said the other, "it is what you call a knack, is it? And that soft hat you wear? Is that a knack, too?"

"I guess 'tis. Do you like it?" timidly.

"I adore it."

There was silence after this. There was a somewhat beatified expression on the elder woman's face as she rested her head on the back of her chair. Perhaps she explained this by saying, presently, with a deep drawn breath:

"I knew I should like your atmosphere."

Rowena had never had her atmosphere praised by any one else, and she felt somewhat confused. She did not attempt any response.

In a moment Miss Phillipps said:

"Did I mention my seal-skin jacket?"

"Yes," responded Rowena, wonderingly. She even thought there was some embarrassment now in her guest's manner.

"May I show it to you?"

"Why, of course," still more wonderingly.

Miss Phillipps rose.

"How do you ring here?"

"We don't ring; we go out in the hall and scream down the stair-way. It is like calling down a well, for nobody hears."

"I certainly shouldn't scream down this stair-way just for amusement."

Rowena had opened the door, and the two stood in the gloom of the upper hall. Miss Phillipps thought she could feel her garments becoming saturated with the combined odors of the place. She wondered what her lungs thought of the air, and how long they would take it in before, in the language of the day, "they went on strike?"

"Where is the jacket?" asked Rowena, innocently.

"In a box in the carriage. Can't you get a servant to go out and get it?"

The girl disappeared down the stairs. The lady left standing there felt a sense of unreasonable disappointment at Rowena's alacrity; and when the girl came back with the box in her hand and a sprinkling of storm on her face and hair, Miss Phillipps was suddenly very cold indeed in her manner.

Rowena felt the change instantly. The two entered the room in silence. Miss Phillipps took the jacket from the box. She said it was too loose for her; she had a curiosity to see it on Rowena; and she helped the girl to put it on.

An irrepressible exclamation of pleasure came from Rowena as she saw a portion of herself in the little mirror. Miss Phillipps seemed to stiffen still more.

"Would you like to wear it?" she asked, icily.

Rowena turned towards her with a radiant face.

"I would like to wear one like it," she said, eagerly; "it fits exactly."

She seemed loath to take it off.

"It will give me pleasure if you will wear this one," remarked Miss Phillipps, in a stately manner.

It was now Rowena's turn to stiffen. She removed the garment and laid it on the bed.

It was odd that Miss Phillipps should look relieved. She had brought the jacket expressly that she might give it to this girl.

"Will you not oblige me," she asked. There was something almost dramatic in the way in which Rowena turned to her companion.

"You meant it as a present?" she inquired.

"Yes."

"Thank you very much. I'm sorry you thought that way of me. I have—a shawl—" here the proud young voice began to tremble. "I know it isn't pretty, but it keeps me warm, and I've got to wear it. I sha'n't take your jacket. I do wish you hadn't offered it to me. I do wish—"

Here the voice stopped altogether. Rowena stood very straight. But she hung her head.

Miss Phillipps put her hands behind her. She seemed to put them there to be sure that they should not touch Rowena. It was plainly no time to touch her now.

"The moths will eat the jacket," said she, smiling.

"Let them," responded the other, still with her head down.

"But I also am not without New England thrift; I hate to see things destroyed."

No answer. Rowena gave a side glance at the jacket. Then she turned her back more decidedly upon it.

"What if I should leave it here while you think about it?" suggested Miss Phillipps. "Where is the disgrace in your acting as a sort of package of camphor and tobacco in regard to this fur jacket? Consider yourself merely as an animated anti-moth packet."

"No."

A deep sigh followed this monosyllable.

Miss Phillipps's spirits were rapidly rising.

"Why not oblige me?"

But Rowena did not feel that she could command her voice sufficiently to try to say anything.

The owner of the garment now rapidly returned it to the box. The odor of camphor was very strong in the little room.

Miss Phillipps went close to the girl. She looked at her a moment in silence, and the high-bred, somewhat mocking face softened a good deal.

"Since you will not wear that, will you do something else for me?"

Rowena lifted her eyes to the face before her. She clasped her hands and said, fervently:

"Oh yes!"

"Will you join our new Browning Club?"

The moment she had made this request Miss Phillipps did not know how she was going to live up to it; but she would not be so weak as to withdraw it.

Rowena's first emotion was one of thankfulness that she could know something further of the man who wrote "One Word More." So she said "Yes," with effusion.

But when her visitor was gone and she sat alone, and the wind and sleet beat on the window, she wondered at herself that she had obeyed any such impulse. Of course she could not go. She wished she had never seen Miss Phillipps. It was horrible to have a glimpse of lovely things. No, she would not go. What a wretch she must be, that she could not help thinking of that jacket! She found it so difficult to put it out of her

mind that she resorted to the desperate remedy
of going down into the parlor to see Mrs. Jarvis.

The supper hour was long since over. She
was greatly astonished to find Ferdinand Foster
and three or four girls engaged in shrill laughter. Mrs. Jarvis was not there. Rowena made
a quick backward movement and would have retreated up the stairs, but one of the girls ran forward and caught her hand, crying out in the
sharp voice that one hears so much in the east
wind here — perhaps it is the east wind which
makes the voice:

"Now don't you go to runnin' right away, 's if
you was too good to stay here. Lemme introduce ye to the rest. We've got an off night.
'Twas so horrid stormy we finally concluded to
stay here 'n' try high jinks in this old parlor. Mr.
Foster got Mrs. Jarvis to say we might have the
room. I'm sure I d'know what we should do
without Mr. Foster. There ain't hardly any gentlemun that's ever at leisure. They're jest bound
up in business. We ladies have to git along with
precious little of gentlemun's society. I tell the
other ladies I guess I shall go West. They say
ladies are so scarce out there that the gentlemun
crowd up to the deepo when the trains come in,
and jest pop the question as the ladies step out
the cars. So you see they're engaged before they
leave the deepo. Now that's what I call an in-

terestin' country to live in. What's Borston to that?"

Shrieks of laughter greeted these words, which were so rapidly spoken that they almost seemed one long word of many syllables. Rowena could not help laughing, though she felt shy and indefinably disgusted. She reproved herself for being disgusted. These were working-girls. She was a working-girl herself.

She was introduced quickly by the girl who had appointed herself her guide, and who was attired in a black dress so tight that it was only by a constantly renewed miracle she could breathe. She had a small face, that made Rowena think of a weasel her father had caught in a trap set near a chicken-coop. She gave the country girl an impression that she would say something decidedly vulgar the next time she opened her lips, and she was continually opening her lips. But there was a kind of good-humor about her which prevented Rowena from positively hating her.

One of the company patronizingly asked if Rowena were learning to color photographs, and if she were going to be paid by the hour or the piece, advising strongly that she try to be paid by the piece. She herself had tried the "touching-up business," as she called it. She had tried 'most everything. She was now in R. H. Black's dry-goods. She'd about as lives be a saleslady 's anything. If you felt cross you could snub folks no end.

Here some one across the room, who had been examining the speaker with the greatest interest, suddenly shouted:

"Mattie, seems to me you've been trimming your bangs, ain't you?"

The girl who had been talking with Rowena quickly put her hand to her forehead.

"No, I ain't trimmed um; I ain't combed um half out. I was kind of saving um; I didn't know but somebody might ask me to the theatre to-night."

Here she gave such a look at young Foster that there was another universal shriek of laughter. Some one clapped her hands and cried:

"That's right! Give it to him!"

Foster looked irritated. He had looked so ever since Rowena's entrance. He did not come near her, but he appeared to find it difficult to keep his eyes from her face.

He was standing by the mantel in front of the register. His face was almost sulky. His hands were thrust far down in his pockets. He was wondering what kind of an ass Miss Tuttle would think he was. Perhaps she would not think of him at all; that would be worse still.

"Ain't there no other gentlemun coming?" asked a new voice. "I thought you said you had two friends that were coming to-night, Mr. Foster. I might just as well have stayed in my own room and had a nap."

Again every one laughed. There were peals of laughter apparently every time anybody spoke. Mr. Foster grinned. He replied that perhaps his friends had found a place where the girls were prettier.

In the hilarity excited by this remark the door-bell rang violently. The girl who had welcomed Rowena ran to open it. She admitted two young men in rough ulsters with the great collars turned up above their ears. A burst of laughter immediately filled the narrow hall.

Mr. Foster remained in the parlor. He turned towards Rowena, who was looking on in a kind of benumbed attention.

"I s'pose you think we're a set of wild beasts, don't you, Miss Tuttle?"

She smiled at her questioner. He appeared so depressed that she wished to cheer him. And it was quite remarkable how much cheered he was immediately.

"Only wild beasts don't laugh," she said.

He laughed now so delightedly that she was surprised. He became animated.

"A set of idiots, then," he said. "But we're really rather of a good sort, only not deep, you know. Don't you go and run away from us.

We ain't going to have a sea-ants. Major Stanger won't be here. My aunt's got a sea-ants up on Harrison Avenoo to-night, and I guess the major 'll be there. Anyway, he won't be here. Do stay; we fellows have ordered some oysters 'n' ice - cream to be brought in about ten. I wanted awfully to ask you, but I couldn't get a glimpse of you, for all I've tried so hard. I thought my aunt would have called on you before this. She was quite taken with you. She said " — here young Foster stopped to laugh again—" she said she thought you'd develop into the best medyum there was in Borston. And that is saying a good deal, for Borston is just stuffed with medyums. What ain't Christian Scientists and Buddhists, and all that, don't you know, are medyums. You've got to be one or the other if you live here. Which shall you choose ?"

Ferd Foster's appearance had become so cheerful, not to say happy, that he did not look like the same youth Rowena had seen when she first came down-stairs that evening. She did not say she would stay, but she lingered until the oysters and cream were brought in from " a caperer's " on Washington Street. This was Foster's joke, and it was laughed at with an abandon that renewed itself and began afresh ; and when Foster said gravely that he knew they'd find the oysters good, for he was very particular as to who capered to him, the girl with the wasp waist went into such convulsions of laughter that Rowena was really alarmed. She had known one girl at home who, in the neighborhood parties, had become celebrated as a "trainer," but secretly Rowena was convinced that this Miss Martin was the greatest trainer she had ever seen.

It was after eleven o'clock before the salesladies went to their lodging-rooms. These rooms were close by. Poor, little, chilly rooms they were, too. The young men walked away with them. Rowena could still hear them training, as they went along the narrow sidewalk; their piercing laughter came back to her on the cold air.

Mrs. Jarvis came out of the back parlor, where she had just pulled out her folding-bed and spread the sheets on it. She looked so weary that again Rowena helped her "trig up" the parlor.

The landlady did not seem to think there had been any unusual noise. She made the startling remark that young folks would be young folks, and she s'posed they must take their good times when they could get 'em.

I hope no one will think any the less of Rowena if I record that the last clear image in her mind before she fell asleep was the image of herself in that seal-skin jacket.

VIII.

PHILIP'S VISIT.

ROWENA was hurrying down Tremont Street. She had been up since six o'clock. At twenty minutes after that hour she had drunk her coffee and eaten a baker's roll. If she had been at home she would have given the roll to the chickens. It had never been good, and now it was stale. Having eaten it, it remained not only heavily present in the digestive tract, but in her mind also. She kept thinking how poor it had been, and how good her mother's hot biscuit always were. She thought she must need some thoroughwort or sarsaparilla, now it had become spring. She felt, as her uncle Reuben had said, "kind of pindlin'."

On his last trip to Boston he had attempted to bring in a squash-pie as an offering from his wife to Rowena. The attempt had resulted in the most disastrous failure. When it arrived it was "jest pig's victuals," as he said, ruefully. It was eventually gathered up in the public cart which stopped at Mrs. Jarvis's.

But the home-made sausages, and the "souse," and the gingerbread from the Tuttle homestead came in good condition. Rowena cried over them, even over the souse. She ate them thankfully. They were gone now. But the letter accompanying them remained. It was a joint production of all the Tuttle family. By this statement I do not mean that it was long. These people could not express themselves with pen and paper. The most terse statement of facts was presented. One sister announced that it was believed that "Georgie Warner had got a beau. He worked winters in the factory at Middle Village. He had red hair. He was called a likely man."

Rowena thought this might account for Georgie's remissness in writing. Another sister wrote that "Philip Barrett's gray horse had died of the botts."

Rowena could repeat the entire epistle from beginning to end. She was doing so as she walked now. She had come out for a long tramp before it was time to go to the studio. As she approached that place she was thinking of her mother's counsel that she "should be sure and not work too hard."

With her mother's words in her mind, and with their effect in her face, making it soft and tremulous, she paused as an object fell at her feet. She had not been noticing anything around her. Mechanically she picked up the object, a short, cane-like whip, such as she had seen in the hands of horseback riders. At the same moment a voice above her said:

"Oh, it is Miss Tuttle! Thanks," for Rowena gave the whip into Miss Phillipps's hand. "Don't dismount, Keats; there is no need."

Now Rowena saw the two riders, Miss Phillipps and a gentleman, who lifted his hat while he looked at the girl rather more markedly than was necessary for the polite salutation of a stranger.

As for the country girl, still quivering with her thoughts of home and the beloved ones there, the sight of these two, mounted on glossy horses, dressed scrupulously, with the indescribable air of wealth and leisure and refinement, the sight of them was like a picture, not as if they were living human beings. Rowena felt remote. She hardly responded to Miss Phillipps's words.

The two rode on. Again the gentleman raised his hat. Miss Phillipps waved her hand and smiled.

Something bitter and rebellious rose in Rowena's heart. It was still there when she reached the studio, and she was late. Breathless, flushed, she walked in among the class of young ladies. The model was already posing. Allestree was moving up and down the long room after his manner, with his big beard held in his left hand.

Hurriedly Rowena took her customary place. She arranged her brushes. She looked at the model, who was a young girl with arms and bust undraped that they might be studied and copied.

Rowena's hands trembled. She had walked too far and too fast, and she had not yet become accustomed to the idea of a model—at least, not a model like this. The girl's face, as she stood there, with all those eyes upon her, was as inexpressive as a bit of wood.

Allestree sometimes walked up to her and slightly touched her neck or arm as he spoke of some muscle that must be well brought out. Every time he did so Rowena shrank and her lips quivered—that is, at first. After a time she forgot that her model was alive. The spirit of her work had entered into her.

It was not until the class broke up and she was putting on that despised shawl that she again thought of the two she had seen on the street. She envied them. As she descended the broad marble stairs, which no longer overawed her with their grandeur, she said, aloud :

"Yes, I envy them. How mean I must be to feel like that !"

She was recalling the man's face, which bore

a slight family resemblance to that of Miss Phillipps. There had been a monocle in the right
eye, and Rowena strongly resented the effect
it gave. She had childishly wished to strike it
out. She did not believe there was any need
of it.

Miss Phillipps was getting careless about coming to the studio. Her group of Indian-pipes on
their moss-bed had not grown of late.

Instead of going to her room, Rowena wandered across the Common and out towards the
Public Gardens. She was senselessly irritated
and despondent. Her art was drudgery.

She did not see that many people turned to
look back at her. The ugly shawl could not hide
the springing grace and style of her carriage. She
did not see some one coming hesitatingly down
the walk that led from the direction of the State
House. She had just decided in her own mind
that the gentleman with Miss Phillipps was the
same she had once seen in the lady's carriage,
when a hesitating, almost deprecating, voice said:

"Ain't that you, Roweny?"

She paused suddenly, the color leaving her face
in the excess of her surprise. It was almost as
if she had looked in at the old kitchen at home
to hear that slow, nasal tone.

She held out her hands, impulsively.

"Oh, Philip!" she exclaimed.

Young Barrett could now hardly speak from sheer joy at the greeting given. Of course he was sufficiently masculine in his appreciation of himself to feel that it was her gladness at seeing him. He could not suspect that all the happiness and freedom of her old life seemed to come back to her at sight of him.

He held her hands. He stammered out rapturously that "he'd ben kinder 'fraid she wouldn't know him."

"Know you? Do you change so rapidly out there?"

She withdrew her hands. She laughed gayly.

Philip laughed also. The two stood looking at each other. The people who hurried by glanced smilingly at them.

Philip had bought a new suit of clothes for this visit. He had bought them at Middle Village, and he had been very proud of them. They bagged where they should have been snug, and were snug where they should have bagged. But he did not know it. Where he lived a new suit was a new suit. The art of dressing is not in the least a complicated affair in remote New England towns.

At last Rowena bethought herself and moved on. Philip walked by her side. He was still smiling broadly. He had never been so happy in his life before. He was glad he had given all that time and labor and those forces of life to writing that letter. He would write another, if necessary. He guessed he could write a letter if he "sut out."

When the two reached the Tremont Street pavement a horseman came slowly close to the curb. It was the man who had, a few moments ago, ridden by with Miss Phillipps. He again looked seriously at Rowena, with a kind of intentness that made Philip ask, quickly:

"Who in time is that feller?" And the girl only said, "I don't know." To which her companion remarked "that he hoped he stared hard enough."

The mere sight of that horseman had somehow quenched Rowena's pleasure in meeting Philip. She tried to keep her face set to its first look. She made an attempt at a sprightly interest in Philip's talk. She asked questions, and did not wait for the answers. But Philip only remembered her greeting.

He said he was going to stay in Boston until the next day. He announced proudly that he had engaged a room at a hotel on Brattle Street, where his uncle Tim used to put up, and he guessed it was a first-rate house. He had left his bag there. He wanted Rowena to go over to Bunker Hill with him that afternoon. In the evening they would go to a theatre. He didn't spend money very often. He guessed he could afford to lay out a little once in a while.

So he talked on eagerly, his honest face earnest, his eyes constantly seeking those of his companion.

He came into the house on Hudson Street. He had already been there once, and had been directed to the studio. Now he sat in the parlor while Rowena went to her own room. He thought the parlor was beautiful. He found no fault with the atmosphere, as Miss Phillipps had done. It seemed to him a fascinating luxury that the apartment should be heated by a furnace. The picture of the "Spirit Friend" on the wall was wonderful, though he could make nothing at all of it, it was so vapory and undefined. But he supposed it was a work of great art, and he hoped Rowena would some time be able to copy it.

He did not dare to walk about in the room. He sat with his feet very near together and his hat on his knees. He inhaled the odor of onions that came up through the furnace and from the basement.

Mrs. Jarvis, in her palm-leaf, wadded morning-gown, came to the door and inquired if he had called to buy meal tickets. At that question, so unexpectedly put, he could hardly tell whether he wanted meal tickets or not. He had in-

tended to disport himself among the various res-
taurants, for he had all the countryman's appreciation of restaurant food.

But now he had a confused sense that it might
be in some way a favor to Rowena to buy tickets
of her landlady. He said he guessed he'd take
some; how much was she selling them for?

It ended by his purchasing twenty-five tickets
for three dollars. As he paid for them he incidentally remarked that he had come in to wait for
Miss Tuttle. At this Mrs. Jarvis said, with some
animation, that she thought, and Madame Van
Benthuysen also thought, that if she would only
let herself be developed Miss Tuttle would make
one of the finest medyums in Borston.

As he heard this, Barrett felt his hair rising
and his hands growing cold. He had heard of
mediums. He knew they were liable at any
moment to find their affinities. What if Rowena
should find her affinity?

He did not dare to say that he hoped Miss
Tuttle would not be a medium for fear Mrs.
Jarvis might, in some mysterious way known
only to spiritualists, cause the girl to be developed at once. Barrett's ideas about spiritualism
were something the same as the generally received notion regarding Salem witchcraft. One
never knew who would next be declared a witch.

So great was his perturbation at the thought

of Rowena's becoming a medium that he would not speak to the girl on the subject when she presently came down-stairs and took a seat near the register.

He sat looking at her yearningly. He now saw she was pale. He also told her she was "kinder pindlin'." She laughed at that. He said "he s'posed she could paint 'n' dror 's good 's anybody now."

At this she laughed again, now with some bitterness. She was learning every day how difficult excellence is, and how much drudgery there is on the road to it. And she had also heard a great deal of talk about the folly of women in trying to be artists. But she could not give up her hope. Once in a while her brush would, apparently of its own volition, make a few strokes that gladdened her like an inspiration. She meant to toil for the time when there would be more such strokes. Once Allestree, looking at her work at such a time, had said in his autocratic way:

"Miss Tuttle, you will do. You have the touch." Then he had added, as if to himself: "if only the confounded feminine limitations do not interfere!"

Miss Phillipps had heard these last words. She had left her easel and walked to Rowena and put her hand on her shoulder as she looked at the picture. She had pressed the hand caressingly.

"Don't believe his heresies," she had remarked. "There are no more insurmountable feminine limitations than masculine. In fact, art is sexless."

"It should be, but it isn't." With this rejoinder Allestree had seized his beard and walked away.

Rowena drank in all this talk and all these influences. She had moments of thinking. She was very wise indeed.

She felt wise now as she sat opposite Philip Barrett. She wished he had not procured a new suit of clothes. All his natural dignity was hidden by that dreadful Middle Village suit. And he looked at her so persistently. Worse than that, he somehow gave her the feeling that she had given him the right to look at her thus.

What had she written him? And what had been her manner just now when she had met him? What made him hold his hat as if it were a basket of eggs?

"I s'pose you've ben to the monument a good many times sence you come to the city, ain't you?"

Barrett put this question rather timidly. He was sensible of some change in Rowena's manner, though he could not account for it.

"What monument?" she asked.

He looked surprised. For him there was but one monument. He had told his mother he was coming to Boston principally to see it.

"Why, Bunker Hill, of course."

"No; I haven't been there," indifferently.

"I wish you'd go with me this afternoon."

He was greatly cheered by her consent. He took her to Copeland's for dinner. He was surprised that he had so little appetite in the midst of such luxury. In the horse-car ride to Charlestown he gave a detailed account of the case of botts which had resulted in the death of his gray horse.

In this recital Rowena showed a good deal of interest. She now became animated and asked many questions about "all the folks." Barrett eagerly replied. He showed an almost pitiable desire to say what would please her. He watched her. He felt there was something in her face he had never seen there before. He wondered what it was. He thought it was miserably foolish in her to study art. Women needn't study art. Of course she would get over it in a little time. But, meanwhile, he found it very hard to bear. She could paint and draw well enough now to make pictures to hang up in the sitting-room. In Philip Barrett's mind it was the very pinnacle of excellence in art to be able to hang something of your own in the sitting-room. He did not understand Rowena, but he meant to do so.

They climbed wearily to the top of the monument on Bunker Hill. When they stood there Philip found it more interesting to look at his companion's face than at the view. But she looked at the view. It was not a clear day. There was an uncertainty of outline that made the outlook peculiarly lovely and which stirred her soul. She uttered one or two exclamations of delight. Barrett had the discretion not to respond. He thought it was "very pretty" to see everything spread out so before them. He would tell his mother about it.

Rowena clasped her hands. The wind blew her hair about the soft hat. Her eyes were radiant.

"That must be the Charles," she said, in a low voice. "And see, where the high light strikes that shore! What a delightful effect!"

Philip's spirits rose again. He wondered what she meant by "high light," but he had a kind of feeling that the beauty of the scene was something he had procured for her. This feeling gave him immense satisfaction.

After a while they crept down within the towering dungeon and emerged into the world with other people again.

Philip pleaded with the girl to go to supper

with him. They rode back to Boston and strolled rather aimlessly along the streets. Rowena
was getting very tired, but Philip did not think
he should ever be tired. He said as much, rather
ardently.

At last they had supper in a place where the
waiter girl was in convulsions of laughter with
another waiter girl. The effect of this hilarity
was such as to dampen Barrett's spirits a great
deal. He could not shake off the idea that they
were laughing at him.

It did not occur to either of these people that
a chaperon was necessary. It was a simple and
ordinary thing that they should go about thus.

Evidently Philip had laid out a plan of battle
to which he would adhere. He was so grieved
when Rowena said she thought she would not go
to the theatre in the evening that she relented.

He went somewhere and returned about seven,
while Mrs. Jarvis's later reg'lars were coming in.
He had orchestra tickets for the Hollis Street
Theatre. He said he guessed one play was the
same as another, but some one had told him the
Kendals were about the thing. Did Rowena
know what the Kendals were? He would have
been perfectly calm and unsurprised if she had
answered that they were a species of gorilla.

Now that the name was mentioned, Rowena
remembered that she had heard Miss Phillipps

say to some one in the studio that there was a
certain strong charm about Mrs. Kendal's acting, but that she could wish the woman did not
"pose so much at virtue" in her private life, it
was wearing—it was protesting too much. No
one suspected her of being otherwise than exem-
plary.

The girl had felt a cynical ring in the voice
that spoke those words, but she had not in the
least understood them.

Now at mention of the Kendals a swift interest sprang up in her mind. She forgot her fa-
tigue. She had never been to a theatre in her
life; neither had her escort. She ran up-stairs
for hat and shawl. When she descended she
met Ferdinand Foster and his aunt, Madame
Van Benthuysen. The latter was in her voluminous circular. Her voice was as rolling as ever.
She threw one arm and part of the circular over
Rowena's shoulder and kissed her. She said
she and Ferd had come to call on her. She had
really been so occupied with one spirit and another for the last week or two that she had not
had a minute of her own.

Inside the parlor Philip was waiting, and heard
these words. He also saw the impressive manner with which Foster looked at Rowena. The
country youth was much struck with the glory
of Ferdinand's necktie and watch-chain. He ex-

perienced a sinking of the heart as he saw them. His own tie was a narrow black ribbon. He wished he had worn the silver chain that belonged to his watch; but he had left it at home lest it might tempt pickpockets.

He stepped forward in time to see Rowena smile at Foster. Almost at the same moment Foster said he and his aunt were going to get up a little party to hear the Kendals and have a supper afterwards. Of course Miss Tuttle would be one of them.

As he finished speaking Foster swung himself round in his big, rough ulster, and saw a fellow in the parlor glaring at him.

IX.

AT THE THEATRE.

YOUNG Foster glared back at young Barrett in the narrow hall on Hudson Street. As they looked the natural antagonism of one to the other sparkled in their eyes.

Rowena hastened to introduce them. She felt that there was thunder in the air, but she could not guess why.

The two men nodded ferociously at each other when she mentioned their names.

Madame Van Benthuysen shook hands in her large, cordial way with Philip. She told him she hoped he would stay over and come to their sea-ants on Harrison Avenue that evening.

As Philip did not know what a sea-ants was he was not alarmed, and only thought this lady was very kind. Her fur circular and her black satin gown made as much impression on him as the necktie and chain of her nephew. His heart sank at the knowledge of what fine friends Rowena had. But did he not desire fine friends for her?

He could not keep his eyes from Foster.   He
was sure that if that person's ulster had been an
inch longer in the skirt or an inch higher in the
collar he could not have refrained from throwing him out into the street.   He vaguely heard
Madame Van Benthuysen talking about a theatre party, "The Queen's Shilling," balcony, supper.   What did it mean?   Was Rowena going
with them?

After a few moments Rowena turned to Philip
and said she was ready to go.   Foster was triumphant and smiling.   He repeated two or three
times that they'd have no end of a jolly evening.   He insisted on shaking hands with the girl
before she left; he bent over her hand with a
good-natured swagger.   He seemed delighted
when she laughed at his rattle.

When she and Philip were in the street she
did not notice that her companion was sulky.
But when they reached the theatre the great interest and novelty of everything absorbed them
both.

There was a pleasure to Rowena in being gently hustled by well-dressed people.   She liked
the semi-darkness, the mingled odors of perfumes.
They both thought they had never seen any
man so wonderfully well dressed as the usher
who came sliding up to them to take their tickets and conduct them to a seat.   Even before

the curtain rose, the gilding, the upholstery, the whole aspect of the place, together with the murmur of music from the unseen orchestra, gave Philip a strong impression that it must be wicked to be there. Anything so pleasant and so unlike anything he had ever known would necessarily be wicked. He recalled with a pang of conscience that the evangelist now preaching in Middle Village had said distinctly that theatres were works of the evil one.

In an awed whisper he gave this information to his companion. But Rowena laughed; she was much further from Middle Village than Philip was. She did not care what the evangelist told those people. Her face showed her pleasure. There was not an attraction, from the dome downward, that did not appeal to her artistic nature with a tingling sense of joy. The strains from the hidden instruments thrilled her. This was her first night. You whose first night in a theatre is involved in the mists of the past, do not laugh at her. How much would you give could you change places with her?

Very soon Philip lapsed into a bewildered silence. All through the evening he was more puzzled than entertained.

They were so near the stage that when the curtain rose on the first scene of the " Iron Master " Rowena felt a shock of almost disillusionment; she saw so plainly how the people were made up, and the pitch of their voices startled her. But when, in a moment, Claire came in, refreshingly unmade up, speaking theatrically, Rowena gave a long sigh of delight, and from the first sight of the heroine she gave herself up to fervent love and admiration for her. She went through with Claire with all her love and all her misery. She longed to rush upon the stage and fling her arms about her. When the husband went out to fight the duel and the wife beat upon the locked door and shrieked in her agony, Rowena sprang up in her seat and made a frantic effort to get away, crying:

"I must let her out!"

The curtain fell. Rowena shrank back to her place and covered her face with her hands. Everybody looked at her. Philip did not know what to do. He did not know but that he ought to aid in the effort to unbar that closed door whereupon Claire had struck in her suffering.

Among those who looked at Rowena when she thus stood were two people in a box at the right. A man and woman sat in front, Miss Phillipps and her cousin, Keats Bradford. The lady's white silk cloak was on the back of her chair; her slightly tinted gown was high in the neck and long in the sleeves, but still it gave with perfect effect the impression of evening dress. She had flowers in her hair and in her hand; her pale face was a little flushed with interest, and her emerald-colored eyes were very brilliant; her lips even more than usually red. The thick fluff of hair, the straight brows, the keenly alive face, made it reasonable that her companion should have deliberately decided that she was in great good looks to-night.

He had just said that Mrs. Kendal was satisfying, that she never overdid things, when he saw Rowena standing there palpitating with the emotion roused by the scene before her. He half rose, as if he would shield the girl, and he paused abruptly in a sentence.

Miss Phillipps followed his glance.

"Rowena Tuttle!" she exclaimed.

The young man breathed a long breath of relief when Rowena sat down and people stopped gazing at her. He polished his glass on his handkerchief and put it to his eye.

"Is she alone with that man?" asked Miss Phillipps. She had, in spite of her unconventional spirit, strict ideas on some topics.

"Not exactly alone," was the answer, "as there are several hundred people with her."

The lady did not reply. She bent forward, and aimed her glass at Rowena so persistently that the girl presently seemed to feel it focussed upon her.

She removed her hands from her face and made a great struggle for composure. She was in terror lest Philip should speak to her. She did not think she could bear the sound of his voice just now. But when she saw the lady in the box she experienced a glow of pleasure. Miss Phillipps removed her opera-glass the instant she had caught Rowena's attention. She gave her a glance that warmed her, but reproved her as well. It is not good form to show emotion in public; but Rowena had forgotten herself. She became painfully crimson.

"If the play were not about over I would send you down, Keats, to bring her here," said Miss Phillipps, autocratically.

Presently the play was done. Claire had been lugged rather unnecessarily to the front of the stage, and it was discovered that the bullet had not injured her seriously; everybody was going to be happy ever after; the handkerchiefs were put away; people bustled towards the door. Rowena tried to wake from her illusions. Philip said he guessed the theatre must be finished, for all the folks were going out.

The two moved with the rest. As they stood on the sidewalk, Miss Phillipps and her cousin came out and entered a carriage. As she sat down, and while Bradford had his foot on the step, the lady saw Rowena and her friend standing near in the lamplight. She beckoned imperatively. People usually obeyed her before they considered whether they needed to do so.

Rowena advanced, with Philip behind her. She vaguely saw the shining white expanse, the low waistcoat and white tie, beneath Bradford's overcoat. He had a pair of gloves in his hand. He fell back with a deferential movement as she approached—but not far back.

"Did you like it?" asked Miss Phillipps, taking the girl's hand closely.

"Oh, I—" began Rowena, when the other bent so near that her breath was on Rowena's face, as she whispered, hurriedly:

"You did not remember that I told you not to show all you feel in your face. You are like a poor little lamb, with no shield nor buckler, and wolves all about. Dear, good-night!"

As she let go the hand she said, aloud:

"Don't forget, it is the Browning Club to-morrow night."

Rowena was very pale as she walked away. She knew her friend was right, but she was hurt, all the same.

"I heard what you said," remarked Bradford, as the carriage rolled on. "Don't you know it is her greatest chawm that her face does miwwor her feelings. You're all wrong."

"I'm right," said the other, positively. "I'm going to protect that girl."

"By all means, pwotect her," sinking back on the cushions. "I'll help you pwotect her."

Miss Phillipps glanced up at him.

"Do wait, Keats, until I ask for your help. And can't you pronounce the letter R?—you are so ridiculous! I suppose you think it is English?"

"To be widiculous? I know it's English."

The next day Rowena experienced a sense of relief when she thought that Philip was going. She was somewhat weary. She told herself that it was all that new suit of clothes. She liked Philip best in his overalls and "jumper." There was a simplicity and manliness about him when he was on his own farm.

His face was very long when she was called down to the parlor to bid him good-bye. He gave her the twenty-five meal tickets he had bought of Mrs. Jarvis. He said he hoped Rowena would use them, for it must be kind of lonesome to take one's victuals all by one's self. When she hesitated he explained that "they wouldn't do him no good, 'n' she might 's well have 'um."

He sat uneasily, holding his hat more than ever as though there were eggs in it. She waited. She had exhausted herself in conversation the day before. There did not seem another thing to say. Something was evidently resting heavily on his mind. At last he got up and stood before her.

"It's not time to go yet," she remarked.

"No, it ain't."

He put his hat on his head, and then, remembering his manners, he took it immediately off, and instantly converted it again into a receptacle for eggs.

"Does that feller git up them sea-antses himself?" he asked, sternly.

"What fellow? Oh, you mean Mr. Foster? No; it is his aunt who is the medium."

Rowena tried not to laugh, remembering how short a time it was since she herself had any knowledge of seances.

Philip suddenly changed his ground.

"I s'pose," he said, "that the feller is very agreeable."

"Oh, I don't know him any—scarcely."

"Be you goin' to the play with him?"

Rowena rose. She was going to reply angrily, when she saw how miserably unhappy her companion was. There was a look in his eyes that went straight to her heart.

"I don't know," she said, feebly.

Philip put his eggs desperately down on the floor. His face was very pale and drawn. He kept his glance upon her a moment in silence.

He wondered blindly what there was different in her; what was it? Then he said aloud, and indignantly:

"It's jest livin' in Borston! You can't live in a thick settled place 'n' be jest the same. I ought to er known it. I ought to er known it!"

His big brown hands shut hard.

"Philip," said the girl, very gently, "don't let's quarrel."

He looked at her so wistfully that she hung her head. She felt that she could not keep the tears back much longer. In some inexplicable way it seemed to her as if in being hard to Philip she was ungrateful to her old home and all in it that she loved.

"I ain't goin' to plague ye," he said. "I wouldn't plague ye for all the world. And I c'n wait. I guess I'll be goin' to the deepo. What sh'll I tell um to home for you?"

Rowena's gratitude made her almost effusive. She was so thankful—for what she hardly knew.

A short time later she stood at the door and saw Philip go down the street. He did not look back, but walked sturdily on.

She went up to her own room and sat down. Immediately her thoughts of Barrett grew warmer. She did not know that when that Middle Village suit was removed from her eyes the wearer of it assumed a different aspect.

Then it occurred to her that this evening she was going to the Browning Club. There was a tumultuous quickening of her pulses at the thought. She was conscious of a shy longing to see this new kind of people. And the prospect of meeting Miss Phillipps was always a distinct pleasure to her.

Does not one who has spent much time in Boston remember the large women with gray curls looped up each side of their large faces? They are ruddy, with a comfortable consciousness of living in Boston diffused through their redundant personality. They always look, as you see them walking on Charles or Beacon Street, as if they had just descended from an intensely Bostonian coupé. If you peer into that coupé you will see the last *Atlantic* in the pocket; perhaps, also, a pamphlet on Nationalism, or a sketch of Confucius as he was, not Confucius as we have thought he was. Somebody in Boston has found out the exact facts concerning him, and to Boston is given the discovery.

The horses in the shafts will not have any check-rein nor any curb-bit, for this kind of woman does not confine herself to theories. She has a very soft spot in her heart for animals, for everything that is abused or that does not have its rights.

Besides *The Atlantic* and the pamphlet, there

is often also in this carriage a dog. He is sitting calmly superior to mere "foot folks." He is a well-groomed King Charley or Yorkshire. Never a fox terrier for this kind of woman. The dog meets your eye with a gentle pity in his expression, a pity for you because you are not a Yorkshire sitting in a coupé belonging to a person like his mistress. He knows there is a sketch of Confucius in the vehicle with him, and he respects himself accordingly. He wags his little stub of a tail if you approach. He is perfectly affable. He knows his position too well not to be so. He is like his dear friend and mistress; it is a good thing that, incidentally, he has wealth, but he is sincere in his conviction that wealth is not to be compared with culture and blood. He probably has clear ideas as to what Buddha preached; anyway, his eyes are bright enough to have such ideas. He is not going to fall into Nirvana when he dies; he confidently expects that in the future state cats will be provided for him to worry.

There were three of these gray-haired ladies in the rooms of the house on Charles Street where Miss Phillipps lived. They put up tortoise-shell-handled eye-glasses and looked at Rowena when she entered, not impertinently, but with the questioning air they gave to everything new.

There were young ladies, also, in the rooms, a few men. There was a murmur of talk and low laughter.

The rooms themselves were, in reality, almost simple, but they seemed magnificent to Rowena. There were low fireplaces, in which smouldered heavy oak logs. There was no gaslight, but queer old lamps shed a mellow light. To this country girl everything appeared in. keeping with Miss Phillipps.

It was enough for Miss Phillipps that she was Miss Phillipps; enough for her house that it was hers.

This hostess when she chose could do some kind things with a grace that made them more than kind.

An almost tender light came into the green-tinted eyes as their owner saw that black-clad, slender, hesitating, and altogether charming figure in the door-way.

Ignorant and unsophisticated as Rowena was, she could not be awkward. There is a hesitancy like that of the flower stalk which hardly knows from which direction the breeze is coming.

A man standing at the end of the first room, with his hands behind him, rather carelessly listening to one of the gray-haired ladies, saw Rowena the instant she appeared. He saw, also, a swift suffusion of gladness go over the girl's face as she met Miss Phillipps's glance. That lady walked quickly to her side and took both her hands in an impressive welcome. This welcome was meant to show her own feelings towards this stranger, and to set an example.

"Who is this that Vanessa has taken up now?" asked Mrs. Sears, with her glass up.

"Weally, I don't know," was the answer from the gentleman whom Rowena had seen riding with Miss Phillipps.

Though he said "weally," he did not look like a man who would say it. Though he had a glass in his eye, he did not look like a man who would have a glass in his eye. There were several incongruities about this individual.

"Vanessa is sometimes very trying," went on Mrs. Sears, as their hostess led Rowena to an old lady who was sitting near the fireplace holding a screen between her face and the heat. "She takes up a person or a theory with ardor, and then—"

"She puts them down with ardor," said the gentleman. "It doesn't hurt the theowy, a theowy can stand it; but a person doesn't like it, naturally."

"That girl is something quite out of the ordinary," said Mrs. Sears. She had removed her glass. Now she lifted it again. "She is—why—"

searching for fitting terms of praise—" she might almost be one of Us."

The man smiled.

" Where did you say she came from ?"

" From Middle Village—or thereabouts."

" But I thought you didn't know anything about her."

" I don't. But I know Vanessa has secured a girl from Middle Village with whom she is now infatuated."

An inarticulate murmur was all the response to this remark.

Miss Phillipps was now bringing Rowena to Mrs. Sears.

Keats Bradford thought he had never admired his cousin Vanessa as strongly as he admired her now. You would have said from her manner it was a princess whom she was conducting, choosing to do this rather than wait for the people to be conducted to the princess.

It must have been a very hard-hearted elderly lady indeed who could resist the desire to greet Rowena warmly. There was about her the penetrating grace of unsullied youth, and nothing is more attractive to age. Moreover, her own indescribable and individual personality, which, perhaps, Miss Phillipps called her " atmosphere," which is born with one, and which makes one beloved or shunned, this was markedly winning.

Mrs. Sears took the girl's hand in her thick, cushiony palm.

"So you have come to study Browning, Miss Tuttle? It is an occupation which never fails."

The words did not mean very much, but they were said with the accompaniment of the kindest smile. Mrs. Sears made room for Rowena on the little couch where she sat.

The young man near her instantly came forward and asked to be presented. The girl remembered him very well, but she tried not to let her face show that she did so. She was beginning to heed the advice Miss Phillipps had given her concerning a reticence of countenance.

The gentleman did not address her, save a few words after his greeting. He continued to converse with Mrs. Sears. But he had the ability to let the girl know that she was in his thoughts; that, though he talked to Mrs. Sears, it was that Miss Tuttle might hear him.

Presently he looked at his watch. He said it was almost time for him to read that selection. He walked away a few steps, then he returned and said to Rowena:

"I have the honor to open the meeting. I shall not wead the extract I selected yesterday. I want you to hear something else the first time you come. I shall ask you what you think of it, so please pay attention."

X.

AT A BROWNING CLUB.

> "Rivals, who...
> Tuned, from Bocafoli's stark-naked psalms,
> To Plara's sonnets spoilt by toying with,
> As knops that stud some almug to the pith
> Pricked for gum, wry thence, and crinkled worse
> Than pursed eyelids of a river-horse
> Sunning himself o' the slime when whirrs the breeze—
> Gad-fly, that is."

"Oh, no; I never go anywhere without my little geological hammer, not even down Washington Street. My hammer and one of Ibsen's plays. One never knows, don't you know, when one may find a specimen; and it is so interesting to get a new one — and then, if I have to wait a few moments in a shop, don't you know, if I have Ibsen with me, I don't lose any time, you see."

"It must be quite dreadful to lose any time," said Mrs. Sears, with an indulgent smile that had a suspicion of irony in it. "Did you bring your hammer with you to-day, Miss Sargeant? You might pound away at 'Childe Roland.' I think it would bear all your strength."

"Is it to be 'Childe Roland' again to-day?"

"Yes."

The owner of the geological hammer tossed her head. She had that type of weasel-face which Rowena had noticed in one of the sales-ladies that evening at Mrs. Jarvis's. She did not look any more refined. She was painfully alert. She tossed her head again. She said for her part she was tired of that poem, if it were a poem. Why didn't they drop Browning and take up Ibsen? She was told that this was not an Ibsen club. She flung her bits of hands out and her bangles tinkled. She gave sharp glances at Rowena, who still kept her place by Mrs. Sears.

"I went out to Diamond Hill the other day," she began. "Rhode Island, you know. Really a curious place; might be a thousand miles away. Natives don't know anything; stand about in overalls—aren't they overalls, Miss Tuttle?"

"They are overalls," replied Rowena, her clear voice contrasting with the chipping noise this Miss Sargeant made in talking, "also jumpers," added Rowena, with a slight laugh.

Miss Sargeant stared an instant. Then repeated: "Also jumpers. Thanks. They stand around in these things, and look at you till you feel their eyes boring like gimlets. I could feel them in the back of my head. They fry their beefsteak there, too—in lard. And they expect you to eat pickles with it — large cucumbers steeped in vinegar."

"Did you get any specimens, Miss Sargeant?"

"Magnificent rough amethysts. I should think there must be a strata of these amethysts somewhere there, a strata upthrown by some subterranean action. Shouldn't you say so, Mrs. Sears?"

The elder lady had shrunk perceptibly at the word "strata," which was spoken as if spelled "strarter."

"Don't you think, Miss Sargeant," she said, with some emphasis, "that you might better use your geological hammer a trifle less, and look into the subject of singular and plural formations a trifle more? Pardon an old woman's advice."

The girl stood an instant in vindictive silence. She was very fond of that word "strarter."

She walked away.

Mrs. Sears glanced at Rowena.

"Do you think I was harsh, my dear?" she asked. "But then, I know Della Sargeant so very well. If I can be the means of teaching her to say stratum when that is what she means, I shall have done an excellent thing. I may confide to you that her friends are very weary of what she does not know about geology. Ah, Mr. Bradford is going to read. Some one usually opens the session by reading a selection. I'm glad it's not Mr. Herndon, for he never reads anything but 'Sardello.' He says we don't meet to discuss what we know, but what we don't know. To tell you the truth, Miss Tuttle, I have reached that age when I like to talk about things I understand."

There was such a whimsical look on the speaker's face that Rowena could not tell if she were speaking as she felt. Before she could make any attempt at a reply some one rapped on a table which held many different copies of the poet they were to study.

A stout man with a very large bald head and English whiskers said in a heavy voice that Mr. Bradford had kindly consented to read for them.

"That is Mr. Herndon," said Mrs. Sears. "He lives to struggle with things he doesn't comprehend. The moment he sees a subject clearly, that moment it ceases to interest him. Odd, isn't it?"

Instead of standing there by the table, which was very far away from the couch which held Mrs. Sears and Rowena, Mr. Bradford sauntered down the room until he came to a window near that couch. He stood in a nonchalant attitude, with his back to the light. As a reader in select companies he was rather of a lion, but this girl from the country could not know that, and she would not have respected him any more had she known it.

The young man began:

> "O lyric Love, half angel and half bird,
> And all a wonder and a wild desire,—"

His voice was not specially musical, but it interpreted the words with a force as if fire ran along with his utterance. Rowena felt her heart burning; every syllable clove its way to her soul. Had there been a human being who could write such words as those? And he had loved. And he had lost. But he could not despair.

She did not think of the reader at all. She did not know that after those two first lines his eyes had left the book and were, though not openly, watching her.

Miss Phillipps thought she had never heard her cousin read so well. There was not the least art about it. He was simply letting himself be borne on by the lines. Even she forgot herself in listening. And she forgot Rowena, until just as Bradford came to the last. Then, as she saw the girl, a cloud came over her face. It was cruel to play on a sensitive and unsophisticated nature in this way. And yet Miss Phillipps knew that she had never loved Rowena as warmly as at this moment. The young face gleamed transparent—the eyes seemed reaching out to heaven itself.

Silently Miss Phillipps glided round behind her guests. Again she was conscious of that desire to protect Rowena.

There was an instant murmur as the reader's voice ceased. Rowena heard some one whisper, "Dear!" close behind her. She knew the tone, and interpreted it.

She so quickly recovered her ordinary look that her friend's estimate of her rose greatly.

Miss Phillipps did not address her again; she made some remark about Browning as a poet of the emotions.

Mr. Herndon rose to read a portion of "Childe Roland."

Miss Sargeant said, when the portion had been read, that she judged that the passage was so "electrically stimulating" that it was not needful to know clearly what it meant.

Another young lady, in an almost man-like severity of costume, said that what had most struck her in this author was his "formative energy." He created, he energized: he said "Let this be," and straightway it was. He was, more than any one who had come before him, a kind of god.

Miss Sargeant now said earnestly that he was, above all else, Bostonian. There were some natures so endowed that, though they had never seen Boston, they were yet Bostonian. She considered Browning so endowed.

Rowena heard in amazement. She saw Miss Phillipps's lips fold tightly together. She saw the smile on Keats Bradford's face. Mrs. Sears turned to her with an impatient movement.

"I wonder why it so often happens," she said, "that people with the least mind are so ready to let us know their limitations."

Mr. Herndon said ponderously that he believed the question now before the club was the question as to what the dark tower was. It was asserted positively that "Childe Roland to the dark tower came," but what was the tower? Symbolical, of course. But symbolical of what?"

"'The round squat tower, blind as a fool's heart,'" recited Miss Sargeant.

"'Built of brownstone'—you see they used brownstone—'without a counterpart in the whole world.'"

This girl sat by a table holding a volume of poems in her hand. She was perfectly sure of herself. She never meant to give up this club. She knew they could not get along without her, and she loved to throw light. She knew that her own ideas were clear.

Rowena rose and walked to the table, taking up one of the copies of the poem that lay there. By this time she was so interested that she had forgotten her surroundings.

She resumed her seat and read the poem for the first time, experiencing a strange, baffled feeling, and that kind of admiration awakened by power, even when it is obscure power. She read the poem again, her face lightening. She looked up with flashing eyes. She leaned forward. She fastened her glance on Mr. Herndon.

"It is glorious endeavor—sticking to your ideal—it is keeping on with the fight—dauntless—courageous—it is—oh, how hard it is to find words!"

A deep red covered her face. She suddenly sank back, almost against Mrs. Sears. But she kept her fiery glance on Mr. Herndon. Before that gentleman could speak Miss Sargeant, in her voice like the rattling of dry sticks, made this remark:

"That is very well. But what is the tower? We are losing sight of the main subject. A brownstone tower—we know that much."

Mr. Bradford advanced from the window where he had remained since he read from *The Ring and the Book*.

"Miss Tuttle is wight," he said.

He looked over at the girl.

"Of course we are glad to know about the brownstone," bowing to Miss Sargeant. "We have Mr. Browning's explicit word for that. I cannot help wishing we could know if there was a bay window, or anything of that sort; but we can only judge by internal evidence. I think from the text it was a plain tower, without any such window. What is your opinion, Miss Sargeant?"

Miss Phillipps had been standing with one hand leaning on a table. She walked forward. Her face did not often flush, but it was flushed now.

"How silly we all are," she exclaimed, with that air she had of being permitted to say anything. She went on rapidly, and with the manner of one who gives an ultimate decision.

"It is just a gloomy phantasy—the sporting of a strong mind. We take it seriously, we try to find what is not there."

She spoke nearly ten minutes, carried on by a kind of strenuous earnestness that often took possession of her when she spoke at any gathering of people. She showed a power which revealed to Rowena why women concerned in any public meetings usually tried to have "that Miss Phillipps" one of the speakers.

After she had ceased, Rowena cared very little for what followed. She hardly listened to it.

10

She sat quietly by Mrs. Sears, and heard vaguely all the talk.

Mr. Bradford came and stood behind the couch where she sat. Sometimes he bent over and said a word or two in an undertone to Mrs. Sears. It was always said so that Rowena might hear it. He always glanced at her. He found it extremely pleasant to stand there, and he liked very much to do things which he found to be pleasant. This girl had gratified a somewhat exacting taste the first time he had seen her on Tremont Street, with her portfolio under her arm. He had been rather surprised at himself that he had remembered her face and figure so well. Young women were usually very flat and unprofitable. They made eyes, they put inflections in the voice, they sidled; they pranced, or they were demure, not because they really were so, but because they chose to appear so. And they were, some of them, painfully intellectual; they kept one's mind strained up to the verge of insanity; they never let one down.

This young man, lounging behind the couch where Rowena sat, was conscious of a delightful feeling of refreshment. He did not speak to her, because it was enough to be there, knowing that he might address her if he chose. Since it was a Browning day, it was appropriate that he should think of that much-quoted line from Evelyn

Hope about "spirit, fire and dew." He even went further than that. His mind suddenly seized upon,

> "There's a woman like a dew-drop,
> She's so purer than the purest."

The whole song murmured itself over, and the sense of it tingled in his veins and diffused itself deliciously through him. He had not thought he was impressionable; certainly he had not been so in these later years. But then, with an inward smile, he told himself a man did not often meet a woman like this one. The city life spoiled women; so did country life spoil them, in its way.

When at last the club broke up and the members were departing, Miss Phillipps detained Rowena.

"Will any one be frightened if you don't go back to that Hudson-Street place to-night?" she asked.

"I don't suppose they will even know whether I'm there or not," was the reply.

"Then, of course, you'll stay. Keats, there is no need for you to linger."

"You are awfully careless about hurting a fellow's self-esteem, Vanessa," said the man. "I don't want to go yet. I want to sit by this fire a minute. I'm so weary of Miss Sargeant and that other little weasel of a girl."

He flung himself down and looked into the fireplace, where the log was now a big coal.

The two girls were standing. "She was just like a weasel," responded Rowena, eagerly; "and there's one at R. H. Black's—a saleslady; only one is a member of a Browning Club, and I guess the other isn't," she laughed. She was in great spirits, better than at any time since she had come to Boston. "Miss Phillipps"— she turned with an impulsively fond movement towards that lady—"you said you had been weeding out your club; why didn't you weed out Miss Sargeant?"

"Yes, why didn't you?" from Bradford.

But Miss Phillipps did not choose to reply. She sat down and drew Rowena to her side. She was silent. She looked thoughtful, even slightly troubled. But she was very tender towards the girl near her. She did not notice her cousin. Still, he was content not to be noticed by her.

"I intended to take Miss Tuttle down to what you call that Hudson-Street place," he said, after a silence. "I thought she might give me privately some of her views of us to-night. But, since I am not to be useful that way, I can be simply ornamental—and comfortable, here."

He stretched his feet towards the fire and thrust his hands into his pockets.

Rowena looked at him with a laugh in her
eyes. The glance was returned. Then she turned her own gaze towards the fire. She felt the
pressure of Miss Phillipps's arm about her shoulders, and the touch gave her happiness. She was
beginning to lose that fear she had had of fickle-
ness in her friend's regard for her. Just now she
had no fear of anything. She had never been so
much at home with any one. Looking back now
she told herself that, of course, she had been at
home with Georgie Warner. But Georgie, though
she loved her, "had not known things." And
then, one slightest touch of Miss Phillipps's hand
was more of a caress than a vigorous hug from
Georgie. Rowena had not known there were
such people in the world as this new friend of
hers. She did not know now but that the world
was full of them, only they did not live out near
Middle Village, or the Corners, or on Hudson
Street.

The silence continued so long that Bradford
rose. There was still humming over in his mind
"There's a woman like a dew-drop." He had
been dangerously near repeating those words
once or twice as he sat there.

"Keats, I do wish you would go," said his
cousin.

"Thank you," he responded, "I don't think I
can stay any longer this evening, though you

urge me so kindly. Good-night, Vanessa. Good-
night, Miss Tuttle."

He held out his hand, a slender hand like that
of his cousin.

He strolled to the door. He came back.

"Are you weally going to pweside at the Psychical Wesearch to-morrow, Vanessa?"

He looked down at the two, but saw only the
younger face with its pure outline and shining
eyes.

"Yes, I am."

"Oh, well," shrugging his shoulders, "they told
me I must pweside if you concluded not to do it
yourself. I wanted to get myself up a bit, don't
you know."

He stood an instant. His cousin did not glance
at him, or she would have been startled by something in his face.

"Your sweetness is very long drawn out to-
night, Keats," she said.

"I know it. I'm weally going now. Good-
night," to Rowena, who bent her head in silence.

This time the young man lifted the curtain at
the entrance, and presently the outer door shut
heavily.

When he reached the pavement he straightened himself and stood still a moment, looking
vaguely about him. Then he smiled. Then he

gave a long, shrill whistle, and started to walk briskly down the street.

In the room he had just left the silence continued for some time.

Rowena, within her companion's arm, looked happily into the fire.

"Was that a country friend with whom I saw you at the theatre?"

The question came like a kind of blow to the girl. She moved uneasily.

"Yes," she answered.

"Are you going to marry him?" Rowena now sat upright.

"No; no, indeed!" she almost cried out.

"He means to marry you. He has a good face; he has also a strong will."

Rowena's heart contracted. She hurriedly rose and stood before her questioner.

"Why do you talk to me like that?" she exclaimed.

Instead of replying, Miss Phillipps said:

"You should not go alone with him to the theatre."

Rowena blushed. "Not go alone with Philip Barrett?" she said. "Not go alone with Philip?"

The eyes of the elder woman were searching the face before her.

"Perhaps, without really knowing it, you love him," she said.

Rowena turned indignantly away from that gaze.

The words opened bewildering possibilities to her. Did she not know herself? She recalled Philip's face as he had said "he didn't want to plague her," and "he could wait." The recollection almost melted her. She could at this moment recall nothing of all that in his appearance which had irritated her. She was only conscious of his noble unselfishness and his devotion.

"I don't think I love him," she said.

Her face took on a wistful expression. She looked down at her companion.

"Don't you know when you love a man?" she asked.

Miss Phillipps laughed slightly. She reached forth and drew the girl down by her again.

"According to the old-fashioned stories," she replied, "we knew when we loved just as we knew when lightning flashed before our eyes. But we have changed all that. Now we are not sure of anything."

Rowena pressed closely. She timidly lifted her face so that her friend could look down into her eyes.

"I think I'm almost sure of one thing," she whispered. She put her lips to the warm palm of the hand that had drawn her near.

"Of what?"

"If I felt to a man as I feel to you I should know I loved him."

Miss Phillipps's eyes flashed through a sudden dew. She smiled as few ever saw her smile.

"My darling!" she said.

XI.

GEORGIE.

WHEN Rowena went back the next day to her attic on Hudson Street she began to work ardently. The old inspiration and love of her art burned within her. She sat at her easel, and her brush made no false move.

And yet it did not seem to her that she was thinking so much of what she was doing as of the Browning Club, and of her friend with whom she had breakfasted. That was ideal life. She smiled as she held her brush over her palette, choosing her colors. She chose the right colors this morning.

She rose and walked away to view her work.

"If I might always drink coffee from a cup like that," she said aloud, laughing like a child, "and always have Miss Phillipps opposite me as I drank it, perhaps then my work would be worth while. Can it be that I am a Sybarite after all? Can Hiram Tuttle's daughter, who was 'sut on goin' to Borston,' be a Sybarite?"

She laughed again.

She approached her canvas and put a few more touches on the face she was sketching.

She had believed that the longer she stayed away from home the more strong would be her desire to return to it. She was surprised to know that the precise opposite might be true.

This thought passed rapidly through her mind, and immediately was superseded by memories of the hours she had just spent in Charles Street. She recalled that Miss Phillipps had quoted to her some words of George Eliot, that "No list of circumstances ever made happiness."

That must be true. Just now Rowena felt that she could be happy anywhere, that

> "God's in His heaven,
> All's right with the world."

Outside the day was balmy and delightful. The fire in the cylinder stove made her room too warm. She knew that in the orchard at home the bluebirds and "Harry-wickets" were singing; that robins were hopping about in the yard; the frogs peeping in the meadow back of the house. Also, sure sign that spring was well advanced, men were coming up from Taunton with new herring for sale; it was now so late that the herring would be cheap enough to buy.

As she thought of all these things her heart did not ache as it had done at such memories;

she was conscious only of a gentle and not unpleasant sadness.

She worked all the forenoon and into the
afternoon, only pausing to eat the chop she
broiled over the coals.

She had actually forgotten that this was the
day of the week when Uncle Reuben usually
came in.

There was a sound on the stairs. A voice
which she did not recognize, but which was
familiar, said:

"I guess I c'n find my way somehow."

Rowena opened her door. Somebody in the
gloom shouted:

"There she is now!"

Somebody sprang at her, and hugged her and
kissed her.

"It's Georgie Warner!" cried Rowena, pulling
the new-comer into the room and shutting the
door.

"Of course it's Georgie Warner," exclaimed
the owner of that name. "I've been calc'latin'
on this for more'n a month, but I wanted to surprise ye, 'n' I guess I've done it. I told mother 's
soon 's the roads got settled I sh'd git a chance
to come in with your uncle Reuben; 'n' here I
am. How be ye, anyway?"

Although Georgie taught school, and could
"talk grammar" when it was necessary, she did

not consider it necessary now. She fell back upon the dialect that slipped so easily from her tongue.

She looked sharply at Rowena as that girl replied that she was perfectly well, and "awful glad" to see Georgie.

After a few moments of incessant talking, Rowena bethought herself that now would be an excellent time to use one of the meal tickets that Philip had left with her. Mrs. Jarvis's dinner extended from twelve until two. They had just time. Georgie tried not to be impressed with the luxury and profuseness before her. It was a strange thing to have a servant come and mention several kinds of meat and fish to her and wait for her to choose. At home, if they had baked sparerib they had no other meat. This variety was princely. But Georgie was not so overcome but that she ate heartily. Rowena sat by her and was hospitable.

There were not many now at the table; but before the two girls left, while Georgie was eating cranberry-pie, and wishing she knew how the lemon-pie tasted, a young man came swaggering round the room and sat down opposite. He seemed so very glad to see Rowena that Georgie was greatly impressed. Of course it was Ferdinand Foster. He was bedecked with his chain; his necktie to-day was not pink, but it was ornate. He had a daffodil in his button-hole.

He eagerly told Rowena that he had secured first-rate seats for to-morrow night—first row in the balcony. His aunt had put off all the spirits, so as to make a sure thing of it. They'd have the jolliest kind of a time. If Miss Tuttle did not think it wicked, he would order some champagne for supper. Would she let him order it?

"Oh no; that would be foolish," said Rowena. "Don't order it."

She rather liked Mr. Foster; he was so good-natured, and such a rattle; she need never take him seriously.

"Just as you say, of course," he answered; "but there's nothing a bit wicked about champagne."

Georgie's amazement grew with every moment. Her last morsel of pie nearly choked her.

When the two were safe up-stairs again she looked solemnly at Rowena.

"I s'pose," she said, "that is your beau. He dresses beautiful, 'n' he seems real pleasant; but—" She did not know how to go on. She went to the small looking-glass and patted her hair. Rowena watched her with eyes full of laughter. Georgie had on her best blue cashmere gown, with imitation Valenciennes about the throat and wrists. Marthy S. had cut this gown, and it bound about the chest and fettered the arms, like all of that lady's fitting. But Georgie was conscious of being very much dressed in it; she had even wondered what Mr. Foster thought of it.

Now, standing at the glass, she wondered again, as she went through small, pigeon-like movements.

"But what?" asked her friend.

"Why, I must say I was as surprised 's I could be when the gentleman mentioned that wine. For my part, I've always considered champagne as the wickedest kind of wine there is. I guess all them horrid, mean women you read about always drink it, don't they?"

"I don't know."

"Mebby you drink it, Roweny?"—in a hushed whisper.

"No; I never tasted it in my life."

Georgie's face showed her relief. She gazed intently at her companion.

"Yes; you be changed, somehow. Philup told me you was kind of dif'runt, somehow; 'n' you be."

"I'm not a particle different. How can you be so foolish?"

Rowena spoke angrily. She could not help asking:

"Did Philip say that? He ought to have known better."

"He told me. He said he shouldn't mention it to another soul. He said you was just as nice, nicer, 'f anything, but you was dif'runt—he couldn't tell how; I can't tell how, either."

"Of course you can't tell. 'Tisn't so!" indignantly.

Georgie and Rowena sat down on the side of the bed. They "took hold hands," as they had done when children.

"Yes; 'tis so, too," responded Georgie, with the persistence that had characterized her when a child. "I was kinder sorry for Philup; he seemed so sorter down. But he said you treated him the best kind, 'n' he had a grand time goin' round with you. Do you go round with Mr. Foster much?"

Rowena's face was burning now with various emotions.

"I don't go round with him at all, and he isn't my — beau!" — flinging out the last word in disgust.

"But you're goin' somewhere with him. What'd he mean by the balcony, 'n' so on?"

"I did say I'd go to the theatre with him and his aunt."

"Oh, his aunt's goin'?"

This fact seemed to modify the aspect of

things, in Georgie's eyes. Where she lived, if a man really admired a girl, no third party ever accompanied the two anywhere. She was bewildered. She shook her head.

"I don't care," she said, emphatically, "he's jest awfully taken with you—even if his aunt is goin'."

"It isn't just as it is at home," said Rowena, somewhat sadly. "Men are not taken with anybody, even if they do appear to be. That Mr. Foster is only a—oh, a fellow who has his meals here," with a laugh, "and has an aunt who is a medium."

Georgie had something to communicate concerning her own history, or she would have given a more extended expression to her horror that Rowena should know a medium. She knew there were mediums as she knew there were hyenas.

She had come in to tell about her own love affair, and to see Rowena. She considered Rowena her most intimate friend, and half the delight of having a love affair would be lost if she could not tell her most intimate friend about it.

She said she did hope she never should know a medium. She never had known one, and mebby she never should.

Having said this she was silent. She gazed

at her friend with a face of mingled curiosity
and importance. The admiration in Mr. Foster's
eyes when he had looked at Rowena, and he had
looked at her all the time, had greatly impressed
Georgie, and raised Rowena in her estimation, if
that were possible.

And what was there "dif'runt" in her companion? She was just as cordial and warm in
her manner, "jest as dear's she could be." She
had nothing to complain of. What was it?

She nestled closer to her as they sat on the
bed. She blushed. She said she s'posed Roweny hadn't heard anything special, had she?

Rowena said promptly that she had received
a despatch about a certain person in Middle Village—a red-headed person, wasn't it—with a
mischievous glance.

Georgie said she must own that she s'posed
his hair was red, but he was real good, and there
wa'n't no likelier man anywhere round. But
she would tell Roweny, though she hadn't let
out a word to any one else that she cared, and
she shouldn't, either; that there was one thing
she wished could be changed, but it couldn't be
changed, and it wa'n't no use cryin' for spilt
milk."

She leaned her head on Rowena's shoulder,
and was held closely there. At last Rowena
said:

"I'm so sorry if something isn't right. Are you going to tell me what it is? Perhaps it won't always be so."

"Yes, it'll always be so, s'long 's the world stands; 'n' the worst of it is everybody else knows it. It'll always be true that Jim Townshend was jilted by that nasty old Jewett girl at the Corners. Homely old thing, with her nose all turned up!"

Georgie sobbed, but directly controlled herself.

"You've seen Mary Jane Jewett, ain't you? She used to come over to evenin' meetin's sometimes. She's one of them kind that always has a beau. I'd know what 'tis, but the fellers are continually running after her. She's as homely as pison, 'n' as bold as brass."

"I've seen her," said Rowena. "It's unaccountable that men like that kind of woman."

"Ain't it?" flashed out Georgie. "You see, I'm takin' her leavin's. Jim was crazy about her. He expected to marry her. All to once't she give him the mitten, and was goin' with Charley Simmons. His mother was mighty glad it was broke off. But she said Jim was in a terrible way for a long time. They 'most lost their crop er medder hay 'cause Jim was so upset. You see it happened 'long the first of last August. Then I got acquainted with Jim. He's ben workin' at the Corners this last winter, 'n' he used to come real often to a place where I had to board in the worst of the weather. He's jest 's good 's he can be. I'd know what did make him like that girl."

Georgie paused, rather breathless, her face red and her eyes full of indignant tears.

"Has he ever said anything about her to you?"

"Oh yes; he said she bewitched him. He said he couldn't help it. He said he guessed it was jest like being drunk. But she wa'n't nothin' to him now, and never would be again. He said he thanked the Lord he had got acquainted with me. He's jest 's good 's he can be."

Here Georgie sobbed once more. Rowena tried to think what to say to her. She sympathized almost too keenly to be able to speak easily. She plainly remembered "that Jewett girl," and the memory of that face was not reassuring. It was an animal face, not pretty, but there had been something in the owner of it that had made Rowena watch her as she talked with her attendant, watch and distrust her, thoroughly repelled.

"I s'pose you think I'm jest as silly 's a goose," at last said Georgie.

"No, I don't."

"But you wouldn't er taken up with her leavin's, would you?"

This fact appeared to be very galling to Georgie.

"I shouldn't worry about that," Rowena answered, cheerfully. "Better be a man's last love than his first," with a laugh. "It's all right if you love each other, and he is good. Not worthy of you, of course," with a hug.

Georgie brightened a great deal. "Oh, I ain't half so good 's he is. He's as stiddy; 'n' he's got something laid up. 'N' I'm makin' the loveliest pattern of a bedquilt you ever see. Ma says it beats all I ever did before, all holler. I shall teach the summer term, for I want to git a little more money, 'n' then in the fall, p'raps—"

She paused and left a blank. She prattled on without pause for the next hour, all about herself and her plans. She said Rowena's folks were all well and gittin' along first-rate. Mr. Tuttle "had taken some sarsaparilla for fear his humor would work, it being spring, so." But Georgie believed his humor hadn't yet worked. There was nothing like sarsaparilla if you steeped it yourself and put a little dandeline root in it. She had been taking some. She had brought a bottleful of it to Rowena. She reckoned humor was as liable to work in Borston as anywhere. The bottle was in her bag, and Uncle Reuben was going to bring the bag along when he came over from "delivering them boats." She was going to stay all night and go back with Mr. Little. "They'd have time to talk over everything, wouldn't they?"

She seemed inclined to go back to the subject of the unusual pattern of the bedquilt she was making, and to the goodness of Jim Townshend.

But Rowena was able to turn the tide somewhat. She was aware of a pricking of conscience because she could not be intensely interested in that bedquilt pattern. She wondered if this lack of interest was because she was "dif'runt." Had there been a time when this subject would have enchained her attention?

She redoubled her efforts to listen absorbedly. She could not conceal from herself that she was getting weary. In a short pause in the monologue she suddenly bethought herself that they would go to walk. Although her window had long been deeply shadowed, she knew the sunlight was warm and bright on the Common. Georgie would like to look in at the shop windows.

It turned out that Georgie was entirely uninterested in the Common and the State House, and wished to give her attention to the things in the windows.

At the corner of Winter Street a gentleman jostled against them. He took off his hat and began an apology. He had a glass in his eye.

"Oh, it is Miss Tuttle," he exclaimed, eagerly.

"I've just been to Hudson Street. They couldn't find you. I left something. My cousin would have come, only she's at the Psychical Wesearch, you know."

He did not linger. The crowd drifted in.

"The land sake!" cried Georgie. "Is that another—"

"Don't say beau!" interrupted Rowena, indignantly.

"Well, I was goin' to say it," confessed the other. "What makes um look so awful glad when they see you? But I don't wonder; I sh'd think they would. There always was something or other 'bout you, Roweny; I never knew what. This feller ain't so dressy as that one we saw to dinner, is he? But he's got kind of a high 'n' mighty look, 's if 'twould do him good to be taken down, somehow. 'N' what a funny little glass that was! How does he keep it in his eye? I sh'd think 'twould fall out. What do you s'pose he's left there where you live?"

Rowena wondered, too. She answered that she did not know, something his cousin, Miss Phillipps, had sent. Miss Phillipps had been very kind to her.

Georgie glanced shrewdly at the girl, whose face was touched by the feeling the thought of Miss Phillipps awakened in her. Georgie's eyes wandered over the figure by her side.

"She's dressed in jest the same clo'es," she said to herself. "I s'pose I sh'd be 'shamed to go round here in that old shawl."

Georgie wore a rough jacket which seemed to have been purchased where Philip Barrett procured his garments, for it produced the same effect on the beholder. "But Roweny c'n carry off things," concluded Georgie in her own mind.

The two girls tramped about until nightfall. Georgie made several small purchases in reference to the fact that she was "fixin'"—that is, fixing to be married. She thoroughly enjoyed herself. She almost felt dissipated.

When they returned Rowena thought it seemed a good time to use two more meal tickets, and they went down to Mrs. Jarvis's table again.

It was now the hour of the greatest crowd. They were obliged to wait a few minutes before they could have seats.

The salesladies with whom Rowena had spent that evening nodded and laughed at her. They sat opposite to where the two found places. They were talking loudly and earnestly. Georgie thought they looked and seemed very stylish. She listened greedily to what they said about the different kinds of goods that were fashionable this spring.

"There's been such a feeling for small checks

along back," said one of them, "but I guess 'tain't going to hold out."

"Yes; 'n' you know there was quite a feeling for large muffs in the first of the winter. Our firm got a lot."

"So did ours. Ain't it funny about the silk mufflers? I give up wearin' one 's soon 's I saw all the girls from the country had 'em. We used to say we could tell what suburb a girl came from by the muffler she wore. If she was from Newton, 'twas blue and brocaded. The Malden girls went into fine stripes."

They laughed shrilly. They gobbled and drank. They talked of the different theatres, and usually called the more noted actors by their first names. They kept an eye on Georgie, who did not try to disguise her admiration for them. She was lost in looking at their slim waists as they left the table. They all wore black frocks, and these frocks encased their waists without a wrinkle, and were as unyielding to any movement of the wearer as if they had been iron. The bangs on their inane foreheads were all of the same length and of the same degree of frizziness. They only varied in color.

Miss Martin, who had "trained" so on the night of the oyster supper, was in excellent spirits. She informed the company that she was going to "the Borston" that night, and she would bet they couldn't guess who had invited her.

Several of the salesladies immediately tried to guess, and each attempt was greeted with volleys of laughter.

When Rowena and her guest were mounting the basement stairs Georgie said, almost enviously, that she hadn't known that Roweny had so much good society; but then she supposed Borston was full of good society.

As they reached the hall Mrs. Jarvis, at her ticket-table, beckoned to them.

"There's been something left for you, Miss Tuttle. I didn't know what to do with it exactly, and so I had one of the girls put it down suller. I guess you'll find it all right."

"Goodness!" exclaimed Georgie, "what on earth can it be? Can't I go with ye to git it?"

XII.

THE ADVENT OF MARMADUKE.

THE two girls turned back and groped their way down into the cellar, the liveliest curiosity animating them.

It was very dark, and very dismal, and very damp down there. In her surprise that what Mr. Bradford had brought should be in the cellar, Rowena had not thought to go up to her own room for her lamp. She did not know of any lamp nearer than her room. She now proposed that she should go for that necessary article, while Georgie should remain exactly where she was until the light was brought. But Georgie protested that "she'd ruther die than stay there a minute alone." She said she had already heard the strangest noise, and if she should hear it again she would not answer for her senses.

She grasped a fold of Rowena's skirt, and thus followed her companion up to where that high and solitary gas-burner in the hall shed light on the incoming and outgoing reg'lars. There Georgie consented to wait. And as she waited she secretly hoped that the splendid Mr. Foster would come in to his supper while she was there. But he did not come.

Presently the two were in the cellar again, Rowena holding her lamp high and walking slowly, Georgie directly behind her.

"There!" said the latter, "I heard that noise agin; do you think it can be rats? Why didn't you ask Mrs. Jarvis what it was that was brought? How awful queer they should have put it here, anyway. Do you think it's flowers, or is it alive?"

The rays of the lamp now fell behind the stairs upon a basket, and the basket moved.

There was a hole in the cover, and from this hole emerged a small, hairy head, with two excessively bright eyes in it. A combination of whine and growl came from this head, and the basket rustled again.

There was a card on the handle. The two girls rushed at the basket. Could this be "it?"

It certainly was it, for the card bore the words, "Miss Rowena Tuttle."

It seemed hardly a moment before Rowena and her friend were in the attic room. The cover was torn off. A blue-and-tan Yorkshire terrier put his very hairy paws on the edge and barked. Then he paused to wag his stub tail. He peered from under his fine, long hair at his companions, who stood back to let him do as he chose, only uttering frantic exclamations of delight. He put up his nose and sniffed, and his nose was exceedingly small and exceedingly black.

He jumped out of the basket and shook himself. Perhaps he weighed five pounds, but his self-appreciation, to judge by his manner, could not have been greater if he had weighed two hundred pounds.

Now that he stood on the floor it was perceived that there was another card fastened to the scarlet ribbon round his neck.

This card was gently removed so that the dignity of the wearer might not be hurt. In close handwriting Rowena read aloud:

"Pardon the whim of an old woman who wishes you to have an entertaining companion who will never bore you, and who wants Marmaduke to have a faithful friend.

"CAROLINE APPLETON SEARS."

At the word "Marmaduke" the terrier pricked up his ears and wagged his tail again. Then he began a minute and exhaustive tour of the room, smelling over and over at every object within his reach.

"It's from Mrs. Sears," remarked Rowena. "I

thought Miss Phillipps sent it. Oh, isn't he a darling! See his little tail! Oh, you precious thing, you! Marmaduke, come here and kiss me!"

She sat down on the floor. Georgie also sat down on the floor. At this moment Marmaduke's explorations had taken him under the bed. They heard him snuffing there. He came to the edge and looked when he heard his name called. He wagged. His eyes shone. He paused a short time, looking from one to the other.

"Do come and kiss me, you darling little love!" pleaded Rowena, holding out her hands.

He wagged again. Then he turned and went back. His two admirers continued to sit there. When he again appeared there was a fuzz of dust on his nose. He came leisurely forward at last, climbed into Rowena's lap, and licked her lips, absolutely refusing to bestow a touch on any other part of her face, but his atom of a red tongue was quite persistent.

He sat down on his haunches and gazed at Georgie, not replying in the least to her blandishments, but retaining a very amiable aspect, as much as to say:

"I'm very fond of incense. But I don't respond if I don't choose, only go right on with the incense; it keeps me in a good-humor."

Rowena retained her position for a long time;

every muscle in her body soon became rigid, but how could she move while Marmaduke chose to sit on his little haunches in her lap and look so awful cunning?

Georgie also remained on the floor. Every time the dog put out his tongue, and every time he didn't put it out, the two girls declared they wanted to squeeze him. His brilliant dark eyes surveyed them with searching discrimination. After a while he curled himself round into a ball and reposed upon Rowena's lap.

"Shall you keep him?" asked Georgie, after having declared that he "was a great deal cunninger asleep than he was awake." She ventured to rise, very carefully, lest he be disturbed; but Rowena kept her position.

"Keep him!" cried she; "I wouldn't part with him for anything. Look at the sweet fluff of hair on his head!—do you think I'd part with that? And I do believe he's almost beginning to love me already."

Georgie stood looking down at the two.

"You know Phil Barrett wanted to give you a setter puppy."

"Yes, I know he did," in a low voice.

"And you wouldn't take it."

"No; I couldn't have a dog as large as that here. I suppose I really ought not to keep this one; but I shall!"—with emphasis.

Georgie turned away. She looked into her satchel. She brushed her hair very gently at the glass, but she did not seem to be thinking of what she was doing. Even the sight of herself in that blue cashmere did not divert her thoughts.

"I declare," she suddenly said, facing round upon her friend, and not sufficiently thoughtful of Marmaduke's slumbers—"I do declare I'm real sorry for Philup."

Rowena answered, almost crossly, that she didn't know why anybody should be sorry for Philip just because a lovely old lady had given her a perfectly bewitching Yorkshire.

Georgie did not retreat. She never did retreat.

"'Tain't that," she said, in her solid way. "You're all taken up with them folks. I s'pose they be terrible fine. But you know we can't keep 'sociating with that kind of folks. They'll stop it when they git ready; 'n' when they stop it they won't be hurt any, but you will."

Rowena did not reply: her heart was like lead. She knew that her friend had common-sense and probability on her side. The knowledge hurt her. In vain she told herself she might take the good the gods provided. The mere thought that Miss Phillipps might become indifferent brought a bitter pang with it.

"Yes; they'll stop it, as you say," she said, tremulously. "I'm expecting it all the time.

And I do love Miss Phillipps so! There isn't anybody like her."

She bent over the dog and gathered him up in her arms.

"But I shall have you, you darling sweetheart, you precious precious!" she cried, rather hysterically.

Marmaduke, thus disturbed, twinkled his eyes at her and yawned, showing a black-roofed mouth and extremely white teeth. Then he extricated himself from her embrace, jumped on the bed and curled up in the centre of the pillow, not without a previous examination, which left it to be inferred that Mrs. Jarvis's pillows were not according to his deserts, and not what he had been accustomed to.

Rowena leaned back against the wall and looked up at her friend with a dreary smile.

"If my friends fail me and my art fails me," she said, "perhaps I can have your school when you leave it to be married. You know I must earn my living some way."

"Why don't you take my school?" asked the other, quickly. "Your folks 'd be jest as glad as they could be."

Rowena sprang up. Enthusiasm blazed suddenly in her eyes. She walked to the easel where was the picture on which she had been at work that day. She turned it about. She had often tried her hand at heads, but never seriously at a likeness before.

This was the head of a woman. It had thick, reddish hair lying profusely on the forehead, green-tinted eyes, and a very red mouth, with a disdainful curve in it. The straight brows lay across a white forehead.

Thus far this, as a whole, was the best she had done. Rowena was sure of that. She wished Allestree might see it. He would not look so much at the expression as at the drawing.

Georgie Warner advanced and gazed with some awe at this object — she said it almost spoke. Then she asked:

"It's her, ain't it?"

Rowena smiled at the picture.

"Yes, it is Miss Phillipps," she answered. "It's only a sketch, you know. She never sat to me. I wish she would. I wanted to do this. But I really love best to paint from nature—fields and hills and sky—meadows, where the scent of white violets comes on the warm wind—anything, almost, in the country. I can learn—I must learn! It's in me!"

She took a brush, but she put it down again.

Her friend could not understand. She herself liked to make bedquilts of a remarkable pattern; that was something that was not only pretty but useful. She wondered if Rowena were not a little unbalanced. If she only ever decided to marry Philip Barrett, things would be all right. Anyway, she loved her the best of any friend she had. Of course she excepted Jim Townshend — Jim was a man. It was the way to love a man best, but Rowena came next.

She did not see her way clear to any reply to Rowena's words, so she said, with a good deal of emphasis:

"I can't bear that face! Does she really look like that — jest as if you was dirt for her to tread on?"

"She does have that expression a good deal," was the answer, the speaker still smiling at the canvas.

"Then I sh'd think you'd hate her."

"Not if she treads on other folks and smiles at me," was the reply, rather mockingly.

"But I sh'd think you'd always be dreadin' when your turn would come," persisted Georgie.

"Don't let's talk like this any more," cried Rowena. She immediately put an artful question about Mr. Townshend.

At the appointed time the next day the two girls walked to Atlantic Avenue, where they found Uncle Reuben just putting his horse into the shafts of the boat-wagon. He had expended his last supply of meal tickets, and his wife had decided that he need not lay out any more money that way, but might "take his victuals with him," which he did. Owing to this arrangement Rowena was not sure of seeing him every time he came in. He usually brought cooked food from Mrs. Tuttle for her daughter, but she often had to go down to Atlantic Avenue for it. As Marthy S. had hinted, Mr. Little had a weakness for "liquor," and there were seasons when in many ways, as his neighbors said, "you couldn't depend on him more'n you could on the wind." Still, he was never so drunk that he could not manage his horse, and come in and go out of Boston safely. Or perhaps his horse was now so wise in this business that he needed no management.

When Rowena and Georgie found him now, his face was so red and he was so conversational that they knew directly that he had "had too much."

He even acknowledged that he had had too much. But he explained at great length that the reason was because "he'd ben havin' a spell of his cussed nooralgy." He was obliged to take something for that. "He guessed he should ride it off long 'fore he got home." He did not say whether "it" referred to the neuralgia or the effect of the liquor.

Rowena tried to persuade her friend to go home by train. She was afraid her Uncle Reuben would think his "nooralgy" needed even more medicament. But Georgie said she wasn't afraid. "If it come to that she could take the reins 'n' drive jest 's well as Mr. Little. Her folks 'd be expectin' her. She had told Jim she should surely come."

At mention of Jim, Rowena refrained from any more urging. The two friends embraced under Uncle Reuben's eyes. He said he was glad to see there was affection somewhere in the world, but there wa'n't much where he lived.

Three young men in the boat-office were much interested in the parting. They bet ten to one that the two would turn back for a second hug, and the two did so.

Marmaduke was under one arm and beneath Rowena's shawl, save for his head. His presence made the embracing more difficult than it would otherwise have been.

When at last Georgie was mounted on the seat beside Mr. Little and the wheels of the cart began slowly to revolve, the terrier bristled his beard and mustache and barked furiously.

Rowena watched the cart out of sight. When the weather was a little milder she would go home for a week. Georgie carried with her a voluminous epistle to Mr. and Mrs. Tuttle. This letter was full of genuine love and longing to see them.

Mrs. Tuttle read it for the third time after she

had put her dried-apple pies into the oven to
bake. The back door was open, and the frogs
were very loud in the meadow there. Blue-
wings were cleaving the air, and the owners of
these wings were saying blithely, over and over,
"Dearie! Dearie!"

"I'm glad she's gittin' kind of weaned from
home," said Mrs. Tuttle, with a sigh; "she won't
suffer so much. But it makes me sorry, too. But
that's nature, I expect. The young ones go. Oh,
I do hope there won't nothin' happen to Roweny! I don't know what her father would do."

Mrs. Tuttle put the letter in the pocket of her
calico skirt. She looked in at her pies. Then
she went to the open door and stood there a
long time, not seeing anything, conscious only of
a dull sense of loss and dejection.

This was the first letter her daughter had written home in which there was something that
showed that new interests were really crowding
upon the old. The mother could not put her
finger upon that something, however. It was
not in words, but it was there.

Mrs. Tuttle furtively passed a corner of her
apron across her eyes. "Yes," she said again,
"I'm real glad she's gittin' weaned from us jest
'nough so't she won't be homesick. Of course
that Miss Phillipps is good to her. I sh'd think
everybody 'd be good to Roweny. I guess I'll

make a jelly cake to send next time Reuben
goes."

She was about turning away from the door
when a rattling of wheels was heard, and a pair
of horses hitched to a farm cart came into the
yard. Standing up in the cart, driving, was
Philip Barrett. A glossy red setter ran nosing
about, then came forward tumultuously to greet
Mrs. Tuttle. She put her hard, thin hand on his
head while she watched his master descend from
the cart.

"Come right in, Philip," she said, cordially;
" I've got a cup of coffee that ain't cold yet.
I've ben expectin' you'd call ever sence you went
to Boston."

The young man walked in slowly, as he did
everything. He had just come from the Corners,
where he had mailed a letter to Rowena. He
had been at work all his spare time on this document since his return.

Rowena's letter, the first and only one she
had yet written him, and which breathed such
a warm friendliness, he carried about with him.
It had been so worn that he had now protected
it by enclosing it in two stout envelopes. When
he was out of doors, busy on his farm, he liked
to put his hand to his pocket where the letter
was. He talked to his dogs about the girl; he
confided to them his hopes and his misgivings.

Now, as he sat down in the "roundabout" chair commonly occupied by Mr. Tuttle, he remarked that the "spring was ruther forrard of the two."

"So 'tis," responded Mrs. Tuttle. "Hiram got in his early pease some time ago."

After this there was a long silence. The woman looked wistfully at her guest while he drank the coffee she had given him. Then he gazed at the cook-stove, from the oven of which Mrs. Tuttle now withdrew the two dried-apple pies.

"I s'pose you seen her, of course," at last said Mrs. Tuttle; "'cause she writes she seen you, and how kind you was. I hope you had a good time."

"Yes, I had a real good time." Philip paused lengthily before he added: "She needn't go to sayin' I was kind. Kind to her!"

Something almost like a flash came to his steady blue eyes.

"Yes; she was jest as nice 's she could be. When she first seen me on the Common I almost made up my mind she was about half 's glad 's I was. Half 's glad would have ben enough—I wouldn't arst for no more."

"Wa'n't she glad afterwards?" anxiously.

"She was jest 's nice 's could be," reiterated Philip; "but I thought she was some absent-minded. You see, Mis' Tuttle, she's got some other friends. There was a feller in a chain 'n' necktie, with a long coat on, real dressy, and with a lot to say for himself. He had an aunt that wore a fur cloak. They come to see Roweny. They wanted to take her to the theatre. I only seen him a minute; but I seen the way he looked at her."

At this intolerable memory Philip rose suddenly from his chair and walked to the window.

"We can't be surprised that folks like Roweny," said Mrs. Tuttle, with a mother's pride.

"No; I ain't surprised," from the window.

After a little hesitation, Mrs. Tuttle walked to Philip and put her hand on his shoulder. This was an action that, in an undemonstrative New England woman, meant a great deal.

"I wish she'd never gone to Borston!" cried Philip, almost violently, turning round and facing his companion.

"I s'pose I hadn't ought to come to you like this; but I've ben thinkin' it all over every minute sence I got home, 'n' I couldn't seem to help comin'; 'n' I made up my mind that I wish she never 'd gone to Borston."

"It ain't no use talkin' like that," returned Mrs. Tuttle, sorrowfully. "She was crazy to go. It wa'n't no notion that would pass off, either. She was sut on it, 'n' has been sence she was half grown up. She's gone without clo'es 'n' saved every cent. Oh, it would er killed her not to gone to Borston to learn how to paint."

Philip took a strong grip on the top of a chair near him. He was very pale, and his eyes were hollow. He looked at his companion piteously.

"If I didn't love her jes' 's I do, if I hadn't loved her all my life, I sh'd try to git over it; but I can't even try. I might's well think I could stop bein" Philip Barrett, as that I could stop lovin' Roweny."

There were tears in the woman's eyes as she heard him. If there was one longing strong within her, it was that her daughter might consent to marry this man. But she had always been wise enough to say nothing on the subject to any one.

"I'd ruther she'd marry you than any other bein' on the footstool, Philip," she said, earnestly; "but what c'n I do?"

"You can't do nothin," returned the other, bracing up visibly. "Things have got to jest take their course. But I won't give up—I can't give up. I've been a good deal down lately. I hope you'll overlook my talkin' so, Mis' Tuttle. 'Tain't my way to, you know; but I've been so down."

"I ain't nothin' to overlook," she said, warmly. "I know how close-mouthed you gen'ly be.

But who should you speak to, if not to Roweny's
mother, I'd like to know?"

Philip went out to his cart. His dog sprang to
greet him. He drove away somewhat cheered.
The very fact that he had spoken to Rowena's
mother cheered him.

XIII.

A LITTLE TALK.

"IF there were such a state of body and mind as being tired, I should say you were in that state."

Miss Phillipps had just taken her seat in Mrs. Jarvis's top-story room, on the afternoon of the day on which Georgie Warner had started home with Mr. Little.

Rowena was mending her stockings. Marmaduke was in the centre of the pillow on the bed. He had been down to investigate the ankles and skirts of the new-comer, and had returned to his pillow. The lady had noticed him, but as yet had not spoken of him.

Rowena looked pale and fagged. She had really exerted herself to entertain Georgie, and she had never known before that a good deal of information in regard to patterns of bedquilts and about Jim Townshend might at last become wearing.

She let her stockings drop unheeded to the floor.

"I am so tired!" she said.

"You mustn't say that," returned her friend, "because there is no such thing as being tired. Looking at everything from the inmost — and that is the only way to look at things—you can't by any possibility be tired."

Rowena stared helplessly. She said nothing in response.

Miss Phillipps leaned back in her usual position in the little rocker. She seemed kind, but rather absent and absorbed.

She wore several rings to-day. She turned them on her fingers.

"Have you formed the habit of looking at all things from the inmost?" she asked.

"No," said Rowena, still more helplessly, "I haven't."

"You must, then. Begin with me from this very hour to form that habit."

Rowena said she would try. Then she exclaimed, boldly, that she didn't know how to try.

"It is in the inmost where God dwells in us. View everything from that stand-point. Then, you see, we shall be charitable in our judgment. It is a great thing to be charitable."

"Yes," said Rowena. She could comprehend that last remark, and was cheered that she could.

"There is, in very truth, no death ; and we are law. God is law, love, wisdom, force. It is disorderly to pray, and, above all things, we must not be disorderly. You dear little thing!" with a sudden warm look at the girl, "do you know what I'm talking about?"

"Not in the least."

"I thought you didn't. But you must learn," more seriously; "it is the principal thing in life. You see, what with my Browning and Psychic Research and Sloyd and painting, and one or two other things that I can't call to mind just now, I've let my mind-cure and my Christian Science fall into the background. I went to one of their lectures this morning. I really must keep up with that, if I let other things go. I've been trying to think what I can best drop. But what has tired you so?" changing her manner again. "That is, if you are still in the old thought, and think you are tired."

But Rowena was not going to admit that the visit of her friend from the country had wearied her.

"One isn't vigorous in the spring," she answered, evasively. "I think I must need some of mother's bitters, made of dandelion root, and such wholesome things."

Saying this, she remembered that Georgie had brought her a bottle of this approved medicine. She would begin to take it the next morning.

"One is vigorous—always vigorous. It is only

that one much choose to be so," said Miss Phillipps, strongly.

" I surely should choose to be so."

Miss Phillipps did not heed the girl's words.
She rose and walked to the bed, where she looked at Marmaduke, who in turn looked at her with
great interest, but did not think it necessary to
rise from his recumbent position.

" Where in the world did you get such a darling as this?" she inquired. " Don't you see he's
a thoroughbred—and a regular angel of a Yorkshire?"

Rowena came to the bed.

" I guess I know he's an angel of a Yorkshire,"
she replied, fervently. " I was going to ask you
how I might have a chance to thank Mrs. Sears.
I don't even know where she lives."

" Did Mrs. Sears send you this dog?"

" Yes; and I want to thank her. Mr. Bradford
brought him yesterday when I was out with
Georgie."

" Mr. Bradford brought him?"

" Yes. It was very kind of him."

" Very."

Miss Phillipps now stooped down and picked up
Marmaduke, who, though thus disturbed, retained his amiability and licked the lady's lips, declin-
ing, as he always did, to caress any other portion
of the human countenance.

She looked over him at Rowena.

"And you wouldn't take my seal-skin jacket!" she said.

Rowena colored deeply.

"A dog seems different, don't you think?"

"Yes, a great deal better. I wish I had given you this one. He will be a comfort to you. He ought to be very happy in being a comfort to you, Miss Tuttle."

These words were accompanied by a soft glance, which the girl felt go straight to her heart.

Marmaduke now leaped back onto the bed.

"You will probably see Mrs. Sears at my house soon. You can thank her then. She lives at No. — Beacon Street. But I am frittering away my time and yours," in a more business-like tone. "You see, I came this afternoon particularly to tell you that you must not live in the old thought any more. You must take up the science."

"With you?"

"Certainly, with me."

"Oh yes, Miss Phillipps, I think I would take up anything with you."

This remark was received with a warm, approving smile.

"That is because you are ignorant. If you knew me better you would not be so charming in your confidence. Supposing we go into theosophy a little at the same time?"

"Is theosophy very hard?" hesitatingly inquired Rowena.

"Well, it is not 'real easy,' like Browning, for instance."

"Don't laugh at me, Miss Phillipps."

But the lady did laugh, and Rowena could not help joining her, until the small, dingy room was full of the sound, and Marmaduke sat up on his haunches and asked what it was all about.

"I don't think I shall have time for theosophy," at last Rowena said. "You know I'm in earnest about my painting. I must succeed in some degree in that."

She spoke with an almost solemn emphasis, and her visitor respected the feeling.

"I won't tempt you. But I shall hold you to the Christian Science. What have you on the easel there? Let me see some of your work. Your lessons should have some effect by this time."

Miss Phillipps spoke with the abruptness and positiveness which she sometimes used.

She walked quickly to the easel and turned it about.

It was the sketch of her own head which she saw.

Rowena watched her face with tremulous anxiety. Her pulses seemed all crowding into her throat. She had unbounded confidence in this woman's judgment of her work.

She thought a faint color came into the pale face which was in profile as she watched it.

"I was too bold, I know," murmured Rowena, deprecatingly.

"You 'hitched your wagon to a star,'" was the sarcastic response.

It was another long moment before Miss Phillipps turned to her companion. When she did speak she used Allestree's very words.

"You have the touch," she said. She looked at the picture again. "Crude as it is, it is absolutely alive."

Rowena's eyes shone. She felt as if she had been drinking wine.

Now her friend turned her back on the canvas and moved nearer the girl.

"Have I really such a cruel expression as that?"

"Sometimes; not now."

"Little truth-teller! But you hurt."

She went back to the sketch as if drawn to it by invisible cords.

"Senour painted my portrait two years ago. I'll show it to you when you come to my house again. He hasn't put a bit of that look in; and I never saw it in my mirror. Is it really so marked?"

The tone in which this question was put was almost wistful. It was hard to reply, as Rowena did reply:

"Yes, it is; but not always."

"Oh, I should hope not always. If I had no different face for a friend I would shoot myself forthwith. And I've been quite set up in my mind when I have looked at Senour's portrait. The only assurance this thing gives me is that I have an aristocratic countenance 'to face the world with.' I should judge that human beings in general were but dirt beneath my feet."

"That is just what—" began Rowena, and then paused in confusion.

Her friend instantly caught her up.

"Just what some one said of it, you were going to say?" She spoke sharply. "Keats—Mr. Bradford has not seen it?"

"Oh no!"

"Who then?"

"Only my friend, Georgie Warner, who went away this morning."

"Your friend, Georgie Warner, knew what she was talking about. I forgive her. I shall forgive you. But I shall not forgive myself for furnishing the material for that look.

"We have talked more than enough about it. Now I am going home. I walked down here. If you did not look so—so 'weeny,' I used to say to my dolls when they were ill, I should ask you to come out for a stroll."

The speaker put on her hat and mantle, which

she always removed if only for a few moments'
stay. She walked to the door. Then she came
back and put her hands on Rowena's shoulders.

"I shall treat you," she said, after an intent
look.

"Treat me?" repeated the girl.

Miss Phillipps gave her a little shake.

"Yes. You must not say my words over after
me. I shall treat you. I shall say—inwardly,
you know—'Rowena'—have you any other Christian name?—no—then I shall say 'Rowena Tuttle, you are not weary, for there is no such thing.
You are fresh and strong.' When I have said
this a few times, with emphasis, and put myself
in the new thought, and in the God-current, you
will be surprised at the delightful sense of well-
being that will come to you."

"You will stay with me to do this?" hesitatingly inquired Rowena.

"Oh no. Thought knows no space. I could
treat you a thousand miles away just as well as
here."

Miss Phillipps looked and seemed quite serious. Rowena felt a trifle uncomfortable.

"Can any one treat me, any one who chooses,"
she asked, anxiously—and I cannot help myself?"

Now Miss Phillipps laughed.

"Why do you talk in that way?" she said.

"Because I should have a choice, decidedly,"

she answered, firmly. "I won't have any one—
not any one—treat me, but you."

There was intense seriousness and almost alarm
in Rowena's face and voice.

Miss Phillipps suddenly put her arms about
the girl and kissed her. Instead of being amused,
she seemed touched.

A moment later Rowena was standing at the
hall door watching the lady as she walked along
the sordid, dingy street. How out of place her
face and figure looked in it! There was still
sunlight in the open spaces and in the country,
but here it was almost twilight. As the girl
looked, there came almost a terror in her heart
that she should care so much for this woman.

She saw one of the salesladies from R. H.
Black's coming for her supper. The two met
and the saleslady turned to look back. She
tossed her head as she came up the steps. She
gave Rowena a disagreeable glance.

"I guess that is that Miss Phillipps that Mrs.
Jarvis tells about, isn't it?" she asked.

"Yes."

"Has she been here to see you? She looks
odd enough on this street, walkin' as if nothin'
was quite good 'nough for her to step on. She'd
better stay where she belongs!"

The saleslady went down into the basement.

A young man in a light suit, with gloves and a

cane, now appeared, walking rapidly. He raised his hat eagerly and with a flourish as he saw the figure at the door. He hastened, but Rowena had disappeared when Ferdinand Foster had reached the steps.

Miss Phillipps had turned onto Essex Street. She was thinking very intently, and not expecting to meet any one she knew, when she was aware of a tall, masculine form approaching. It was very familiar.

"Why, Keats! How came you here?" she asked, as her cousin gravely lifted his hat.

"How came you here?" he responded. He turned and walked with her.

"I came here in the interest of Christian Science," she answered. "Can you give as reasonable an explanation?"

He fancied she was looking at him sharply, and he was annoyed.

"I'm not sure I shall explain at all," was the cool response. "I weally suppose a man may stroll on Essex Street and not be guilty of engagement in any very sewious intwigue."

"Oh, if you are going to take that tone," and Miss Phillipps walked faster. He kept beside her. He swung his stick; he adjusted his glass to his eye. At last he laughed. But she was very serious. She did not glance at him.

"You have been to see your latest and strongest fad," he remarked.

"I am so tired of that word!" she said.

"What word? I used several."

"Fad."

He laughed again. She frowned distinctly.

The two turned into Washington Street. He kept beside her, and said cheerfully that he knew she did not want him, but that he was bound to walk home with her; he had something particular to say. She might better become resigned at once. Whereupon she assumed a pleasant aspect immediately, but walked even faster than before.

Neither spoke until they struck across the Common. They did not appear to wish to go directly to Charles Street. Now, with the roar of the city somewhat removed, Miss Phillipps turned to her companion.

"Well?" she said.

But Mr. Bradford did not seem quite ready to speak. He gazed about him vacantly.

"You had an air as if you were going to arraign me before the bar of justice," she continued, after a moment.

"I am."

"Go right on. Don't mind hurting my feelings."

The man turned to her with sudden sternness.

"I object to your latest fad," he said.

Miss Phillipps paused in her walk.

"So you will use that word," she responded, and then continued, frivolously: "Let me think—do you mean Sloyd, or hypnotism, or Ibsen? I'm interested in all, but I can't tell you positively which is the latest."

She looked quite scornful and disagreeable. All the unpleasant possibilities in her face became accentuated.

But Mr. Bradford was not intimidated. He rather assumed a more masterful manner.

"I mean Miss Tuttle," he said.

"Oh, you don't call her a fad? You must have very few words from which to choose in your vocabulary, Keats, when you are reduced to calling Miss Tuttle a fad."

"I am sorry for her—I mean, I shall be sorry for her."

"You shall be sorry for her?" Miss Phillipps glanced up at him and smiled very exasperatingly. "Do you know precisely at what period this sorrow is to begin?"

"That depends upon you."

"Really, you are crediting me with a great deal of power."

"I want to pwotect her. She is going to need pwotection."

"Hardly—if you are her champion."

"Vanessa, be sewious, be humane."

Miss Phillipps looked about her.

"He asks me to be humane," she said to the surrounding air.

"I am in earnest. You are the cruelest woman I ever knew, Vanessa, sometimes. I even think you capable of being unkind to that girl; and if you ever do make her suffer you will be a howwible bwute. I shall hate you."

Miss Phillipps suddenly turned aside and said, sweetly,

"Let us sit down here a moment."

The two sat down on one of the iron benches. The woman's face was much changed and softened. Her lips were slightly tremulous as she said:

"How could you think I would hurt her?" with a stress upon the last word.

"Oh, you won't hurt her until you are weary of her. I have known you since I've known anybody, Vanessa."

"But she appeals to something strange, unused in me, Keats. You don't believe it. But it is true. When I am with her it is almost as if I also were unhackneyed, unsullied by the world. You can't be near her and not breathe pure air. She is a tonic. She is something better. When I look in her eyes I feel once more as if I might keep true to the dreams of my youth."

The speaker's voice ceased almost inarticulately.

The man did not reply. He had averted his face, and appeared to be gazing out towards the pond.

"I want to protect her, too," went on Miss Phillipps, hurriedly. "She will suffer so much, I am afraid. I want to take care of her. Keats," turning upon him with a most unexpected savageness, "are you going to make love to her?"

"Why shouldn't I do what you are doing?"

"For the best of reasons—because you are a man."

"You have given just the weason why I should do it; it is a man's glowious pwivilege to make love to a woman. Vanessa, you are usurping masculine rights."

For some inscrutable reason Mr. Bradford dropped his earnest manner with the utmost abruptness. He rose and stood before his cousin, looking down at her whimsically.

"Miss Tuttle comes very near adoring you, Vanessa, and I know you like to be adored. Shall we walk on?"

"I wish you would let me go home alone, now, Keats," responded the other. "I want to think, and you confuse me."

Mr. Bradford went away in silence.

"I was foolish enough," he said to himself.

"Rowena Tuttle must take her expewience in life as we all must, and when Vanessa is weally in earnest why—she is in earnest."

The young man strolled along aimlessly until he found himself opposite Mrs. Sears's house.

He rang. He was allowed to go into a small apartment on the ground floor, which Mrs. Sears was in the habit of calling her "withdrawing room," because she said she withdrew there from bores.

She was knitting and reading. She was of the opinion that women over sixty ought to knit stockings occasionally. One could always give them to the poor.

"I hope you know it is a great favor to be permitted to enter here," she said, as Bradford came forward.

A small dog, almost exactly like Marmaduke, slowly lifted himself from the skirt of her dress where he had been reposing, shook back the hair from his eyes, and then sprang forward. Bradford picked him up and put him comfortably on his knee at he took the chair his hostess moved towards him.

This young man was fully aware that he had called now upon this old lady because she had said some very nice things of Miss Tuttle, and because she had sent Miss Tuttle a terrier.

XIV.

MR. FOSTER'S SISTER.

"I NEVER did see such a flirt in all my life, I declare!"

Rowena was slowly descending the stairs from her room. It was not yet eight o'clock, but she considered it extremely late. She had a small tin pail in her hand. She was going out to the corner for some milk for her morning coffee. It was raining. Two girls were hanging dripping water-proofs on the pegs of the hat-rack in the hall; one of them was Miss Martin, and it was she who now cried out shrilly that she "hated a man flirt above ground."

At this stage in the conversation they saw Rowena.

"Holloa, is that you?" said Miss Martin. "We were talkin' about Mr. Foster. Did you know he's an awful flirt?"

Rowena wondered why the two looked so closely at her as this question was put. She paused at the last step and rested her pail on the top of the post.

" No ; I didn't know it," she said.

" Well, he is ; he's jest awful. They do say now he's got a girl out in Malden and one in Roxbury. I d'know how many he's got in Boston."

They still gazed sharply at her.

" I hope none of them are inclined to be jealous," she remarked, somewhat embarrassed by their scrutiny ; resenting it, but feeling helpless.

Miss Martin laughed boisterously.

" I pity um if they be," she said ; " I guess they'd have to take it out in being jealous, don't you, Jen ?"

Jen said she guessed they would, too.

Rowena had a sensation of disgust, and of self-reproof that she was disgusted, a feeling she had known when in Miss Martin's company before. She knew that all working-girls were not like this. She made a movement to go. They appeared disposed to linger a little before going down to breakfast.

" Ain't to-night the night you're going to the theatre ?" inquired Miss Martin.

Rowena could not tell why she should feel somehow ashamed that she must reply " Yes."

" The medyum's goin', ain't she ?"

" Yes."

The two girls giggled. Miss Martin said she hoped she wouldn't go into a trance. Then she informed Rowena that she, Miss Martin, and a "gentleman friend" had been asked to join the party, but "they'd ben otherwise engaged. Besides," she added, with another laugh, "she didn't know's 'twas necessary to have a dooenna along; there couldn't be half as much fun."

Now Rowena opened the hall door and stepped out into the street. She could not tell why she was conscious of a sense of humiliation. Her cheeks burned as she recalled the talk and the glances she had just heard and seen. She wished she were not going to the theatre. She tried to think of some excuse she could offer. The more she thought of the subject the stronger was her disinclination.

She walked by the grocery where she was to get her milk, and hurried back to it. She bought an extra pint every day now because Marmaduke had shown a liking for that kind of food, and she had learned that he was rather particular. She never dared to have him on the street without a string attached to him. She scrupulously took him a long walk in this manner every day. She was already absurdly fond of him. She conversed with him as she sat in her room painting hour after hour.

She considered that she had had a piece of great good-luck lately. She had sold two little water-color sketches, both of them bits of the up-

land pasture back of her home. The small sum
she received she put away in the bottom of her
trunk to be sacredly reserved for the use of Marmaduke; if he wanted a scrap of something good
he must have it. He was a person who quite ap-
preciated a scrap of something good.

Now, if Marmaduke had not been waiting for
her in her room, Rowena felt that she would
have liked to prolong her stroll indefinitely. It
was spring. It was raining gently. Even the
town could not avoid letting one know that it
was spring. And how busy the sparrows were!
How they fought! A few bunches of fading,
trailing arbutus were in a shop-window that she
passed. She thought the housatonia must be
thick in the lane that led from the cow-yard,
and the saxifrage among the rocks in the orchard. She sighed. But though she sighed she
did not feel that poignant pang which she had
known so many times in the first weeks of her
stay.

She now hurried along with her tin pail. When
she came in sight of her house she grew hot again
and thought of the interview with those girls. A
sudden fear came to her that she would meet
Mr. Foster before she could possibly get to her
room. She ran up the steps and did not slack-
en her pace until she was at the top of the first
flight. Marmaduke began to bark when he heard

her coming, and when she opened the door of her room she set down her milk that he might leap into her arms. She hugged him and confided to him the fact that she had not half lived until he came; that she should not half live if he should go away. She had a joy in the knowledge that it is so safe to love a dog.

In a short time she was drinking her coffee, and Marmaduke was lapping milk and greatly dabbling his beard and mustache in the liquid. He kindly ate, also, a small quantity of boiled egg, then went and sat on the window-ledge lest some stray cat should walk over the roof below and he should not see her.

Rowena tried to settle calmly to her work; she was thinking all the time of the theatre-party. At last she rose and went down-stairs, taking the terrier under her arm. She liked to feel his little warm body held closely to her, and he looked out from this position as if he were thoroughly used to it.

Mrs. Jarvis had just risen from her ticket-table. Since spring had really come she wore until noon a palm-leaf loose gown that had precisely the same effect as the wadded gown, only it was not wadded. Her pompadour roll never varied by as much as a hair. Her shabby face lighted a little at sight of the girl.

"I'm jest going down for my breakfast," she

said. "They've all gone, finally, and I hope I c'n have a minute's peace. Don't you want a cup of coffee with me?"

Rowena went to the dining-room with her. The girl had almost come to have a sort of liking for the always-tired hack of a woman by whom she sat now.

"Nothing tastes good," said Mrs. Jarvis, after trying to eat some lukewarm ham-and-eggs. She pushed the plate from her. She now glanced at Rowena. "Seems to me you look kind of worried yourself."

"I don't want to go to the theatre to-night. I'm worrying about that now," replied the girl, with a smile.

"Goodness! I hope you won't have anything worse'n that to worry about. Most girls 'd be fretting 'cause they couldn't go. Madame Van Benthuysen's going, ain't she?"

"Yes," said Rowena; "she has put off the spirits for one night I'm sorry I said I'd go. Can't you think of an excuse for me, Mrs. Jarvis?"

The young voice fell very sweetly on the woman's ears. The elder woman turned and met the young, questioning eyes.

"I guess you'd better go," she counselled. "You'll have a real good time. They like you first-rate, and they'll be awful disappointed if you don't go. Ferdinand's sister is comin' in

14

from Newton on purpose to go. You'll like her. She's a book-keeper, only she's out of health now. Her firm thought so much of her that they're keeping her place for her. Oh, you'd better go."

Rowena sighed, and offered Marmaduke a bit of ham, which he refused. He had his front paws on the extreme edge of the table, and was looking leisurely and thoroughly about him. Possibly he was thinking that Mrs. Sears's dining-room did not in the least resemble this one.

"I suppose I shall go, then," said Rowena.

"Oh yes, of course. They did it jest for you, I guess. Madame was real taken with you. Have you thought any more about being developed?"

"Oh no."

"Well, there's time enough. You'll get used to the idea after a while."

When it was time to begin to get ready for the evening Rowena needed a great deal of moral courage to enable her to rise above the thought of her clothes. She did not quite succeed in the effort, but she did not give up the attempt. She felt, however, that it was contemptible to be conscious of one's apparel.

It was not more than seven o'clock when one of Mrs. Jarvis's servants called her down to the parlor. She said there was a lady there.

Rowena's heart began to beat as it always did

when she thought that Miss Phillipps was near. She hurried down.

But it was not Miss Phillipps. A very different person rose from the horse-hair couch beneath the "spirit friend." A small person in gray gown and gray spring jacket, very neatly and yet cheaply dressed. Rowena hesitated. She thought there had been a mistake.

"Miss Tuttle?" said the stranger.

"I am Miss Tuttle," said Rowena.

"I asked for Mrs. Jarvis," went on the girl, with some shyness, "but she is out. I thought it might not be so awkward if she could introduce us. I am Miss Foster, Ferdinand's sister. He suggested that I make you a little call before the theatre; and I was glad to come."

Rowena now held out her hand cordially. She was pleased with Miss Foster. She told her so earnestly that it was kind of her to come that Miss Foster felt her sincerity with a curious pleasure. Rowena's voice, also, gave her almost a thrill, it was so clear and sweet and honest. She held her hand an instant longer than was necessary. Then she dropped it and blushed. She was not self-possessed like her brother. She did not look like him either.

"I should have liked real well to call on you before," she began, "but I've been so out of health I haven't been much of anywhere. Ferdinand has mentioned you several times, and he doesn't often mention his acquaintances; he thinks I won't be interested in 'em, usually. And I don't think I should, either. Ferdinand is quite gay."

She said the last phrase as if, while she deprecated the fact of her brother's gayety, she was still somewhat proud of it. She coughed, and put her handkerchief to her lips bashfully.

Rowena sat down near her.

"You are not well?" she said, sympathetically.

"Oh, I'm a great deal better than I was a month ago. I shall go back to my work soon. And I owe it all to the science. If it hadn't been for the science I don't know what would have become of me."

Rowena leaned forward eagerly.

"The science?" she repeated.

"Yes, indeed," was the almost feverish response. "Don't you know about the science? You see, I've been living in the new thought, and I'm so thankful to Mrs. Jones-Burt that I don't know what to do. If it hadn't been for her I should have been thinking now that there was such a thing as disease."

"But there is disease, you know," said Rowena, with innocent conviction.

"Oh no, no! That's the old thought; that's because you have fear. You must drop fear.

Now, for instance, one cause of a cold is being in the draught, but the main cause is fear. It is all cured by putting yourself into the mind of God. Just be borne by the current. Face the light instead of the dark. You have only to hold yourself still and let God, who dwells in you, do the work. You know you can be all that God is. If you keep yourself in that thought, all evil drops. Don't you see?"

Miss Foster's eyes were sparkling, and her thin face was red with excitement.

Rowena was excited, also. She sighed. She must be very stupid. She said, "No, she could not see."

"Oh, it's all so clear to me!" exclaimed Miss Foster. "Just as clear!"

The two looked at each other a moment.

"You must hear Mrs. Jones-Burt; you certainly must."

"I should like to hear her," responded Rowena.

Miss Foster gave a short, nervous laugh.

"Here I have been going on about Christian Science just as if I had known you ever so long, Miss Tuttle. I hope you'll excuse me. Ferdinand says I'm about crazy on the subject. He laughs at it. He laughs at a good many things. But it's done just everything for me, just everything for me."

Miss Foster coughed, and again put her handkerchief to her lips with the same nervous motion. Then she said, with a polite assumption of interest:

"I understand you are studying art, Miss Tuttle?"

As Rowena was replying, the door-bell rang. After a long time a large Irishwoman came lumbering up from the kitchen and opened the door.

Madame Van Benthuysen entered, followed by her nephew. She was in a plaid suit with a plaid cape, and in this guise she seemed to be even larger than she had been in her fur circular. The nephew was in great spirits.

"So you're here, Sis," he said, after they had greeted Rowena. "Told her all about the science, I expect. What does Miss Tuttle think of it? But you are better and no mistake."

"If the science has helped her, let the science have the credit," remarked Madame Van Benthuysen, largely. It was as if she had said that she was willing to acknowledge that there were things in this world as effectual as the spirits in the other world.

Mr. Foster looked at his watch and said that there was no hurry. The rest of the party, consisting of two, would be at the theatre. After a short time the young man's face underwent a change: it was no longer so gay. In truth, he did not feel so happy. He could not tell precisely why. He had, as he would have said, "reckoned" on this evening ever since the appointment. Rowena smiled at him and talked with him, but there was a certain remoteness about her that had a very disastrous effect upon his spirits.

This effect continued all the evening. In thinking over these hours afterwards, the young man could not, to quote him once more, "put his finger on a thing." Rowena never had been particularly kind to him, he owned, but she had never been so very far away from him.

She and Miss Foster talked with an appearance almost of intimacy. At last, after the oysters and the ice-cream, and after Rowena had been safely left at Mrs. Jarvis's, Ferdinand was alone with his sister at Madame Van Benthuysen's residence on Harrison Avenue. She exclaimed enthusiastically that she knew "she should like Miss Tuttle awfully." Ferdinand only grunted inarticulately.

He did not remain. He went out and slammed the door with extreme violence. He twitched out the small bunch of violets from his coat and flung them into the street. He swore he had had a devilish poor time, and he hoped the rest hadn't had any better. He was not in a good-humor.

Rowena, on the contrary, was in a very good-humor. She had liked Miss Foster, though she had wished she was not quite so nervous. She had been greatly interested in the way she lived when she was book-keeping in Boston. She kept house in a room up at the South End.

The two girls found a common ground here. They told their experiences between the acts. Of course, Rowena had not much time to give to Mr. Foster, although she tried to attend to his remarks. Miss Foster was to resume her work next week, and Rowena was going up to her room to visit her.

Marmaduke was very sleepy when Rowena returned; but he waked thoroughly, and from that time on until the morning he was continually springing off his cushion to rush at the walls of the rooms, behind which was a great scuffling of rats.

Therefore his mistress slept very little. Once, at about three, Marmaduke was so violent, and squealed and scratched so, that Rowena almost believed he had caught a rat.

She lighted her little lamp, having a dreadful feeling that she was surrounded. But there was nothing but Marmaduke wagging and dancing on his hind-legs for joy at seeing her up. The light, however, revealed a letter which she had not seen when she had come in.

The envelope bore Eunice Warner's handwriting. It was a childish hand. In one corner was the word "imediate," deeply underlined. The lack of the usual number of letters seemed to make the word stand out more urgently.

Rowena wrapped her shawl about her and opened the envelope, while the terrier jumped in her lap to investigate.

"Georgie's been just crazy for me to send for you," the missive began abruptly, "and I'm goin' to, anyway. She's sick. She's got a fever, I guess. And she's terrible odd. Mar says she must have something on her mind, but Georgie says she ain't got a thing on her mind ; but she does wish you'd come out if you possibly can. She sets up some, but she don't eat nothing scarcely; don't nothing taste good. We thought mebby as you was talking some of coming home 'fore long, you could come out to-morrer with Mr. Little. He said he'd take this and he could bring you 's well 's not. Mother said I was to be sure and not scare you about Georgie, but she couldn't help feeling kinder worried. Jim Townshend's been here every day. He seems all used up about Georgie. He's just 's good 's he can be. Yours respectfully,   EUNICE WARNER."

Rowena read the letter through twice. She crept back to bed, with the terrier in her arms.

"We shall have to go, Marmaduke," she said. "It will only be a little earlier, anyway. I must send word to Miss Phillipps that I can't go to Mrs. Jones-Burt's lecture on the science. And I can't finish that sketch of the brook by the birches. Allestree calls that good work. Of course, it isn't anything about Jim Townshend. I shall go right home first."

Rowena liked to talk to the dog. It had been a privation not to speak in the long hours when she was alone.

She could not go to sleep again. The thought of seeing her father and mother and the others made her restless. Now she wondered how she had stayed away all these weeks. She could hardly wait for the time when she should be on the way. She cried at thought of the meeting. She had stuck to her work; she was glad of that. But she deserved no praise; she loved it so well she could not neglect it.

As soon as it was light she dressed. It was too early to go out. Uncle Reuben would not start for several hours.

Rowena put the portrait of Miss Phillipps on the easel and looked at it.

XV.

A HORSEMAN.

IT was a fortunate thing that Reuben Little was not what is called "in liquor" the day Rowena was to go home with him. He was very melancholy and despondent. He said the girl might ride with him if she thought he was good enough. He said he hadn't taken the pladge yet, but he should before he was twenty-four hours older. This was an assertion that he was in the habit of making, so it did not greatly impress his companion.

The two were sitting on an uncomfortable seat placed on the narrow platform which connected the two pair of wheels on which the boats were fastened. Now an arrangement made exclusively for the transportation of boats is not supremely comfortable for the human being. But Rowena thought she should not mind it. She was somewhat cramped, but she could get out and walk occasionally. She was afraid Marmaduke would not like his accommodations. The terrier was rather particular. He had not been used to travelling by means of wheels arranged for row-boats. It was not nearly as comfortable as if the boat had been along and they in it.

When the horse went uphill Rowena thought she should slide backward, and when he went downhill she knew she should go forward between the animal's hind-legs. There was nothing visible to prevent her doing these two things. Uncle Reuben, who to-day took a black view of everything, said there wasn't much chance that he could see why she shouldn't slip off both ways a dozen times before they got home.

And Marmaduke was seized with a desire to stand upright in her lap and lurch this way and that, barking ferociously at every carriage they met. This peculiarity of his made the situation still more complicated, for Rowena was obliged to have a firm hold on the terrier's hind-legs lest in his intensity he should precipitate himself on the ground and be trampled on or run over. And for the first few miles they were constantly meeting all kinds of teams.

When they had traversed a distance of five or six miles matters in regard to Marmaduke began to grow calmer. He sat down on his haunches and put out his adorable little red tongue to pant.

Rowena was beginning to rest somewhat when all at once Marmaduke stood up in order to wag his stub-tail, and his diminutive self vibrated as it did when he saw a friend. A man on horseback had cantered from a side street. This man would not have looked at the equipage moving at a foot-pace had he not heard the dog's sharp bark of welcome. But once looking he glanced again. He wheeled quickly round and raised his cap, exclaiming:

"It is Miss Tuttle!"

Miss Tuttle, keeping her terrier in her lap by main force, met Mr. Keats Bradford's surprised eyes with a smile.

"Are you leaving Boston?" he asked, quickly.

"Yes."

"Does Miss Phillipps know it?"

He was prepared to be very angry with his cousin if she had known and kept the knowledge from him.

"She will know it when she gets my note to-day."

"But you are coming back?" with more eagerness than he usually displayed.

His face showed unmistakable relief when she replied. He did not turn his horse towards the city. Into his air and attitude there came a sudden gayety. His eyes, in color and capability of expression so much like those of Miss Phillipps, took on a certain look which somehow Rowena found it difficult, nay, almost impossible, to meet.

Without suspecting in the least why, she also was conscious of a sense something like exhilaration.

Mr. Bradford had pity on Marmaduke's excited condition. He leaned forward from his horse, skilfully took the dog from the girl and placed him in front of him, keeping gentle but firm hold of one hairy hind-leg. Marmaduke seemed absolutely to grin in the superlativeness of his content with this arrangement. He gave Rowena a glance of kindly commiseration because she could not come also.

"He and I are old friends," said Mr. Bradford. "We understand each other perfectly."

Rowena was in an exceedingly pleasant frame of mind; she even laughed at this man's inability to pronounce some words correctly.

She thought that to see him was something like seeing his cousin, without that occasional sense of insecurity which she knew when with Miss Phillipps.

The suburbs of the city were left behind. They were in the open country where farms began to stretch out over the hills and fields. It was May. People were planting. There was the scent of the earth in the air. There were dandelions by the road-side, where the grass was growing strongly. The robins and blue-birds were wildly happy. The little song sparrows swelled their tiny throats with their delicious songs.

Mr. Reuben Little was mostly silent. This gentleman had been duly introduced to him by his niece, and he had looked him over very sharply, Mr. Bradford being perfectly conscious of the scrutiny, and even going so far as to wish it might bring a favorable conclusion.

For the first ten miles Mr. Bradford thought that in a few moments he would say "good-bye" and turn back. But he went on. Really, how marvellously lovely the country was in May! It was different from the suburbs, altogether different. He said a few ardent words to this effect. He did not quite know himself in this ardor, which seemed to be present in his most commonplace remarks. Or rather, to be strictly true, perhaps he did know himself, vaguely, as being under the influence of that girl who sat there in that rubbishing old cart, and who now and then glanced up at him for one swift instant. He began to cast about in his mind for subjects which should have the effect of making her look at him. All other subjects appeared very flat, indeed.

But I hope it is not understood that Keats Bradford did not know what he was about. He knew extremely well, no man better, and when he said, after a dozen miles had been gone over,

that he believed he would continue right on to
the end of Miss Tuttle's journey, he had most
thoroughly made up his mind to let himself go.
He knew there was a rush and a swing and an
intoxication about letting one's self go that was
comparable to nothing else in the world.

"I've been wondering what little trip to take,"
he remarked, in explanation, "and a fortunate
chance has decided me. Don't tell me it will
annoy you, Miss Tuttle; be kind and say you'll
like to have me along."

"Yes, indeed," replied Rowena, almost too
readily to please Mr. Bradford thoroughly, "it
will be pleasant."

And it was extremely pleasant. Sometimes
the girl alighted from the cart and walked up a
long hill, Mr. Bradford walking beside her with
the bridle over his arm, and Marmaduke career-
ing madly everywhere.

Mr. Reuben Little did not once change his position. He said he was used to it. He sat there
while the two went on ahead, for anything that
could move at all moved faster than Mr. Little's
horse when it was going uphill.

"Thunder and lightning!" remarked Reuben
once to himself; "I wonder what Roweny thinks
of him. Gals is so mortal queer you can't make
'em out more'n you can a riddle. 'N' Roweny
never was in the least sut on beaux. She never

seems to perk 'n' twist herself jest 'cause a man
speaks to her kinder pleasant. Cluck! Git up!"

Mr. Little languidly slapped the right line on
the horse's back. The horse in response turned
his right ear backward, and he made no other response.

This man entertained himself by studying for
a long time the riding costume worn by Mr. Bradford. He made an estimate of the cost of those
leather leggings, leather always being " mighty
high ;" but he was rather baffled by some other
articles of the suit. Then he gave himself up to
stolid watching of the man and to listening to
every word he said.

Mr. Bradford was particularly gifted in many
respects, but in none more than in the ability to
put a great deal of meaning into words that in
themselves meant very little.

For instance, he could say " Thanks" with eye
and tongue in such a way that the most sensible
and reasonable girl might be pardoned for blushing and for remembering the moment with a
tremor. But Keats Bradford was not fully aware
of this power of his. It was only one of the re-
sults of the process of " letting himself go."
When he spoke and looked in this kind of a
way it was only because he felt strongly. He
was not that sort of a creature who tries exper-
iments. If he was deeply moved, the result

15

often was that some one else became deeply moved also, and generally in a way similar.

Even Reuben Little had a dim sense of something rather out of the ordinary in this person in the leather leggings. He could not, as he told his wife afterwards, when he discussed the matter with her, he could not make out as "that feller" said a word to Rowena all the way out but what he might have said himself; but he vowed it was the tallest and by far the most superior kind of courtin' he ever saw done in his life. If he'd "been a gal he should have jest been pleased 'nough."

And praise from Reuben Little, when he was not "in liquor," was praise indeed.

At last the way began to seem familiar to Rowena. There was the "third district school-house;" there was the old pine-tree which had been struck by lightning and riven down the middle of the trunk. Even the horse-briers by the way-side had a different look to them. At the top of a hill she could see the spire of the Baptist Church at the Corners. In two miles more she would be at home. She grew silent with the sudden rising of the emotions which had been kept in the background.

Mr. Bradford presently asked Mr. Little to direct him to the hotel of the nearest village. He told Rowena he might be in the vicinity a couple of days; in that case he should call on her, if she gave him permission. Then he rode down a cross road. Rowena was glad he was gone. Now that she was so near her home his presence confused her. She drew a long breath and looked eagerly at every object; every birch-tree spoke to her in the old language, but was it as sweet a language as she had thought? Was there really a hint of dreariness and desolation in the rocky farms and the low-browed, solemn-looking houses near which she sometimes saw a man slouching and gazing intently at them?

Everybody they saw now nodded at them. Rowena knew they would all tell that " they seen Roweny Tuttle goin' 'long with Little." She knew also that they would wonder among each other as to whether she had "come home for good or not." Delegates from different directions would appear soon at Mr. Tuttle's to learn whether her arrival was for good. There was a very well-defined feeling of hostility towards her plan of " studyin' in Borston." They did not understand it. If she wanted to study, why not have her paints and things at home? You could get real good paints at Middle Village; and one of the stores there had for sale those thin brass disks on which some women painted daisies and pansies. Philip Barrett had long had it in his mind that he would present Rowena with one of these brass objects so that she might paint what she chose on it. But he had never yet resolved to do it. To him there was some mystery in the way she thought about painting—"art," as she called it.

Rowena could hardly wait for the movements of Uncle Reuben's horse to take her over the road. They had now climbed to the top of that long hill, near the foot of which was the turn, and opposite the Warner house.

Rowena felt as if she could not stop, even for the time necessary to inquire about Georgie. She must get home to her father and mother. But she knew she would be expected to stop. She had asked Uncle Reuben about Georgie. He had said she was probably going into a decline, or "failing," as he expressed it. But Rowena knew too well what a view her uncle took of all subjects when he was contemplating signing the pledge. Therefore she did not greatly heed his opinion.

The long cart rattled tumultuously down the hill and round the corner.

Eunice was in the yard with an apron hastily pinned over her head. Rowena hurriedly alighted with Marmaduke under her arm.

Eunice precipitated herself so furiously upon her that the terrier deemed it incumbent upon him to growl and bristle up his mustache.

While Rowena was endeavoring to return the embrace, and before she could say a word about Georgie, a young man came walking slowly round from the back of the house. He had his hands in his pockets and his hat pushed far back on his head. A thin, reddish beard covered the lower part of his face, leaving fully revealed a mouth which was shaped in a way that was both handsome and weak. His eyes also were handsome, and of that light, limpid blue which frequently accompanies sandy hair and skin. His shoulders were bent and very broad. He gazed with great interest at Rowena, whom he had never seen before.

Eunice turned quickly to him and seized his arm.

"Oh, Jim," she cried, "she's come! I knew she'd come! Now I guess Georgie 'll begin to pick up, don't you?"

"I do hope so," was the earnest response. "I d'know what we shall do if she don't pick up soon now."

With a great deal of pride in her ability to perform an introduction, the child now introduced Mr. Townshend to Miss Tuttle. The two shook hands. She had a decided impression that she should like Jim Townshend. The troubled, drawn look on his face was due, of course, to his anxiety. Rowena hastened to say that she would go home now. She must see her mother. She would come right over that very afternoon and sit with Georgie.

As she was about to climb back into the wagon Mrs. Warner hurried out, rolling down her sleeves as she came. She gave Rowena a loud kiss. She said she hoped Roweny'd make up her mind to stay to home. She'd had a real good chance to learn to dror 'n' paint now.

Rowena could not reply to this. Marmaduke peered at them all from the folds of her shawl. They exclaimed at him. Mrs. Warner said she thought he was real cunning, but she s'posed he wa'n't good for an earthly thing, and how much had he cost? The Tifts on the pine road had some kind of puppies that they sold for two dollars a-piece.

Rowena said, rather coldly, that this dog was a gift to her.

Mrs. Warner said she didn't see why Georgie didn't git 'long, only she didn't. Roweny must come right straight over.

When Rowena drove on she held the terrier close. She told him she supposed the Warners had always been just like that, but she had forgotten.

After a few rods they met Marthy S. walking. In her hand she had the bag which Rowena remembered so well, the flat, square twine bag in which were carried a tape-measure, scissors, thimble, and sometimes a roll of work to be taken home.

"Don't stop," whispered Rowena to her uncle. He nodded. But when Marthy S. stepped right up almost in front of the wheel he was obliged to stop.

Marthy S. put up her little, hard hand, and when Marmaduke reached forward she sprang back, exclaiming:

"Gracious! Does he bite? How dy do, Roweny? I s'pose you've come home for good now. Your mother needs ye. She ain't first-rate. Her humor's ben workin' some, she told me, when I seen her last week. I guess you know all 'bout paintin' 'n' dorin', now, don't ye? Mr. Lapham's daughter Julie's ben takin' lessons of a woman that comes to the Corners. She was good enough for Julie. But I guess she wouldn't do for you. She's painted something on a piece of slate. They say you c'n paint on most anything nowadays. I s'pose you've had a first-rate time. But your mother needs ye. She didn't say so, but I knew if her humor was workin' she must need ye."

Rowena was growing more and more angry. The old animosity this woman always roused in her sprang up again.

"I've been very busy, Miss Hancock." she said. "I didn't go to have a good time."

Marthy S. drew back so that Uncle Reuben could safely slap the lines and cluck. The horse moved forward, and the dress-maker went on her way.

"She's just the same stuck-up thing she always was," she said, aloud. "I don't care if I did give her a dab."

Over Rowena's face the heat was rising in waves, each wave hotter than the last. Her eyes burned so that she could not see very well. The narrow white road glimmered and seemed to rise up and down before her.

"I wouldn't mind that critter one grain, Roweny," her uncle said, roughly.

The girl almost sobbed.

"She made me feel as if she thought I was careless about my mother—my own mother!" she cried, in a smothered voice.

Rowena put her face down on Marmaduke's back.

"Dumb her!" responded Uncle Reuben; "of course she made you feel bad if she could. It's jest like her."

The girl was not going to yield to this emotion. In a few moments she would be at home.

She raised her head and tried to believe that "things looked natural." Certainly they had not changed. Everything was as it usually was at this time in May. Nevertheless, there was a sense that everything was alien. Rowena was impatient with herself that it was so. She could not understand it at all.

"There's somebody comin' down the road."

Mr. Little's voice brought back the girl's eyes from the fields where the savins were growing and where the clear air so sharply defined the outlines.

She looked down the road. A tall, thin figure with a plaid shawl round it and a cloud on its head was walking rapidly.

Rowena's face and eyes suffused. Her heart gave a great bound.

"It's mother!" she cried, in a loud whisper.

She began to climb down from her seat before the horse stopped. She put Marmaduke on the ground and began to run, the terrier at her heels.

Almost in a moment she was in her mother's arms. Those arms closed so tightly, so tightly about her.

"I couldn't help comin' to meet ye," said Mrs. Tuttle, huskily. "My bread was almost riz, but I couldn't help comin'.

XVI.

SOMETHING ON HER MIND.

THE girl and her mother hurried towards the house, while the boat-wagon rattled slowly homeward. Marmaduke's progress was very deliberate, for he was obliged to smell of every shrub and every tuft of grass.

Sometimes a bluebird came swooping down close to the two women.

The frogs were "hollering" in all the low places.

"You see, I've got to git right back," said Mrs. Tuttle, gazing in an almost famished way at her daughter. "My bread was almost riz," she repeated; "but I thought you must have got round Warner's Corner, and I couldn't help coming."

She put one hand over her eyes for a moment. Her lips trembled. Now that Rowena had actually come, she could hardly struggle against the reaction from that long waiting and longing. Her other hand clutched tightly that of the girl.

"Oh, mother, it was wrong of me to go, wasn't it? Have I been so wicked?"

Rowena's breath caught. Her words roused Mrs. Tuttle as nothing else would have done.

"It wa'n't wrong, neither—not an atom," she exclaimed. "You can't expect me to jest love to have you gone, Roweny; but I guess you've got a right to your life 's much 's I had to mine when I married your father 'n' left my home. I ain't goin' to be foolish another minute. The children are all to school. They've missed you a lot. Your father was 'bliged to go to the Corners, but he expected to be back by this time; 'n' there he is now."

An old gray horse attached to an ancient covered wagon, of the kind locally called "bedrooms," was now seen coming from the opposite direction. Mr. Tuttle bent over and whipped his horse, which gave a lurch and then seemed to retrace its steps.

Rowena ran forward. Mr. Tuttle hurriedly stepped on top of the wheel and jumped to the ground.

"Well, I am glad," he said, after he had kissed her. "I declare, the days have been awful long, Roweny. How's your drorin'?"

The terrier allowed himself to be greeted warmly. It was plain that he approved of this part of the world; it was much better than pavements and city streets. He followed Rowena as she went about to every nook and corner of the house and barns. She strolled up the lane. Apparently the same woodpecker was pounding on the immense old chestnut-tree that stood by the bars at the brook. Absolutely nothing had changed, and yet—

Rowena did not know what it was. She was so glad, so very glad to be there. She knew that if she had returned within a week or two after she had left, her happiness would have been greater. She did not understand it at all. Perhaps it would all come to her at last; she was waiting for absolutely the same feeling. There was no one to tell her that absolutely the same feeling would never come to her again.

Presently she heard her mother's voice calling to her from the back door of the barn.

She ate a lunch, with her father and mother sitting and looking at her. Their faces shone. They tried to be staid and calm.

Rowena was obliged to eat before supper-time, because she was going directly to see Georgie Warner.

"It does seem as if Georgie had something on her mind," Mrs. Tuttle had just said. "'Tain't natural for a girl to take all the bitters she's taken without havin' some appetite, 'less there was something on her mind. But she keeps sayin' there ain't."

"She ought to know," remarked Rowena, trying to eat a seed-cake. "I'm sure I should know if I had anything on my mind," she laughed. "Who's going to know, if you don't know yourself? What is it supposed to be?"

"I guess it ain't supposed," replied Mrs. Tuttle, giving lavish morsels of very sweet gingerbread to Marmaduke, who partook approvingly. "She's had to git a substitoot for her school. Jim Townshend's there every day. It can't be no trouble about him. P'raps she'll tell you something."

"Oh, well," said Mr. Tuttle, in his usual optimistic way, "I guess Georgie 'll weather it fast enough. I s'pose she's got kind of er spring fever; 'n' mebby her humor's workin' some."

Mrs. Tuttle shook her head.

"Hiram, you know there ain't nobody equil to Mis' Warner for doct'rin' a humor. It's mor'n a humor."

Very soon Rowena was hurrying along the road alone. She could hear Marmaduke's shrill remonstrance against being left behind. As she walked through the pines she recalled that day she had walked there before she went to Boston. How long ago was that? She had known Miss Phillipps since then—and Mr. Bradford. She walked still faster.

Eunice was lurking among the pines nearest her home. She had an apron pinned over her head, and the long, broad strings of it fluttered like pennons as she now ran forward.

"She's expectin' ye!" she shouted, when still at some distance. "She's ben cryin'. She cries a lot. She cries if you speak to her, 'n' if you don't. 'Tain't very pleasant to our house now."

The latter sentences were spoken after the child had reached Rowena and was walking by her, holding her hand.

Although Georgie was so impatient, Eunice was disposed to linger. She had a great deal she wished to say; she wished to tell Rowena, among other things, what Marthy S. had been saying about her.

But Rowena would not linger. She was somewhat excited when she began to ascend the stairs that led to the chamber where Georgie was. She went alone. It had been Georgie's desire that she come alone.

She stopped an instant at the broad, top stair. Then she softly opened the door.

Georgie was dressed in a pink calico wrapper. She was lying on a lounge that was drawn to the window. There was a small air-tight stove in the room, and the air was close and warm.

She half raised herself and eagerly held out her arms, her thin, flushed face looking strange to Rowena, who had never seen it save when it was plump and commonplace.

The new-comer sat quickly down on the side of the couch and encircled her friend in her own arms, putting her cool face to the hot, weary one.

Georgie began to tremble and to sob.

"Don't cry—don't cry," murmured Rowena, holding the trembling form more closely.

Her presence and her voice appeared to soothe the sick girl. She became more quiet.

"I shall take you out in our old 'bedroom,'" said Rowena, after a while. "You must have the air."

Georgie shuddered.

"I don't want the air," she said, with her head on Rowena's shoulder. She turned her face into the folds of Rowena's shawl and cried out in a fierce, muffled tone:

"It's her! It's her! I knew 'twould be, 'n' 'tis! But I ain't lisped it to anybody else. I couldn't!"

The other girl remained silent a moment. She was trying to recall a name.

"Do you mean Mary Jane Jewett? The one you told me about?"

A kind of convulsion shook poor Georgie as she heard.

"Yes," she said. "He's all carried away with her. And he wants to do right. He suffers awful. 'N' I love him so! Oh, dear me!"

Georgie's shoulders heaved; she gasped hysterically.

"But everybody says Mr. Townshend is perfectly devoted to you, Georgie; that he is here every day. Aren't you mistaken? Isn't this a notion of yours?"

Georgie lifted her head. Her eyes were dry and staring.

"I wish 'twas a notion. But 'tain't. I guess I know. Yes, he is here every day. He's tryin' to do right, I tell ye. 'N' I've been so silly I jest let him come. I can't give him up! I can't! I couldn't tell nobody. It's killin' of me?"

Georgie put out her hot hands and shut them hard. "Oh, how I hate her! Do you think I c'n let her have him? I hate her! I d'know but I could try to give him up if it wasn't to her. But I can't! I can't!"

She spoke as one does who has been long denied speech on a certain subject, and now the words came in torrents, incoherent, sometimes ambiguous, running into each other.

"She's ben after him agin. She's made him believe she loves him. He says he can't seem to help himself; he says he's mad for her; he says it's like bein' drunk. But he's tryin' to do right."

Thus, after her wild talk had calmed a little, there seemed nothing for Rowena to say. She was bewildered. She could only hold her friend closely and wait.

At last the stream of words ceased entirely. Georgie lay still on Rowena's shoulder. She was both exhausted and relieved. She fell asleep.

The afternoon was almost gone when Rowena had come. Now, as she sat there motionless, the sun went down and the long spring twilight began. The robins sang their evening song. The sound of the frogs was louder than ever. She grew stiff, and her limbs ached. When it was very dusky in the room the door opened softly, and Mrs. Warner looked in. Seeing that still group she noiselessly closed the door and crept down the stairs.

"I do hope Georgie's goin' to be better," she said to her husband as she stole about her evening work. "She's fast asleep with her head on Roweny's shoulder."

"I do hope so, too," was the response. "It's ben mighty hard on you. Sh'll I bring home some herrin' from the Corners? I'm goin' to hitch up 'n' see 'bout them seed p'taters."

Eunice and her mother continued to creep about the lower rooms for a half hour longer.

At the end of that time Rowena came downstairs for a glass of fresh water.

Georgie had wakened. She wanted Rowena to stay all night with her. Would Eunice go over and tell Mrs. Tuttle, so that nobody need to worry? Whereupon that child started off on a run to do her errand.

Mrs. Warner drew a bucket of water from the well. As she dipped a tumbler in it she looked wistfully at the girl before her.

"How do you think she is, Roweny?" she asked, in a whisper.

"I'm too ignorant about sickness," answered Rowena, "but it doesn't seem to me she is dangerously ill—and yet she suffers."

Mrs. Warner set the glass by the sink instead of giving it to her companion. There was in-tensest curiosity as well as concern in her face as she said, in a still lower whisper,

"She's got something on her mind, ain't she?"

The girl hesitated. She resented the question; but she thought she must give some answer to Georgie's mother.

"I'm afraid she has," she said.

"There!" exclaimed Mrs. Warner, but still whispering, "I told um it wa'n't all humor, 'n' 'tain't. Is what she's got on her mind 'bout Jim?"

"You must ask Georgie, Mrs. Warner."

The woman now remarked that she didn't see how under the canopy it could be about Jim. Jim was the best fellow in the world, 'n' he'd ben near crazed 'cause Georgie was sick. She did hope Georgie hadn't got any other feller in her mind, looking sharply at Rowena as she said these last words. The girl was thankful it was so dark. She hurried back up the steep stairs with the water. She helped Georgie take off the pink wrapper and prepare for bed. She found her friend to be pitiably weak and full of fancies, so different from the sturdy, commonplace girl she was when in health.

At last Rowena lay down beside her and held the feverish hands closely. She was surprised that Georgie soon dropped asleep.

But it was long before she herself could sleep. Strange thoughts trooped with almost painful vividness through her mind. Now that she was alone she could recall the face and voice and manner of the man who had ridden so many miles by the side of the boat-cart that day. She could think of Miss Phillipps.

She must go back next week. She must not lose too much time before the long summer vacation, when her lessons would cease and she would be at home. She almost dreaded being at home so long. Where would Miss Phillipps spend the Summer?

Finally, long after the clock down-stairs had struck twelve, she also fell asleep.

She was awakened while it was still dark by a spasmodic clutch around her neck, and by Georgie whispering shrilly:

"I'll tell you what you must do—you must see her."

Rowena thought at first that her friend was dreaming. She tried to soothe her.

"You jest promise you'll see her—promise!" persisted Georgie, "and don't you let no mortal know it."

Rowena hesitated. She could guess very well what person she was to see. But how could she do it?

"Ain't you goin' to promise?" asked Georgie. "Don't you care nothin' 'bout me? I've ben dependin' on ye. I thought you wouldn't fail me."

The girl's chest began to heave, and she began to tremble.

"I'll see her," said Rowena.

"I want you to see her to-day—this very day."

"I'll see her to-day—if I can have father's horse and wagon."

Georgie stopped trembling.

Rowena felt herself in a very humiliating position, but she could not retreat.

"You must give me some idea of what I am to say to her. If she is what you think, she won't be agreeable."

Georgie replied in rather a strong voice:

"Tell her," she began, "tell her I'm dyin'—"

"But you are not."

"I be, too! I guess I know when I'm dyin'.

And I want her to stop tryin' to git Jim away from me. If she stops her nasty, mean tricks he'll git over it. I know he will. He told me solemnly that he believed I was the best girl, and would make him the best wife. He said he wanted to throw off her influence, but he couldn't seem to. Jim's real good, but he ain't got so much resolution 's some folks have; he ain't to blame for that."

Rowena was silent for so long a time that her companion broke forth into a long-drawn whine. Georgie Warner was completely unstrung with the nervous strain and the slow fever which her lover's conduct had induced. She had also learned that the more she gave way the greater became the facilities for giving way. She had discovered what others had discovered before her, that there is a strange, perverted kind of enjoyment in a "fit of the nerves." She was really ill; but not nearly so ill as she believed herself to be.

"What you so still for?" she asked, in her sharply feeble voice.

"Georgie, don't do that—don't do it," exclaimed Rowena, earnestly. "Let Jim go, if he must. You can't furnish him with resolution. You'll despise yourself if you try to keep him that way."

"Oh, dear me!" cried Georgie. "You said you'd see her! You said you would!"

"I will.   But I'm ashamed to do it."

Georgie did not care; if her errand were done, no matter what the cost to the doer of it.

She now began to hug her friend and to weep softly. Notwithstanding this, Rowena could not help remaining rather cold and impassive.

She made one more attempt to bring her friend to reason.   She tried to persuade her to wait until she was stronger, when she might look at the matter differently. At this Georgie tossed about violently, and protested that she should never get stronger, never, until Mary Jane Jewett had been seen and made to stop her nasty, mean tricks.

Rowena rose and dressed.   She wanted all the time she could have to herself before she should seek Miss Jewett.   She had not the remotest idea as to how she should state the case.

As she walked along the solitary road, now flooded with the level, new rays of the sun, she made a resolution which she felt was rash.   She would see Mary Jane Jewett; but she would see Jim Townshend first.   That man's winning face, with its indeterminate mouth and chin, came very strongly before her.

When she came within sight of her home she saw the terrier nosing about in the yard.   Her father walked across to the barn, a milk-pail in each hand.   A thick smoke was going straight up from the immense mouth of the old chimney.

Now Marmaduke saw her and raced furiously towards her. She caught him joyfully in her arms. The sight of him rested her; and his presence also brought pictures of her Boston life. Had she really lived that life, and known Miss Phillipps and—Mr. Bradford? How very odd it was that Mr. Bradford should have happened to come out with her yesterday! She remembered now that she had not mentioned this fact, even to her mother. Was it because she had forgotten it? Doubtless he was already starting back to Boston. It was pleasant to know him, he was so much like his cousin in many ways.

At breakfast Rowena announced that she had an errand to do for Georgie. She should need the horse perhaps all the forenoon.

Mrs. Tuttle inquired with the keenest curiosity if Rowena thought Georgie Warner had anything on her mind. She said she was sure she didn't know why it had got round so that Georgie had something on her mind, when Jim Townshend was so attentive. It was perfectly evident that it was not thought for a moment that a young woman could have anything on her mind unless this thing were connected with some past or present or possible lover. Rowena replied that she thought Georgie was rather worried about some matters. Mrs. Tuttle knew her daughter's face too well to press her question.

Rowena took her place on the narrow seat in the covered wagon. She gathered up the worn leather lines, and the old gray horse walked out of the yard. At this moment it seemed to her as if she had never been away. As she turned the corner on the road that led towards Middle Village, and by the Townshend farm, she wondered if Mr. Bradford would really call on his way to Boston. Perhaps she ought to have warned her mother of the possibility of such a call. Then she forgot Mr. Bradford, and, for the moment, her disagreeable errand, in the beauty of the hills and vales before her. Their loveliness penetrated with a subtle exhilaration.

The horse walked on unheeded. The girl's eyes and soul drank in the enchanting vistas where tints of green and gray, and all the colors of unfolding leaves, stretched away in every direction.

"Oh!" she murmured, in a kind of ecstasy, "I can paint all this! I must! I will!"

She forgot where she was going. When the horse stopped to bite off the top leaves from a scrub-oak she did not notice. She was leaning forward; she was setting up her palette; the canvas was before her. The high light should come just there, then the shadows.

The horse did not care where the high light would come. There were some tender leaves just over the wall. He pulled forward to reach them. The two right wheels of the " bedroom " lurched and strained, and finally rose up on some large stones. It was too much for the ancient axle. It snapped ; so did something in the front wheel. Then the front wheel collapsed, and Rowena stopped thinking about how she would paint the scene before her. She slipped down from her seat onto the ground. As soon as she could she hurried to the horse's head, fearing he might have a fancy to go on. She had forgotten that the gray never had a fancy to go on. He looked round benignly at her and continued to eat twigs.

XVII.

THE EPISODE OF MARY JANE JEWETT.

THE girl and the horse and wagon were on a hill nearly two miles from any house. It was not a convenient place for a wheel to collapse. It was hardly a convenient place for anything, save fresh air and scenery.

Having recalled the fact that the horse would be the last to make any kind of a movement, Rowena stopped holding his bridle and stumbled back over the stones to the road.

She sat down on a rock to think for a few moments. The road was not much travelled; she might wait there for half a day before any one came. But it was a very lovely place. Before she knew it her artist eyes were again absorbed in gazing. She made an effort and roused herself. She walked round the turnout. She wished Marmaduke were with her. Things were always so much more cheerful where Marmaduke was. It was very vexatious. There was nothing for it but to go back home. She had ridden bareback as a child, but later she had an old side-saddle. She must try bareback again. She went up a few rods to the very summit of the hill. She looked both ways along the road. It wound on beneath the clear blue of the sky. Nobody was in sight.

"Yes," said Rowena, aloud, "I shall have to ride the old gray home."

Instead of unharnessing the animal directly, however, she fell again to gazing about her. She had been shut up in Boston for so long she had half forgotten the vigorous, bounding sweep of the country.

Finally she began to take the tugs from the whiffletree. It was hard work to pull them from the hooks in the position now occupied by the wagon.

Rowena's hat fell off, and she began to grow red and to pant.

She did not see a narrow, dingy-top buggy reach the brow of the hill and then come slowly towards her. The buggy stopped, and the horse attached reached its head far out and tossed it up and down, trying to get at the road-side grass.

"I guess something's happened to your ex, ain't there?" asked a voice.

Rowena stopped pulling on the strap so suddenly that she nearly fell over.

The occupant of the buggy got lightly out of it and walked to the other side of the old gray.

"Let's get this tug out first, and then the oth-er 'll have a chance to give a little," she said.

This person was a young woman, rather large and rather plump. She had a somewhat coarse-featured, handsome face, with immense black eyes under heavy brows. She spoke in a good-humored voice, and she put her red, strong hands very effectively upon the strap and unfastened it from the whiffletree. She had judged rightly. Rowena was now enabled to release the tug on her side. The two girls worked together until the horse was free and Rowena had led him out into the middle of the road.

"I guess that wagon ain't wuth mendin', is it?" asked the stranger; then she said, more quickly, "Why, it's the old gray Tuttle hoss, ain't it?"

"Yes," said Rowena.

The girl looked full at Rowena an instant now. She smiled, showing white, even teeth.

"Then you must be Roweny Tuttle."

"Yes, I am. And you are Mary Jane Jewett, aren't you?"

"Of course. But how'd you come to know me, I sh'd like to know?"

She was evidently much interested in this girl, who would go to Boston to learn to paint when she might have received instruction of a woman who came to Middle Village for the express pur-pose of giving lessons.

"I've seen you once at an evening meeting," said Rowena, rather stiffly, "and I saw you at a picnic last summer with James Townshend."

Miss Jewett laughed.

"Yes, I've been round with Jim consid'able. I c'n generally find some feller to go round with me. Hadn't you better git right in 'n' lemme take you home? You c'n hitch the hoss on behind. 'Twon't be no trouble to me; not a speck."

Miss Jewett had looked Rowena over. As she spoke she had decided to ask her for a pattern of her dress. She did not know what there was about it, but it just suited her. She didn't believe Martha S. cut it, "never in the world."

Rowena stood for a moment leaning against her horse. She asked herself if Providence were not aiding her to an interview with Mary Jane Jewett. She must go with her. She cast a side-glance at the girl as she stood there waiting. There was something in that personality so thoroughly antagonistic to her that Rowena's anger rose high against Georgie Warner for having placed her in such a position.

"You are very kind," said Rowena, even more stiffly than she had yet spoken. "I shall be glad to go with you."

She tied the gray horse by a rein to the axle of the buggy behind. She stepped up and sat

down on the seat.   As Miss Jewett put her foot
on the step she gave a short laugh and said that
she had seen folks before that had swallowed
ramrods and had um stick in their backs.

Miss Jewett had felt very kindly and very help-
ful when she had arrived upon the scene.   She
had been favorably impressed also by Hiram Tuttle's daughter.   She resented Rowena's manner.
Rowena knew it, and thought she did not have
it in her power to try to conciliate her companion.

The two drove on in silence.   Suddenly the
silence was broken by Rowena's saying, desperately,

"I was on my way to see you."

Miss Jewett stared.

"The land!" she cried.   "You don't mean it!
Well, I am beat."

"Yes," went on Rowena, hurriedly, "I wanted
to see you about—about Georgie Warner."

Rowena blushed uncomfortably as she said
this.   She added that Georgie was a dear friend
of hers.

Mary Jane Jewett had turned, and was looking
squarely and unblinkingly at the speaker.   There
was a hint of a smile on the large mouth, and a
malicious amusement in the black eyes.

"Well," she said, "I'm a listenin'."

"Mr. Townshend is engaged to Georgie," said

Rowena, now beginning to feel so actively hostile that she was ready to fight.

"I want to know!" responded Miss Jewett. "Is she a holdin' on to him yet? I guess she finds him kinder slippery, don't she?"

Rowena turned savagely upon the other. Her eyes burned; her voice trembled with fury.

"Do you think it honorable to try to get a poor sick girl's lover away from her?"

"It don't take much tryin', you'd better believe," was the answer.

"But you do try. If you hadn't tried he wouldn't have gone back to you again. You know that. It isn't fair. It's mean; and she ill and half crazed just with this trouble about him. And she loves him so!"

Rowena paused, nearly breathless. She did not know why the vivid picture of Georgie lying in that little, close room all at once removed all her anger. With one of the sudden transitions which were characteristic of her she bent near the girl beside her. She put her bare hand on the bare hands that were holding the lines.

"Don't do it! Don't do it!" she said, so softly and pleadingly that Miss Jewett, who had been "real mad," as she would have said, a moment ago, was now conscious of an unaccountable revulsion of feeling.

Rowena's hand pressed upon hers. Perhaps

Miss Phillipps could have analyzed what there was in Rowena's touch, and often in her glance, that so won upon people. Whatever it was it had its effect now.

Miss Jewett met Rowena's eyes. Her face changed.

"I declare," she cried; "what makes you care so much? I shouldn't think she'd care neither for a fellew that was bewitched with somebody else. 'N' Jim is jest bewitched 'bout me, 'n' that's a fact."

The girl laughed, but not too triumphantly.

She withdrew one hand and placed it on Rowena's with a strong pressure.

"You wouldn't want to keep a beau that way, would ye, now?" she asked.

Rowena recoiled.

"No," she said; "but Georgie is ill and weak, and so unhappy. Do you care for him?"

"Oh, land, no; not particular, you know. It's amusin', though, to keep him on. 'N' I like him first-rate. Is she really sick?" with interest.

"Yes, really."

Miss Jewett laughed again.

"Odd, ain't it, that any one should git real sick about Jim Townshend? There ain't a man on the face of the earth wuth gettin' sick about."

The idea seemed to amuse Miss Jewett greatly. She shook her broad shoulders and broke into a loud laugh. Then she said, apologetically, that "she was laughin' at what she was thinkin' on."

Nothing at this juncture occurring to Rowena to say, she said nothing. She knew that she could do very little more. She began to wonder why her companion continued to laugh. She was not quite so disagreeable now as she had been at first.

"I s'pose Jim's hangin' round there, ain't he?"

"Yes."

"I thought 's likely 's not. He's hangin' round me, too. Betwixt Miss Warner 'n' me it's a wonder how he gits a chance to do his work, ain't it?"

More laughter.

At last Mary Jane became somewhat composed. She turned round on the circumscribed buggy seat that she might face Rowena.

"I'm sure I don't know what there is about you, Miss Tuttle," she began, with broad frankness, "but I was mad 'nough a few minutes ago to throw you out of the buggy, 'n' now I ain't mad a bit. I kinder like you. 'N' I wish I knew how you git such a fit on your dress. Have you got a pattern?"

She seemed disappointed when she learned there was no pattern.

Rowena was now very much depressed. She

17

felt that she had accomplished nothing; and still there was hope lurking in her heart.

Miss Jewett spent a short time in urging the horse and remonstrating with it, with no effect whatever.   Then she sat back.

"Now I'm goin' to tell ye something; it's a secret.   I ain't even told mar yet.   It's something Georgie Warner 'll give her ears to hear. You may tell her, but you needn't lisp it to another soul.   Promise me you won't."

"No, I won't."

"Well, then, I'm ingaged."

"Oh!"

Rowena could say no more.   She felt a great load lifted from her heart.   She already pictured herself as giving the good news to Georgie.

"I s'pose you don't know him.   It's Charley Simmons.   He's got er place in a grocery store in Borston, 'n' we expect to be married in the fall, 'n' I sh'll live in Borston!   Mebby it'll be near you."

The glow of exultation and satisfaction on Miss Jewett's face was superlative.

"Will you tell Mr. Townshend?"

"Won't he be cut up, though?" responded Miss Jewett.

"Will you tell him?" persisted Rowena, almost feverishly.

"Oh yes; of course I will."

"The first time you see him?"

"How you go on! Yes, I will. That's a promise; 'n' I'll keep it, too. But there couldn't anybody else have made me do it, I tell you."

"Thank you—thank you, so much!" said Rowena, warmly.

"Mebby you'll jest kiss me for that," said Miss Jewett, almost shyly, and coloring faintly as she spoke.

"Now we're real friendly, ain't we?" she remarked, after the kiss had been given. "You jest tell Georgie Warner I wouldn't have done it for anybody but you. She's a bright one to send you."

Miss Jewett went on talking in the same startlingly frank manner. She was telling some peculiarities of an admirer who had threatened to kill himself unless she "had him," when she interrupted her recital to exclaim:

"Mercy! Who is that, anyway? Ain't he jest got up fit to kill, and no mistake? Did you ever see anything beat that little dorg he's got?"

Coming slowly up the hill down which Miss Jewett's horse was walking, with the old gray stumbling behind, was a man on horseback. Of course, it was Keats Bradford. Sitting quite calmly in front of him, just as if one hind leg were not held lest he might fall, was Marmaduke, surveying the landscape with approving eyes.

Mr. Bradford was not looking to find Rowena in this buggy with a companion. He was in pursuit of the covered wagon and the gray horse. He was very near the two before he looked at them with any interest. Then his face lightened brilliantly. He stopped his horse and, lifting his cap, said:

"Miss Tuttle, Marmaduke knew you before I did. Will you have him? He was happy with me until he saw you."

The terrier was wriggling with joy. With very small aid he leaped from the saddle into Rowena's arms.

Miss Jewett was staring with undisguised interest and admiration. She was absolutely sure that she had never seen leather leggings like these now before her. Her never-sleeping instinct of coquetry became instantly active. Her opinion of Rowena rose still higher. She could not help respecting a girl who knew a man who had such leggings, who had a glass in his eye, or rather dangling from a cord, and who could take off his cap with such a manner as that. This was no common beau. Charley Simmons seemed, for the moment, to recede very far into the background.

Bradford had turned his horse, and the animal was now walking by the side of the carriage.

"I called at your home, Miss Tuttle," he said. "Your mother told me in which direction you had gone. Marmaduke was frantic to come with me. If we intrude, send us away."

The young man's face was radiant. There was no more any languor on it. He had gone to sleep the night before with the resolution to see Miss Tuttle at every possible moment. The carrying out of this resolution was already as full of enjoyment as he had anticipated it would be. He now looked down at the girl with a reckless pleasure in his eyes. He felt that he would not deny himself a single glance.

Miss Jewett's shrewd observation was upon him. She was fully capable of interpreting the expression on the man's face.

She changed her mind about exercising any of her arts upon him. She did not wish to waste any ammunition. But she pushed a powerful elbow against Rowena, and whispered:

"Do introduce him!"

Rowena obeyed. Bradford could be polite, but he thought it was time lost to look long at any other face when he might see Rowena. He was gratefully aware that his cousin Vanessa was a good many miles away, and that she did not know where he was at this moment.

He did not know that she had the slightest influence upon him, but he did know that she knew him almost as well as he knew himself. And there are occasions in life when the absence of such a person is desirable.

There was a bitterness in his thoughts of his cousin that was very like the bitterness of jealousy. Later, he acted under a different feeling.

Perhaps this was the first time that Mary Jane Jewett had, since she was grown, been in the company of a gentleman and not been first in his eyes. She was one of those women who seem to change in manner and looks the moment a man appears. But now she came nearer effacing herself than she had ever come before. She watched the two; she had a sharp curiosity to know Rowena's attitude towards this man, and she was wise in such matters. But she could not decide. The girl was unaffectedly glad to see Mr. Bradford; her eyes shone at him; sometimes she blushed beneath his look. She laughed gayly; she talked with a naïve freedom; or she was sometimes silent.

"Well, I am beat," said Miss Jewett more than once to herself during the next quarter of an hour.

When she parted from the two at a corner near the Tuttle place she sat a moment watching them.

Bradford was leading his horse and the old gray. He was walking between the two animals. Rowena and the terrier were strolling behind.

Rowena turned and waved her hand. She cried out, joyously,

"I shall go right and tell Georgie!"

"Go ahead!" shouted Miss Jewett. "I'll keep my promise."

And now she saw Rowena hurry forward. She left Bradford far behind, the dog caracoling about her.

Mary Jane Jewett, as she went on her way, told herself that this was the first girl she had ever seen that wa'n't as flat as dish-water. Girls was usually so uninterestin' it wa'n't no use spendin' time with um. It wa'n't 'cause that Tuttle girl had said anything bright, either; she didn't know what 'twas.

Keats Bradford did not know what it was, either, and he was not in the mood to analyze. He remained most fully in the mood to let himself go.

He put up the old gray in the barn and hitched his own horse, while Rowena hastened over to Georgie Warner's with her good news. She would not let him go with her. He went in the house and sat in the kitchen, while Mrs. Tuttle was frying doughnuts. He successfully concealed his great surprise when he discovered that Mrs. Tuttle called these fried cakes "sim-balls." He had never heard that word before, and it affected him almost to the verge of hysteria. He ate a sim-ball and was able to thank the giver of it. When Rowena returned she also ate a doughnut. While partaking of this lunch she asked Mr. Bradford what her mother had called this food, putting the question as simply as a child would have done.

When he had gravely replied, she looked at her mother fondly as she said :

"I've been trying to teach mother not to call these cakes that way. There's something so ridiculous in that word, don't you think? There was a piece in our old reading-book which we children always thought meant doughnuts. I shall never forget when Georgie Warner stood up one examination day and began, 'Heaven hung no symbol there.' She said sim-ball. I've always believed that the committeemen didn't know the difference. We don't know as much in this deestrict as we do in Borston, Mr. Bradford."

Her eyes sparkled as she looked at Bradford. He felt a most idiotic gladness that he had already eaten two sim-balls.

Perhaps you do not believe that a man who was born and reared in Boston, who has spent more than a year in London, don't you know; who tries to wear a monocle, and who says " weally," could be as much in love as another man without such advantages.

But Keats Bradford was capable of being extremely in love. At this present time he is living most thoroughly up to his capabilities. He has reached that stage when he acknowledges this to be the truth.

XVIII.

ON LOVE.

WHEN a Boston Brahmin falls in love the spectacle presented to the outer world must be very impressive.

Keats Bradford, however, was not thinking at all of the spectacle he presented. It did not seem to him that he was thinking anything; he was only feeling. But he was man of the world enough to be able to offer a sane front to people whom he met.

He had to go back to Boston on the third day after his arrival in Middle Village. He was now capable of the bravado of calling upon his cousin Vanessa. She was not alone. There was with her a gentleman of imposing appearance, and large, clean-shaven face. He was introduced as Professor Vacci, the great hypnotist. He seemed hardly to see Mr. Bradford, save in the general, comprehensive view which took him in as a speck in the field of vision.

Incidentally, there was present also Madame Vacci, the professor's wife, and she appeared to be a still smaller speck in the outlook taken by her husband.

The two guests were standing, and apparently about to go. Miss Phillipps was greatly interested in what had been said. Her face was vividly animated.

When her guests had departed she turned to her cousin.

"Keats, you ought to have been here. The professor was superb. You should have seen the sudden and wonderfully complete way in which he gained control of his wife."

"Oh, I can believe that easily enough."

"Don't scoff. I do hate to have any one scoff in the presence of science."

"I came not here to scoff," said the young man, sitting down and taking up a book. "Nevertheless, I would challenge that man to hypnotize me or you."

Miss Phillipps was walking back and forth in the room. She was absorbed. Mr. Bradford presently looked at his watch.

He had an hour to spare before he need go to his rooms preparatory to returning to Middle Village that afternoon.

He laid down his book.

"I am going to wait here sixty minutes, Vanessa," he said. "If you 'come to' before the end of that time I shall be very glad."

He crossed his legs. His attitude was very calm. Nevertheless there was a life and excitement in his face that made it possible that he might say some very strange things.

Miss Phillipps continued to walk.

"You know I've never really looked into this; it is a vast subject. This and telepathy appear to me kindred; I have an idea—but I cannot give the thing real attention until after the theosophy session. You know Mrs. Besant is coming. I am going to preside at one of the meetings; I want to make a little speech. I want that bold spirit to be welcomed properly. We Boston women owe her a great deal. You heard her in London, didn't you, Keats?"

"Yes."

Miss Phillipps casually looked at her cousin as she asked this question. The casual look was arrested and changed from vagueness to keenness. She stood still in front of him.

"Where have you been? What has happened to you?" she asked, imperatively.

"So glad you have ' come to,' " said Bradford.

He rose also. He stood up before her. He was smiling absently.

She took him by the arm and turned him more towards the light, scrutinizing him in silence.

"Does any one of your sciences tell what has happened to me?" he inquired.

"I know you rather well, Keats," she said, still keeping her hand on his arm, and her eyes upon him. "I think, yes, I am almost positive, that you are in love. Are you?" Now looking at him in a wondering way, as if he were under the dominion of some miraculous power which she had not yet thorougly studied and classified.

The man moved suddenly away, and in his turn began walking back and forth.

"I want you to do me a great favor, Vanessa," he said, earnestly.

"Haven't I always been willing to do you favors?"

"Yes, yes. I don't think you'll find this very difficult."

Still he hesitated. He could not quite define the expression in his cousin's face.

"I am waiting."

"Do you think Miss Tuttle ought to live in that Hudson Street place?" suddenly asked Bradford.

"Miss Tuttle? Oh!"

There was so much meaning in that exclamation that the young man reddened slightly.

"I cannot prevent her living there," remarked Miss Phillipps. "She is a proud girl. I cannot say to her, 'Let me support you in some more fitting locality.'"

There was an accuracy about this utterance that almost made it sound cold.

" I don't expect you to say that," said the man. "I only wanted to suggest that you invite her here for a visit. I dislike to think of her on Hudson Street. She is coming back. She is going to keep on with her work until summer. You will not leave here at present—you said—"

Here that indefinable something in the woman's face became so marked that Bradford stopped abruptly.

" It will be pleasanter for you to visit Miss Tuttle here, you think?" Miss Phillipps said.

" Pleasanter for me? I was not thinking of myself. I can stand Hudson Street. Pardon me, Vanessa. I ought not to ask so much of you. I suppose you have wecovered from what fancy you had for Miss Tuttle. Perhaps the fancy is transferred to Pwofessor Vacci, or is awaiting the pwesence of Mrs. Besant. I only hope Miss Tuttle will not be too much wounded. She loves you."

There was something in the speaker's voice as he pronounced those last words, or in the words themselves, that made Miss Phillipps's face tremulous for an instant. She turned away. Thus removed from her companion's eyes she asked, quite steadily,

" Does she love you?"

" I don't know."

Bradford made a movement towards the door.

In spite of all his knowledge of his cousin, he was puzzled and indignant.

"I will ask her here. I will write to her to-day."

Miss Phillipps came forward now to her cousin's side. She held out her hand.

"It is too early to congratulate you," she said, cordially.

"You are weally kind, Vanessa," exclaimed Bradford, eagerly. "But don't do this if it interferes with any plans. You see, I was hoping you still cared for her. Oh, don't hurt her by coldness when you see her!"

"Indeed, Keats, what kind of a wild beast do you think I am? Now go; tell her—no, I will write. Good-bye. I am due at the Christian Science in a quarter of an hour."

Bradford left the room. Miss Phillipps heard him leave the house. She lingered a moment. She looked at some tablets she drew from her pocket. She wrote a few words on them, then gazed at the words as if she could not see them.

That afternoon when Bradford went out to Middle Village he went again on horseback. He was not going to tell Rowena that he had been to Boston and had seen Miss Phillipps.

He was a good walker. He could travel easily the miles which separated the hotel from the Tuttle farm, and still reach that place by twilight. He laughed at his own impatience, while he greatly enjoyed it. He swung rapidly forward. He wondered if the girl would be out-of-doors—would she be standing or sitting when he first saw her? Would her eyes become radiant in that enchanting way they had? Would she smile?—or have that serious look which, perhaps, was sweeter than a smile? Was it sweeter, after all? Her very simplicity perplexed him. What did she think when she met his glance with those clear eyes? and when she flushed—

You perceive that Mr. Bradford's mind was very much occupied as he walked over from Middle Village.

He hoped the Tuttles would have had their supper. He wondered if they had "Johnny cake" and milk and herring every night in the year. He had survived seeing Rowena partake of that fare. He had even partaken of it with her and found it delicious. But when removed from her presence he could not honestly say he liked the odor of herring. He did not know that this fish was only eaten for a certain time in the spring.

It was not a lover's fancy that made it seem as if Rowena were possessed of a simple and entirely unconscious dignity that enabled her to do what others could not do in the same way.

Bradford was within a couple of miles of the

Tuttle farm. He was thinking of trying a cut across a pasture, when he saw a pair of horses attached to a light wagon coming briskly along the road.

He thought he heard a shrill bark proceed from the carriage. He hesitated, leaning on the fence he had been going to jump.

Now he saw that the occupants of the wagon were Rowena, with Marmaduke standing on her lap and barking at him in great excitement, and a young man whom Bradford recognized as the one whom he had seen at the theatre with Miss Tuttle. It was Philip Barrett, who now stared at him as he went by. Rowena returned Bradford's greeting in a manner that he could not dislike. The dust flew round him from the turnout. He felt ignored and slighted. It had not once occurred to him that Rowena might have some other employment than that of being ready to receive him when he came. He was furious. His imagination had not gone so far as this. He struck his stick violently against the post. I am almost afraid he swore. He felt as if a bucket of cold water had been flung in his face. He could not tell himself at first that it might be only a natural thing that Miss Tuttle should go out driving with an old acquaintance.

But Bradford was possessed of perception enough to discover that Barrett was not a mere

18

acquaintance. He remembered the fellow's face at the theatre.

"Here's Philup, Roweny," Mrs. Tuttle had said while the family were at the supper-table. "I guess he's come to take you out. There ain't no better feller'n Philup. Of course you'll go."

And Rowena went. But she took Marmaduke. The terrier had a way of barking or of suddenly rising to lick her face that might be very exasperating to her companion, but that she found to be protective and comforting. Marmaduke generally desired to caress her at the most inopportune moment, in the eyes of some one else.

Young Barrett, well as he liked dogs, could have found it in his heart to fling this small specimen over the wheel before the first mile had been passed over. But he tried to control himself. He had come over filled with a desperate resolution. Everybody was talking about that "city feller" that had come out "from Borston" and who was hanging round Roweny Tuttle. Of course she would take up with him; and who knew anything about him, anyway? He might be a gambler.

That very morning Philip's mother had talked all breakfast-time on the subject. She said "Roweny was actin' shameful. She guessed Philip wouldn't write any more letters to a girl like that, she wa'n't deservin' of such letters."

At last the long-suffering Philip had risen from the table. He stood a moment looking fiercely at his mother.

"If you ever speak like that agin 'bout Roweny, I'll clear out. She couldn't do anything shameful. I mean what I say."

He had then gone to the barn, leaving his mother cowering. She was sickeningly subservient all the rest of the day. She made no remark when her son appeared towards night in that suit he had bought before he went to Boston. Yes, it is true that he arrayed himself in those garments, and that no intuition told him not to do so.

When the horses were hitched to the carriage he walked into the kitchen where his mother was just taking the herring from the oven.

"I sha'n't want any supper," he said. He stood with the door in his hand. "I'm goin' over to ask Roweny to marry me," he continued, "and I want you to understand that if she don't, 'tain't no fault of hern. 'Tain't no crime not to want to marry me."

Mrs. Barrett opened her lips to speak, but she did not quite dare to say the words that came to her.

It was in this resolved condition of mind that Philip drove over to the Tuttle house. His mood was such that really it did seem a pity that Rowena should assume that Marmaduke was in-cluded in the invitation. But there sat the ter-rier perched on the girl's knee, and he kept such a very sharp watch that Philip almost began to think that the dog knew the whole state of affairs.

Every time the young man turned particularly towards his companion he met the terrier's bright eyes, or the terrier would give a lurch and a bark, and immediately absorb Rowena's entire atten-tion.

This party had not driven many rods before the girl had divined Philip's intention. Indeed, it required no particular power to divine this, for in some inexplicable way Philip's present deter-mination was written boldly all over him, even in the creases of those dreadful clothes.

Rowena tried to converse on topics quite for-eign to anything in her companion's mind. Each attempt was very much like throwing a stone into an extremely deep well; you suppose the stone reaches the water, but you cannot see nor hear anything to hint that it does.

Finally, in despair, Rowena became silent. She was now convinced that she could do nothing towards averting the inevitable.

With all his will and nerve, poor Philip from moment to moment put off the fatal question. He grew more and more depressed and silent.

With the cruelty with which fate seems to like
to afflict a man, never had he thought Rowena
so entirely what he longed for as now.

He had been a blind fool to think of her. Useless to tell himself that. He had thought of her
and loved her ever since he was a boy. If he
could not drag Rowena Tuttle home from school
on his sled on winter afternoons he would not
have anybody. But he usually could take her.
She had always liked him; surely she had always
liked him. And in those days there had been
few competitors. He had almost considered it a
settled thing.

But now, now her life appeared to branch out
far away from his.

Philip took a long, deep breath. He turned
towards Rowena.

Marmaduke immediately was seized with an
irresistible desire to caress his mistress.

Philip grew red, then nearly purple.

"I do almost wish that terrier hadn't come,"
he said.

"But I can't go anywhere without Marmaduke," responded the girl, effusively.

"I was going to say," continued Philip, "that
it's a mighty pity you ever went to Borston, I
think. You can't live in a thick-settled place 'n'
be jest the same; you can't do it."

He returned thus to this old conclusion of his.

"I'm just the same," said Rowena, with quiet emphasis.

"No you ain't, either," he cried. "You ain't. You're all taken up with that paintin' notion of your'n; you're—"

"Yes," interrupted Rowena, "I am all taken up with it; I shall always be taken up with it; I love it beyond words. I don't know as I should want to live if I thought I couldn't work at painting, and try to do better and better work. Do you understand me, Philip?"

She turned to him with beseeching eyes.

But if he understood, he would not own that he did so. He would rush to his fate. He thought that a fellow never was exactly sure how to know what a woman meant. He believed that the only manly way to put things beyond a doubt was to ask her.

But his heart sank very low. The terrier considerately remained quiet for an instant. But one never knows precisely how long a Yorkshire may continue to be considerate.

Philip met Rowena's eyes with such a look that her own dropped, and she had a wild feeling that perhaps she pitied him almost enough to love him.

But she did not love him. She would certainly know it if she did. Miss Phillipps's assertion that we know nothing positively in these days

came back to her, and with that memory came
the recollection of Miss Phillipps's presence. A
curious glow and thrill went through the girl's
heart.

"You know what I'm going to ask ye, Roweny," now said Philip, visibly bracing himself.

His voice trembled pitiably. It was really terrible that Marmaduke should have chosen this
instant to make a furious attempt to fling himself from Rowena's arms upon a stray hound
which had just emerged from the woods at the
right.

Philip shut his teeth hard, while his companion
reasoned with Marmaduke, and at last quiet-
ed him.

When peace was restored, and the terrier had
nobly offered to kiss Philip himself but had been
restrained, the young man repeated his words.

" I s'pose you know what I'm goin' to ask you,
Roweny?"

She did not reply. Probably he did not expect
a reply.

There was a somewhat long and painful silence.

Philip cut his horses with a whip. They were
so surprised that they sprang forward furiously.
As they sprang their driver turned to the girl.

"Will you have me, Roweny? I love you with
all my heart. I'll take awful good care of you.

You sh'll paint all you want to. You sh'll do whatever you please."

It was said now. Rowena's lips appeared stiff to her as she spoke.

"I can't marry you, Philip."

She wondered if it hurt him any more to hear those words than it hurt her to speak them. It was dreadful to her to seem cruel to Philip Barrett.

He sat without moving, with his eyes fixed straight ahead. He had got his blow. He had been almost sure it would be like this. Now there was no more doubt, and no more hope.

He was to live without Rowena Tuttle. How was he going to do it? He hoped no one would tell him he would get over it and marry some one else. He should want to kill any one who said that.

His mind went groping dully among various probabilities. What did Rowena think of that "city feller" who was staying at that hotel in Middle Village? And there was that person, and his aunt who was a medium—that person who was so "dressy." What did she think of him?

He could not ask her. He did not think it would be exactly "the thing" to put such questions.

The twilight was now fast merging into evening. It was half a dozen miles to Rowena's home.

"I guess we'll go round by the Corners," at last Philip said, and turned his horse into a well-travelled road.

It was useless to try to talk. Marmaduke was the only one who was quite himself.

They drew up at the post-office, where the late mail had just arrived. The two sat there in the mild, sweet air of the spring gloaming until the mail was distributed. Then Philip brought out all the papers and letters for his neighbors. They made but a small package.

There was one letter for Rowena. She could not see the writing plainly enough to guess the author of it. Who would write to her now she was at home? She had very few letters. She was interested and excited about this one.

Philip had involuntarily glanced at the envelope as it had been handed to him. It was a large, flowing superscription. He was sure that no one but a man would write in that way. He thought, with a heavy bitternesss of spirit, that this epistle was from that man who had the aunt who was a medium.

XIX.

FERDINAND IN TROUBLE.

As soon as she reached home Rowena took her little hand-lamp and went up to her room where the one window looked over the wide stretch of pasture-land. The moon lighted up the pasture now.

The girl sat down a moment with the letter in her hand. Philip had gone. He had not lingered a moment, save to take her hand and say in an unsteady voice that "he didn't know when he should see her again. He should try not to see her; he didn't think he could stan' it to keep meetin' her."

Mrs. Tuttle was standing in the open door when her daughter walked slowly up to the house.

"Oh, Roweny!" she exclaimed. "I do hope you ain't done nothin' you'll be sorry for."

"I hope so, too," returned Rowena. "I've done what I had to do. Don't stop me, mother, I can't talk about it."

Then she had taken her lamp and gone upstairs. Her sisters looked at her wonderingly.

Mrs. Tuttle stepped out to the barn, where her husband was looking after a sick cow.

"I guess it's all over, Hiram," she said, stopping in the yard, where she found him cutting up fodder.

"What's over?" in an alarmed tone.

"All our plans 'bout Roweny 'n' Philup. She's jest come home."

"Oh, well," returned Mr. Tuttle, "we can't manage them things, you know. The young folks have their own notions. I hope it'll all come out right, 'n' I guess 'twill. Do you think"—pausing in pushing the fodder through the cutter, "do you think she's got a fancy for this feller that's round, 'n' that can't say 'r' only once 'n' a while?"

"I've ben tryin' to make up my mind, but I can't. Well's I know her, I can't seem to tell. What do you think of him?"

"I like him first-rate. He ain't no fool, I tell ye. I've been watchin' him. He's in love with her."

Mr. Tuttle spoke rather proudly. He had taken to Bradford more than his wife had done. It was a recommendation for the young man that he had fallen in love with Rowena.

At last the girl detached her thoughts from Philip sufficiently to recall her interest in the letter she had just received.

It was not from the young man whose aunt was a medium. It was from Miss Phillipps. She had lost no time in keeping her promise to her cousin Keats. Her note to Rowena had gone out the same day on which he had gone. There were not many lines. The girl's eyes flashed eagerly down the page, then back again for a second reading. Surely there was more than that. No, there was not.

The letter seemed to be cordial. It asked Rowena to come to Charles Street for a visit of a week or two on her return to Boston. The writer would not leave town quite as early as she had once intended.

It was in vain for Rowena to read the words again. She was chilled. But she did not know why. Her very fingers grew cold as they held the paper and felt the message from her heart. And yet it seemed a cordial, sincere invitation.

She would not go to Miss Phillipps's house. Even if she had felt differently she would not go, because she was in Boston to work. She was to leave home the following Monday. She could spare no more time before the long summer when she would be in the country, and would feel as if everybody were looking at her and condemning her because, if she must take lessons, she did not take them of that woman who came out from some place—it was not known where—

only "she came out." She made a person an artist in six easy lessons.

Rowena was very much depressed when at last she lay down for the night. In the background of all her reflections was the face of Philip Barrett when he had bidden her good-bye. There was also a feeling that she might not have money enough. She supposed people always spent more than they intended to spend. She felt that she had been saving of her pennies to the verge of meanness. And they were getting so low. She must decide whether she would apply for the school Georgie Warner would give up in the fall. She should dislike it; but she might be obliged to teach a term or two so that she might still go to Allestree for lessons. She could not conceive any stress of circumstances beyond an interference by Providence that would make her give up her learning to paint. It had been a dear triumph for her to know that, since her study, she had far more control of her hand when she made sketches from nature. There was a something she could catch and hold now which had always eluded her before.

Mr. Bradford praised while he criticised. He had many ways like his cousin. Rowena had almost fallen into a habit of watching for those ways. When they came she would suddenly look up at the young man and smile. On such occasions the responsive smile upon his face was becoming so ardently warm that Rowena was vaguely moved by it.

The next day was Saturday. On the Monday, early, she would go back to Boston in a boat with Uncle Reuben. To ride thus would not be tedious now that the days were sweet and warm with the near presence of summer. Besides, she saved a car fare by going this way. She would send Miss Phillipps a note from Hudson Street.

Lying there, close to the roof of the old house, she began to compose the note to Miss Phillipps. But her mind wandered ; she no longer heard the frogs. She was asleep.

Georgie Warner was already mending rapidly. The news that Mary Jane Jewett was really going to marry Charlie Simmons and " live in Borston," was now widely disseminated. Miss Jewett had kept her promise. She had told Jim Townshend. He had struggled manfully under the blow, and he was resolved that Georgie should comfort him—as resolved as he could be with his kind of a mouth and chin.

Miss Jewett, to facilitate further the distribution of the news, had imparted it to Marthy S.

When Rowena walked over to see Georgie, late Saturday afternoon, she had found that invalid sitting in a rocker, with a pillow at her back, looking over strips of patchwork. She even had visions of a new kind of pattern of a bedquilt that should outdo anything ever yet made.

Georgie was still weak, however. She was melted to tears at sight of her friend, who had not been afraid to speak to that Jewett girl.

She hugged Rowena with hysterical fervor. She asserted that if it had not been for her she "should have ben in her grave 'fore the Fourth of July."

Rowena could not dispute this assertion. She sat down and put her arm round Georgie. She listened, a little absently, to a great deal of talk of Jim and Jim's goodness, now he was "really red of that awful Jewett girl." Georgie almost hinted that Jim would probably have taken measures himself to be "red of her," if things hadn't turned out exactly as they had.

It was not many days since this change of circumstances had occurred, but it seemed rather long ago. Georgie's intensity of interest in bedquilts at last wearied even Rowena. She must go back. She rose. She skilfully parried or ignored any references to the city feller, also to Philip Barrett. She thought she could not hear Philip's name mentioned. She was in terror lest Georgie might speak it.

She caught up Marmaduke under her arm and hurried away. She would stop and say good-bye on Monday.

She walked through the small pine wood, the odorous dusk soothing her. She was almost ashamed and wholly astonished that she was eager to get away from home again.

She believed her home and its surroundings must have changed. Only her mother and father were the same always. At thought of them, all that she feared must be a wicked hardness in her nature melted suddenly and flooded her eyes.

It was full of black shadows among the pines there, though the moonlight was bright beyond the trees. Rowena could hear the terrier rustling about in the sweet-smelling pine-needles, sniffing and sometimes growling under his breath. He was as protective as if he were a very large dog.

Suddenly he ran forward and barked in such a tumultuous way that each explosion raised his fore-feet from the ground.

Rowena stood still, hidden in the shadows. It was a lonely place, but the girl had traversed it many a dark night and never thought of fear. It was a part of her home to her. But she was startled.

She could not see Marmaduke at all, but he kept up his clamor as he never did save at some kind of an intruder.

After waiting a moment, Rowena walked forward towards the dog. Now she saw in the moon-

light the figure of a woman, hesitating, and looking about her doubtfully.

"Come here, Marmaduke! Be still, sir!"

Rowena advanced as she spoke, and so did the
stranger.

"Is it Miss Tuttle?" inquired a voice which
Rowena had heard before, but which she could
not really recognize.

She went swiftly forward.

"Did you want me?" she asked, alarmed and
surprised.

The stranger, who wore a long, gray cloak and
a close bonnet, clasped her hands nervously together.

"Oh, I'm so thankful to find you!" she cried,
in a subdued voice. "It seems as if I'd been
looking for you for ages, though I only left Boston this afternoon. You know me, don't you,
Miss Tuttle?"

Rowena held out her hand.

"Why, it's Miss Foster!" she said, in strong
surprise.

Miss Foster moved a few steps until she came
to a tree; she leaned heavily against it.

"I'm just as nervous 's I can be," she said, dis-
tressfully. "We drove over from the next town.
Ferdinand would have it so. He said he didn't
care what did happen; he would see you before
he went; and he made me come with him. He

19

said he shouldn't dare to come without me. He took a notion that you seemed to like me. You know we said we'd go to see each other in Borston."

"Yes," said Rowena. She was becoming excited herself now. She wanted to question the girl, but she hardly knew how to do so. She tried to be quiet, and wait. Meanwhile the moonlight revealed Miss Foster's face to be more pallid than usual, and full of the keenest suffering. Her eyes were wild and dilated. She was continually looking behind her, and often she stopped in the middle of a sentence and seemed to listen.

She left the tree and came close to Rowena.

"You see," she said, almost whispering, and speaking so rapidly it was difficult for her listener to follow her, " Ferdinand's got into trouble. He made me promise to tell you. He's so generous and so good-hearted, you know, that he's been spending too much money. He's the most generous fellow in the world; money just slips out of his hands. Oh, Miss Tuttle, don't you go and think he's bad! I d'know what I should have done if it hadn't been for him since I've been sick, him and the Science. He's got into debt. Oh, I mustn't stop to tell you all about it. You know he's head book-keeper for Nichols Brothers. He's been taking money, now and then, for some time. He was going to pay it back, you know.

He fixed up the books so it didn't show. He
says in a few months more, he thinks, he should
have had a chance to pay it all back. But they've
found it out, or Ferd is almost sure they suspect.
He says he's got to skip; he says he'll go out of
the country; he says he sh'll find some way to
pay um; he's sure he shall. He's out there,
round the turn, the other side of those savins.
Will you come?   He's waiting."

Rowena could not, for the moment, reply. She
gazed in silence at the girl, who kept twisting
her hands together.

"We can't waste time," said Miss Foster.
"We've got to be over to Hibbard's Station to
catch the midnight train, and our horse 's been
getting lame for the last mile or two. It's a
stable horse from the town here, and I've got to
drive it back. You see he might have gone
right on in the train, but he was bound to see
you. He said he'd risk it. Oh, do come! How
can it harm you?"

Rowena did not hesitate any longer. Miss
Foster took her hand eagerly, and together the
two girls ran along the dusty, moonlit road.

Not far, however. The terrier, racing on ahead,
came to a place where he began to bark again.
A form detached itself from the darkness under
the savins. There was a horse and buggy standing near.

Rowena had not a single word at her command as young Foster came out into the moonlight. She held fast to her companion's hand lest she might try to leave her.

Ferdinand Foster took off his hat without any of his old flourish. He had no display of necktie and no flower in his button-hole. He fixed his eyes eagerly on Rowena. She held out her hand. There was something so desolate and appealing in Foster's face and attitude, something so entirely different from the way she had remembered him, that she obeyed her kindly impulse and put out her hand.

"It is awfully good of you," he stammered. "You see, I had to see you. I—"

He stopped suddenly. He turned and walked away a few steps, his hat still in his hand, his head bent.

Rowena hardly knew him. She was so sorry that her face was almost tender.

He returned and stood in front of her, his back to the light, which was upon her in full radiance.

"Since I've seen you, Miss Tuttle," he began again, "I've meant to be a better fellow. I'd got into kind of bad ways, you know. But from the minute I saw you I felt different. I've left off doing a lot of things that I knew you wouldn't like. I meant to tell you all about it some time, when I knew you better. But I couldn't see you much, somehow. I wish I could have seen you more. I don't see how a fellow could be very bad that saw you often. Yes, I do wish I could have seen you more."

Rowena was silent. She was trying to recognize the man before her. Even his voice seemed unfamiliar. She could not quite realize that these words were spoken by Mr. Foster—and to her. It was all unreal. The moonlight, the two people, the shadowy carriage and horse; even the terrier, now sitting silently close to her feet, might have been some other terrier.

"You ain't going to be angry with me, are you?" asked Foster, coming still nearer. "I know I was cheeky in tryin' to see you; but you'll overlook it, won't you? I guess you don't know how I've been thinkin' of you. To tell you the truth, if you were a friend to a fellow I don't see how he could help being good. I wish I'd known you a good while ago."

Still Rowena did not speak. But she was touched. She did not understand very well how he could really mean that a man would be better if she were his friend. She thought it was only a way of speaking.

Foster was looking at her intently, longingly. His commonplace face received a little dignity from his earnestness.

His sister drew out her watch and looked at it.

"There ain't much more time, Ferd," she said.

He turned almost savagely upon her.

"I can't help it," he cried. "I don't see how I'm going to get that train, anyway. Look at that horse. He can't put that foot to the ground now. I'm just up a tree—that's what I am."

Miss Foster began to wring her hands.

"Don't do that," he went on. "What's the use of it? If I can get away I shall. If I don't they'll nab me, that's all."

He seemed ashamed of this outburst, for he went on directly, looking at Rowena and then back to his sister:

"You see, I ain't slept much lately. I'm a regular brute, Miss Tuttle—"

Here he appeared unable to control his voice directly. He put his hand to his necktie, as if he must loosen it. All the time he was gazing intently at Rowena, whose feelings were a mixture of pity and a desire to turn and run away.

"I don't suppose I shall ever see you again," he said. "I can't ever tell you—you wouldn't want me to tell you how I—"

"Oh no, no!" cried Rowena, in a kind of fright, suddenly feeling that the expression in the man's eyes had all at once become unendurable. She could not be looked at in that way by Ferdinand Foster.

She retreated a few steps. Perhaps uncon-
sciously, Foster followed her.

"I tell you I shall never see you again," he repeated, passionately. "Haven't you any pity to
throw to me?"

The pleading in his voice touched her now.
She put out both her hands.

"Oh, I am sorry! I am sorry!" she said, with
pathetic earnestness.

He seized her hands and held them despair-
ingly.

He could not say any different words from
those he had already used.

"I do wish I could have seen you oftener!"

"Ferdinand!"

His sister called his name. She was trying to
lead the horse forward; but the animal could not
step; he could not put his foot to the ground.

"What shall we do? What shall we do?"
moaned Miss Foster.

Her brother stamped furiously. He ran to the
horse and looked down at the leg which was held
from the ground, the toe just resting.

"What will become of you? You must catch
that train!"

Miss Foster seemed beside herself. Rowena
tried not to be too excited to think clearly. There
was no neighbor who had a horse that could go
beyond a slow trot. Useless to think of them.

She knew that Mr. Bradford's horse was fleet. She had thought he would come over this evening, because it had been his habit to come over. Perhaps he was at her house now. But could they have all the time necessary to walk that distance?

It is true that things sometimes happen opportunely. One of these things happened now. The sound of a quick gallop came down the road. Rowena knew that gallop very well. She ran along to meet the coming horseman. He saw her and came yet more rapidly. He sprang to the ground. She hardly looked at him. She seized the horse's bridle.

"Come, Mr. Foster! Quick! This horse 'll take you!"

Foster ran forward. He caught Rowena's other hand and kissed it. He jumped into the saddle and rode away.

Rowena now turned to Keats Bradford.

"You'll lend your horse for a few hours, won't you, Mr. Bradford? The case is very urgent."

Bradford's face was rather black. He was thinking of the kiss upon Rowena's hand.

"I think I shall lend him," he answered, "since you ask me, and since he is already gone."

XX.

MARMADUKE AND MARTHY S. MAKE THEM-
SELVES USEFUL.

THE two stood in the middle of the dusty road just where Foster had left them.

"Were you alone here with that man?"

Mr. Bradford put the question with so much asperity that Rowena's eyes flashed.

"I have been alone here with you," she said. Then she seemed to think it not worth while to be angry, and added, quickly, "Do you consider it being alone if you have a buggy and a terrier and a girl and a horse with you? But the horse is so lame that perhaps he doesn't count. Do you think we can get him anywhere, Mr. Bradford? Please look at him. Perhaps you can lead him. This is Mr. Bradford, Miss Foster," as the two came to the place where Foster's sister was standing desolately by the buggy, hardly taking it in that her brother had really gone.

Mr. Keats Bradford needed all his self-possession to enable him to be as nonchalantly calm as he was now. He greeted this new young lady as if he were meeting her in a drawing-room. He asked if he could help her in any way. In five minutes he found himself first in a procession which consisted of himself, leading that other young man's lame horse, while two young women and a dog followed on behind.

Bradford was not wearing his eye-glass so much in these days, but he was still as helpless concerning his pronunciation.

He was swearing occasionally now with a great deal of earnestness. He had ridden over this evening with the intention of having a short time alone with Miss Tuttle. He did not know when he should have another opportunity. It would not be so easy to meet her in Boston. He felt that it was an absolute necessity for him to see her.

He glanced back at her now. She was walking somewhat by herself. Her hat was pushed back. He saw the outline of her face and that her lips were close shut, as if she were thinking steadily. Was she thinking of that man who had just ridden away? It was all very odd. How did the fellow come here? And were the police after him? It seemed to Bradford as if there was a flavor of the police in the way the escape had been made; for it must be an escape. He would have it out with Rowena at the first possible moment. He looked back again. This time Rowena looked at him; she smiled. He could not comprehend why this country girl should have a smile that might mean nothing—or everything. He had spent a great many hours of late thinking of that smile. Just at this moment he asked himself if it were likely she had ever bestowed it upon that person to whom he had just now lent his horse.

It was a great trial to Keats Bradford that a stranger should ride his horse. He winced now as he thought of it. He had not an acquaintance whom he would willingly have mount that intimate equine friend of his. What if that fellow should strike him? What if he should make him go too far and too fast? And when and where was the owner to have him again?

Having asked these questions irritatedly of himself, Bradford fell to planning precisely what he should do if he ever succeeded in leading this atrociously lame beast as far as Mr. Tuttle's. He made his plans very distinctly, and he adhered to them.

At last the company had entered the yard of the Tuttle house. Rowena ran forward and soon returned with her father. What explanation she had given him was not known. Mrs. Tuttle appeared on the porch with an apron over her head. She invited Miss Foster to come in and rest. Rowena was following her. There could be no question about the farther travel of the lame horse.

Bradford's face was set to a resolution.

Rowena heard a voice close behind her say,

"Miss Tuttle."

She paused, and half turned her head. The others went on.

"I am devoured by curiosity," said Bradford.

"Oh," said the girl.

"I am also devoured by anxiety lest something happen to my horse. I love my horse."

She turned fully round towards him.

"If you are devoured by two such feelings, there will soon be nothing left of you," she responded. Then she added, quickly and earnestly, "I know what it was for you to lend your horse thus. It was so good of you."

"Are you weally very grateful?"

"Indeed I am."

"Prove it."

She blushed and hesitated. He tried to speak calmly.

"Must I prove it," she asked.

"Yes; you must. I hope it won't cost you much to walk down the road with me."

"But if I meet some one who asks, 'Are you alone with that man?'"

"I will answer such a person. Come."

Rowena again hesitated. Something whispered to her not to go. She was afraid.

"But Miss Foster—"

"She can wait."

Why should she not go? There really was no reason.

She turned and whistled for Marmaduke, who had followed Miss Foster into the house, and who was now deeply engaged in smelling of her skirts. He felt that there was something of which he did not fully approve about this new-comer, and he was trying to decide precisely what it was.

He galloped out at the door, however, when he heard his mistress whistle.

"Are you going to take him?" asked Bradford.

"You would not separate me from Marmaduke?"

She glanced up at him as she lifted the terrier and put him under her arm.

Bradford groaned aloud. He would perhaps learn, as Philip Barrett had learned, that a small dog is not always a source of unmixed pleasure to all parties concerned. There was an especially strong desire on Rowena's part to have Marmaduke with her. He was a third person, a shield, a protection. He was usually discriminating as to the times when he ought to assert himself; but it must be owned that he sometimes asserted himself when he ought not, thus resembling many human beings. He never erred on the side of self-suppression; again resembling many human beings.

Bradford and his companions walked slowly out of the yard and down the road in a different direction from that in which they had just come. The young man was still thinking of the fact that another man had kissed Rowena's hand a short time ago, and that he might have been in the habit of doing so.

He broke out in a startling manner.

"Was that person your lover?"

Rowena reddened furiously. She did not like to think of that kiss. It made her shudder to remember it.

"No," she answered.

"Did you want him to kiss your hand?"

"No."

Bradford straightened himself and opened his lips to speak. He was conscious of an ecstatic gratitude. But he hesitated to say what had rushed from his heart to be said.

Instead, he remarked that he supposed his companion had not been expecting those people.

But Rowena did not choose to be catechized any more on the subject. She did not reply at all.

Bradford bent his head towards her.

"Pardon me," he murmured. "I know I have no right. I—"

Here Marmaduke made a furious leap out of his mistress's arm at a squirrel that ran across the way. She started after him.

"I would not have him catch a squirrel for worlds!" she cried.

Bradford stood still. His eyes glittered with something like ferocity. At that instant the terrier could not have confided in him as a friend.

After a delay of rather a long time, and after a wrestle in the underbrush, Rowena captured Marmaduke and again put him under her arm.

"I believe you took that dog purposely," remarked Bradford, with no amiability in his voice.

"Of course I took him purposely," she replied. "You did not think it was accidental, did you? And when you speak of Marmaduke as 'that dog' I feel as if you did not respect him, and as if you were not friendly to us."

Bradford now offered to prove his respect and friendship by carrying the terrier, if he were not going to run; "but why not let him run?" looking with ill-subdued eagerness at Rowena.

The girl answered that she could not tell exactly why she did not want him to run: he might catch a squirrel, or frighten one, and he was so small that if a horse and carriage came along he might be run over; and she should never get over it if—

Here Bradford mutely held out his arms, and Marmaduke was transferred to them. It occurred to the young man that Mrs. Sears might better have presented this animal to some one else; or have waited before giving him to Miss Tuttle until— Bradford did not formulate this thought very clearly in his mind.

The two walked on. Bradford had a sense that he could not adequately say what he wished to say while he was carrying a dog; and since the dog was not to run, he had believed that he would prefer to have him rather than to allow his companion to have him. But now he was not sure that he did prefer this alternative. He frowned as he walked. Marmaduke appeared to be perfectly contented. There was not the slightest excuse to change his position.

"I almost believe he likes you as well as he likes me," remarked Rowena, after a while.

"Then he is not the discriminating dog I thought him. I could dispense with his company just now."

"Can you say that when you look at that distracting fluff of sweet hair on his head?"

"Miss Tuttle, I am not here to talk of Marmaduke."

"But Marmaduke being here, how can you help talking about him? Oh, Mr. Bradford, are you hurting him?"

"Good heavens! Don't you suppose he would cry out if I injured him?"

"He looked as if he were just going to cry out," said Rowena. "Perhaps his little feelings were hurt by something you were thinking about him."

"Perhaps they were."

At this point in the conversation the two looked at each other. There was a mischievous shining in the girl's eyes. They both burst out laughing. In the midst of the laughter the terrier made a dexterous struggle and jumped to the ground.

"You did not mean to carry him, and he felt it."

For answer Bradford turned rather triumphantly towards his companion.

He put out his hand, and with the tips of his fingers touched her arm. These fingers were not quite steady. She shrank involuntarily. She felt the fire of his eyes on her face. A tumultuous rebellion rose in her heart. Why could she not have warded off this moment? In her mind she groped wildly for some means, even now, of averting what seemed inevitable.

Where was Marmaduke? His shrill voice responded to her mental question.

She stopped suddenly and looked back. A woman was coming rapidly behind them. In an-

other moment Rowena saw that the woman was
Marthy S. with her hemp bag in her hand.

"I've ben hurryin' 's fast 's I could to git up
to ye 'fore I got to that strip er woods between
here 'n' old Mr. Gray's," she said, panting as she
spoke and peering sharply at both the faces near
her. "I thought I shouldn't be afraid, 'twas so
mooney, but I am kind er 'fraid after all. I s'pose
you're goin' right along. You'd better intro-
dooce me, Roweny. I ain't acquainted with the
gentleman."

Rowena introduced Mr. Bradford, who found
it very difficult to be civil. If he had done precisely what he was tempted to do he would have
lifted Marthy S. and thrown her over the wall
among the brakes that were growing there. He
now thought of Marmaduke's presence with something like pleasure.

Rowena was walking with great demureness
the other side of Marthy S. The terrier was
pacing deliberately just ahead of her. Bradford
thrust his hands deep in his pockets and clinched
them there.

Martha S. gave them a minute account of the
reason why Mary Jane Jewett had given her own
dress-maker the slip and had decided to employ
Martha S. while she (Miss Jewett) was "fixin'."
She told how many dress-makers there were to
be, and that one of the waists was to be shirred

all up and down the front, and that the effect was beyond anything she had ever dreamed of.

"But then Mary Jane was one of them as could carry most anything off."

The dress-maker expressed the conviction that that shirred waist would be very much liked in Borston, where the bride was going to reside. Marthy S. said "reside" for the first time in her life. She said it out of deference to the city feller, and she was conscious of a certain feeling of respect towards herself as a woman capable of using such a word.

Her spirits rose. She thought Rowena had never been so pleasant, and her usual estimate of Hiram Tuttle's daughter was that she was "too stuck up for anything."

She had a strong sense of exultation in the prospect of relating. the particulars of this interview at the place where she was going to dress-make Monday morning. It was a trial to her that a Sunday must intervene. But she would go to meeting. There were many ways in which a woman like Marthy S. could utilize going to meeting. And the dress-maker was one who never wasted an opportunity in her line.

This party had not walked more than a quarter of a mile when Rowena paused. She began to think of Miss Foster with compunction. She must return. That piece of wood was now visible ahead of them.

"I think I will go back," said the girl, steadily ignoring the imploring look which Bradford fixed upon her. She glanced superficially at him as she went on to say that perhaps Mr. Bradford would be so kind as to walk with Miss Hancock through the wood.

Then she said good-night, and hurried away from them.

Bradford, in spite of his social training, was for the moment absolutely inarticulate with disappointment and rage. He raised his hat in silence and was left alone with Marthy S., who involuntarily began to bridle somewhat in acknowledgment on her part of being left alone with "a gentlemun."

This gentleman was thinking that to-morrow would be Sunday, and that he had been let to know unmistakably by Mrs. Tuttle that she did not approve of having visitors on Sunday.

He supposed an exception would be made in favor of a regular accredited admirer who came for Sunday evenings. But he was not occupying that enviable position in regard to Rowena Tuttle.

No; he could not call the next day. And here he was, stranded as it were, on a lonely road in the moonlight with a woman who had a hemp bag, and who kept smirking and appearing as if she were going to make a remark, but who had not yet made one.

Of course, on Monday he meant to ride his horse to Boston beside the boat-cart. But there were a great many drawbacks to be anticipated in that journey. It is true that Bradford had been only too thankful for the opportunity to ride beside the boat-cart some days ago. But he had got beyond that period now. He demanded a great deal more than that at this stage of his malady.

Mr. Reuben Little would be present. It was uncertain whether Mr. Little would be in liquor or not; probably not, as it would be the day after Sunday. There was, however, the chance of a stroll on foot along some lovely bit of road with Rowena.

All these thoughts went flashing through Bradford's mind as he stood there with the dress-maker.

He wondered why she did not walk on. He offered to carry her bag. She was confused at his offer, but did eventually relinquish the bag, telling him it had the lining of Mary Jane Jewett's wedding basque in it.

She appeared to be uncertain whether it was proper for her, under the circumstances, to continue her walk or to wait for "the gentlemun" to propose it.

Bradford, after a few moments of doubt as to her intentions, asked if they should not go on. So they went on.

He did not try to talk. He was too deeply irritated. But he was kind; he could not be otherwise.

Marthy S. made a few confused observations, to which he replied as well as he could.

He accompanied her to her destination. He delivered up the bag and left her with deferential respect.

From that time on the dress-maker was absolutely sure that "that Tuttle girl would ketch that feller if she possibly could do it. It wouldn't be no fault of her'n if she didn't ketch him."

Among all the people for whom she worked that season Marthy S. held the proud position of one who was acquainted with the man that was hanging round Roweny Tuttle. She came to be rather an authority concerning him. She told what she thought he would be likely to do, and what he would not be likely to do.

The Monday morning was clear and beautiful and full of the scents of late spring. Rowena had a companion in the boat with her besides her Uncle Reuben. See invited Miss Foster to stay over Sunday and go to Boston with her. She thought such an unusual trip would do the girl good. The lame horse was left in charge of Mr. Tuttle, who was to go to the stable and report.

"It's only a very few weeks now before I shall be home for a couple of months, mother," Rowena had said.

She spoke with apparent gayety, and her mother replied with apparent cheerfulness.

So she went back for the second time. She felt a score of years older.

In her thoughts there was constantly the letter from Miss Phillipps. The memory of it was like a sore place in her consciousness.

You can imagine the sensation which Keats Bradford experienced when he cantered up alongside the boat and saw Rowena's companion. He was obliged immediately to give up all thought of the strolls along solitary bits of road. This renunciation made him very silent and very unresponsive when both girls eagerly inquired how he found his horse, and if it had been injured in any way.

When Rowena at last encountered Bradford's eyes she felt sorry for him. Without looking at him, without speaking to him, how did she yet console him somewhat? It must have been by a process in connection with some science kindred to thought transference. Was there a subtle brain-wave set in motion?

As she came nearer and nearer to Boston, Rowena's resolution to write to Miss Phillipps an answer to her letter of invitation gradually changed to a resolution to call on that lady. She had never been to that house on Charles Street save by special invitation. She would go there. She must know if Miss Phillipps herself would now repel her as her written words—or, rather, the words she had not written—had done.

XXI.

ON CHARLES STREET.

THE girl returned to her work with an enthusiasm which sustained and animated her. While she sat at her easel in Allestree's studio on Tremont Street she found that she could think with more calmness of Miss Phillipps's fancied coldness.

"If I may only work," she whispered to herself. "It must be true that a woman may be happy that way. Miss Phillipps says it is true. I wonder how much she really knows about it. She makes you feel as if she knew, and that is something."

Rowena was surprised at the warmth of Allestree's greeting.

"It is worth while to teach a pupil like you," he had remarked, after shaking hands with her. "It makes a master's life endurable. You made some sketches out there in the country? Ah! Let me see them."

He instantly selected one from the three she gave him. His face lighted. He seized his beard after his manner when interested.

After a long glance at the sketch of some birches standing beside a narrow brook, he put the paper down and held out both his hands.

"You'll do, Miss Tuttle ; you'll do, if you only keep on. Take courage. How good your drawing is getting! I didn't dare to praise you too much before. Girls are such very strange beings—they can't take praise or blame—they fly off at the strangest tangents. I've been watching you. You mean business. Painting is not merely a means with you—'tis an end. You really love it."

Rowena looked up at the man with a glowing face. She could hardly speak for pride and joy.

"Oh, indeed, I love it!" she exclaimed, in an uneven voice.

"I know—I know. Now if you were a young man, I should have no hesitation in predicting your future. Being a girl—"

Rowena glanced indignantly at him. He smiled indulgently. He was in a pleasant frame of mind.

"Don't you know what it is to be a girl? It is to love some man and marry him, and put your easel up in the attic."

"I shall not put my easel in the attic," she replied, angrily.

"We shall see. I hope not. If you do, I shall want to choke the man. You have no business to marry."

Rowena worked in a state of exaltation much of that day. It was the first after her return from her home.

In the afternoon she walked out across the Common. She lingered there, longing, and yet afraid, to seek Miss Phillipps.

The reaction from that exalted condition was now beginning. As she went aimlessly down a mall she felt desolate and depressed. If it were not that she rarely failed to adhere to a resolution she would have gone back to Hudson Street.

She had also to contend against the wish, which was now almost intolerable, to see Miss Phillipps, and to have her the same as she had been. What if she should not be? What if that note was like what the writer of it now was?

When she could bear these thoughts no longer Rowena started rapidly for Charles Street. She kept up her pace until she reached the very door of the house.

When she had rung, it occurred to her for the first time that it was very probable that Miss Phillipps would not be at home. She was interested in so many things: she attended so many meetings.

The servant who opened the door conducted Rowena to a room which was strange to her. On the wall of this room the girl immediately saw a portrait of the mistress of the house. This must be Senour's portrait, which Miss Phillipps had mentioned. Rowena was held fast before it. It was just as the original of that portrait had said: it was the face without the disdain and the suggestion of cruelty in it; a refined countenance, aristocratic, but somehow lacking in a certain incisive power which was characteristic of the woman herself.

Rowena was standing thus absorbed when Miss Phillipps appeared at the open door, coming noiselessly over the thick carpet. She paused on the threshold and gazed at the girlish figure. As she gazed a slight contraction stirred her features. Then she walked forward and held out her hand.

"I am glad to see you, Miss Tuttle," she said. "Did you have a pleasant visit in the country?"

Rowena turned. She could hardly extend her hand in response. She needed no more than the inflection of that voice. She could not look at the speaker. But the girl was not without something in her character which came to her aid now. With the knife-thrust in her heart, she held herself upright.

"Thank you," she answered. "I enjoyed my visit. But I am glad to be at work again."

Miss Phillipps motioned her guest to a seat. She sat down near.

"Yes, work is a great thing," she said. "I

sometimes wish I were compelled to labor in some way for my bread. It would at least be a new sensation, and I like new sensations."

"I received a note from you," said Rowena, after a little pause. "As I was coming directly to Boston, I waited to see you to tell you that I shall not be able to accept your kind invitation to spend a week or two with you."

'She uttered these commonplace words in a steady voice. She could not imagine why that invitation had been given.

She rose.

"You think you will not come?" remarked Miss Phillipps. "Don't go yet. It seems to me that there was something I wished to say to you. Please sit down."

Rowena obeyed, and waited silently.

Miss Phillipps was not leaning back in her chair as usual, but was sitting erect. The young girl glanced at her. The lady was always pale, but she was very pale now. Rowena looked quickly away. She hoped she would not be kept there long. She felt a wild, sharp feeling of thankfulness that she had her work.

There came a knock on the door which Miss Phillipps had closed when she entered. A servant announced that Professor Vacci was in the reception-room.

"Tell him I cannot see him," peremptorily.

Again Rowena rose.   Her hostess put out her hand.

"Stay," she said.

"Professor Vacci says he came by appointment," remarked the servant.

"Tell him I cannot see him," repeated Miss Phillipps, and the door was closed again.

Rowena had not resumed her seat.   Now the lady rose also and stood gazing at the girl whose eyes were lowered, for she needed all her forces to aid in the struggle of this moment.

"I asked you to visit me now, because it was Mr. Bradford's wish that I do so."

Miss Phillipps spoke in her clearest voice.

A color rose over Rowena's tense face.   She did not think it necessary to reply.

The woman watching her saw the color, and it had a curious effect upon her.   She seemed to throw away, with a sudden gesture of both hands, the somewhat icy calmness which had been hers.

"When a man," she exclaimed, "chooses to assert himself, he is always the victor.   See! Because my cousin Keats fancies this or that, I must yield.   It were indeed a waste of strength for a woman to contend with a man, and that man Keats Bradford.   I thought it must be my duty to retreat; but I have changed my mind; I won't retreat."

Miss Phillipps's eyes were flaming.

"I am used to having what I want," she said, "but I thought it was for your good not to try to place a straw in the way of his love. I won't now, if you return it. I distrusted myself. I tried to make myself believe I was really like your portrait of me. Perhaps I am. Yes, I think I am. But I never saw any one like you before. It may be I have seen better people, but never one who was to me what you are. It is not what a person is, but what he is to you, that tells. You may read a thousand hearts, but if you cannot read mine, if I cannot read yours, what is it all worth? Do you know he told me not to hurt you? Not to hurt you!"

Gradually Rowena's face had been changing. The terrible grip upon her had been relaxing and giving place to something which she was afraid could not be real.

At the moment when Miss Phillipps had spoken the last words some one entered and paused just within the room.

"They said I should find you here, Vanessa," said Bradford.

He stopped abruptly.

"You need not go," said his cousin, as the young man now turned, with a murmured apology.

But he could not stay. The jealousy, he could

not call the feeling anything else, which Vanessa had awakened in him became just now very powerful. He had wished to ignore that emotion as something unworthy of him. He had resolutely acted up to that resolve and confided in his cousin.

As well as any man could understand, he believed that he understood the charm which acted and reacted between these two women. But how long would it last? At what time would his moment arrive? Surely it must arrive. Was it not right and just to believe that, with a woman, it is the masculine element which at last prevails?

And there was the art which so dominated the woman he loved.

Bradford walked rather blindly down the street. He wanted to get away from everybody. He realized that he had a great deal to contend with. He was conscious that he should have an opportunity to test his waiting powers to their fullest capabilities. And the end of it?

He could still see Rowena's face as she had been looking at his cousin when he had entered the room just now. When would she look at him like that? There must come a time when she would do it. He also was used to having what he wanted. Yes, there must come a time.

Vanessa must have been thoroughly in earnest in what she had said to him on the Common of her interest in that girl. But Vanessa could not change her nature. Had he misunderstood his cousin all these years? Impossible, he told himself. Still one never knows precisely when something latent will suddenly start into life and rule one; had Rowena's touch roused in her friend something which should modify what she had once been?

Bradford's thoughts ran on with a miserable, confused haste.

Within the room the two stood in silence. The younger woman almost feared that she could not bear this swift change from misery to happiness. She clasped her hands tightly together. She was looking at her friend, who returned her gaze.

Miss Phillipps came nearer. She put her hand on Rowena's shoulder.

"I almost thought you loved him," she said.

"I was greatly attracted to him," Rowena answered, "because—"

Here she paused, again absorbed in the eyes meeting hers.

"Because—" repeated Miss Phillipps.

"Because he reminded me so much of you."

The girl's lips trembled under the stress of her feeling.

"Ah!" said Miss Phillipps, in her softest tone.

Late that evening a messenger boy brought a note from Bradford to his cousin.

"I am leaving town for an indefinite time," he wrote. "But I give nothing up. I can wait. Do you remember what the French say:

"'To-day to thee.
To-morrow to me?'"

XXII.

ALLESTREE'S PROPOSITION.

PERHAPS it was simply because human nature, particularly feminine human nature, has so many phases, that Rowena, when at last she left Charles Street that afternoon, was conscious of some feeling besides that of supreme happiness.

Still she was so happy that she was almost successful in ignoring that emotion to which she gave no name.

Miss Phillipps had never been more tenderly charming. She may also have been a trifle triumphant.

Rowena had never more entirely surrendered her fancy, and perhaps her heart, to the woman whose wish it was to enthrall her.

The girl had listened eagerly as she sat at the lady's feet in that half-lighted, elegant room. The portrait by Senour had looked down upon them.

Miss Phillipps had talked of many plans, and in all of them Rowena filled a part. The voice was at its softest, the face at its gentlest and best. But with that caution which is so often a characteristic of New England rural nature, Rowena could not give an unreserved affirmative to the words she heard. But they charmed her.

The long June twilight was gone, and a dusk, odorous even here in the city, was coming among the trees on the Common when Rowena rose to go back to her shabby little room and to the Yorkshire. This latter individual had been trying to beguile his ennui by a complete destruction of a pin-cushion which Georgie Warner had made and presented to the friend who had gone to Boston to learn to paint.

This article was constructed of infinitesimal fragments of silk, laboriously sewed together and stuffed with bran. It was in the midst of this bran that Marmaduke was lying in peaceful slumber, awaiting the return of his mistress.

It was not until Rowena had strolled somewhat vaguely two or three times up and down the Beacon Street Mall, and not until she had been some time out of Miss Phillipps's presence, that she suddenly became aware that she was thinking of Bradford's face as it had been at that moment when he had stood within the door of the room and looked at the two women. Rowena had not known she had seen him so plainly, but now he came before her with a vividness

which made a red color rise even to her forehead.

The love and the disappointment in the man's
eyes were working an effect. It is a curious truth
that pity really has so much to do with that feeling which is said to be akin to it.

And now Rowena was sorry for Bradford. It
cannot be expected that a girl can imagine that
a man may possibly find some consolations, or
that he may occasionally think on subjects un-
connected with her.

She began to walk very fast. She crossed
Tremont Street and almost ran down Winter
Street. Her mind was hurrying like her feet,
but, unlike them, that was hurrying blindly.

How unspeakably shabby Hudson Street looked under the light of the lamps! And how out
of place the sweet June sky seemed, bending
above that thoroughfare.

When she drew nearer the house, Rowena began to walk more slowly. She attempted to arrange and classify the tumult in her mind. She
found, as is generally the case, that tumult will
not be arranged and classified.

Three girls who were very late were just giving their supper tickets to Mrs. Jarvis at her
small table. It made Rowena sick to see the
girls and the tickets and the table.

She hastened up the stairs and entered her room.

Marmaduke rose from the bureau and from the bran which had once been a pin-cushion. He stretched himself, yawned, and then frantically vibrated his short tail and his little body.

His mistress caught him up to her neck.

"Oh, my sweetheart! My darling! My only Yorkshire love!" she exclaimed.

He enthusiastically licked her face. He knew very well that he was her only Yorkshire love. He would have been very dull indeed if he had not known, having been told a great many times since his residence with her. He was doubtless conscious that there was now an extraordinary fervor in this assurance, for his response was proportionately ardent.

Rowena spent a feverish night, in which she was not able to distinguish between her waking and sleeping visions.

She was very glad when the time came for her to go to the studio. Whatever confusion there might be in her thoughts about other matters, there was no confusion about her work. Her devotion to that was clear as ever.

After some of the drudgery of learning has been gone through there are days when one seems to work as if by inspiration. Ideas are lucid, and the hand unerringly follows their guidance. It was so with Rowena for the next few days. And she was so young and had had so little experience that she almost believed that she could continue to work thus. There was no outward occurrence to intrude itself. She did not see Miss Phillipps, who had been called out of town, and who would remain a week.

Allestree, walking about ·among the few students that the early summer had left with him, was continually stopping by Rowena's easel. His glance was warm with approval, but he refrained from speaking until just as the hour had expired. He saw the girl linger, loath to leave her canvas.

"Stay a moment, Miss Tuttle," he said, "I have something to say to you."

She began cleaning her brushes, trying not to be too eager to know what he would speak about. There was a deep flush on her cheeks, but her hands, as an artist's hands should be, were perfectly steady.

When the two were alone the master said, abruptly,

"I suppose you would like to study in Paris?"

The girl looked at him. She grew pale. Then she said :

"Yes. But I cannot do it. I don't wish to talk about it."

"But we will talk about it," was the autocratic response. "I have decided. A pupil whom I recommend, as I shall recommend you, is to be sent abroad by a fund which was placed in my hands for the purpose of furthering worthy art study. Mind you, it is an impersonal affair. It is for art. The thing is often done. Recall the scholarships in colleges. You need not look so proud, Miss Tuttle. This is no charity. And you would have to live as economically as you do now—possibly more so. But think of the opportunities!"

"Is all this just as you tell me, about the fund?"

The voice was, by a great effort, made steady as it put this question.

"Just as I tell you. If you care, if you really care, young woman, you may be an artist. But to be one you must work, work, work. Do you care?"

Allestree seized his beard firmly in his left hand, and the diamond on his finger sent a spark right into Rowena's eyes. She stood up very straight. Her head was flung back. Her eyes were a great deal brighter than the diamond.

"Do I care?" she cried out, sharply.

Allestree gave a short laugh, and walked half down the studio and back again.

"When will you go?" he questioned.

"To-morrow—to-day," was the answer.

All at once her brilliant glance softened. Her face quivered.

"What is the matter?" he asked.

"I was thinking of my mother—my father," she said, brokenly. "It is very far away—that Paris."

She put a hand over her eyes.

"Now don't be womanish!" he said, angrily.

"Yes, I will be womanish, too!" she answered. "But I will go all the same."

The man laughed again, well pleased.

It was all she could do not to begin to weep tempestuously. But she did not weep.

"We will talk about this to-morrow," remarked Allestree, with more consideration. "You will not go till the early fall. There will be time to arrange everything."

There was time to arrange everything—time even for Marthy S. to call on the Tuttle family, ostensibly as a delegate from the entire respectable portion of the neighborhood, and remonstrate with Mrs. Tuttle for letting her daughter go into foreign parts. They had all heard of Paris, Marthy S. said. It was a place where every woman was bad and every man worse. She suggested for the hundredth time that if Roweny must still continue to learn to paint, though if she had common faculties she must know how by this time, then, that she take lessons of that woman who came out to the Corners "on purpose to teach girls like Roweny." And this woman was known to paint hollyhocks beyond everything.

Mrs. Tuttle listened with a pale and patient face to all this talk. But her cheeks burned when Marthy S. incidentally remarked that everybody thought that "if Roweny could have caught that Borston feller that pretended to want her, there never'd ben no talk 'bout goin' to Paris to learn to paint."

Thus the dress-maker kindly related to the Tuttles the prevailing gossip, and the Tuttles suffered therefrom.

When Rowena informed Miss Phillipps of the good-fortune which had befallen her through Allestree's commendation, she looked with uncontrollable suspicion at that lady. But Miss Phillipps bore her look with a perfectly innocent air. She did not seem to see it. And it was not until midsummer that she wrote that she had made up her mind to go abroad with Rowena. She had long been thinking of going again, and when could she hope to be so happy as in making the journey in such company?

Mrs. Tuttle felt a load lifted from her heart at this news. It had been dreadful to her that her daughter should go; still more dreadful that she should go alone, or in the care of some stranger.

Before this proposition of Allestree's, Miss Phillipps had asked that the girl might spend part of the summer with her, but now she said it was no more than just that the mother should have her.

Frequent letters, brief but telling, came hurrying out to the remote hamlet from the mountains and the sea-side. Rowena read them eagerly. Everything seemed unreal to her now. She used to ask the terrier if he were her own terrier, or if he would suddenly vanish. He replied by not vanishing.

The girl and the dog would walk down that road where they had walked with Keats Bradford when that gentleman had been so irritatingly treated by both the girl and the dog. In these walks the girl would recall that the gentleman had been very forbearing. She would also recall some of the glances which had come from his eyes. Whether Marmaduke also thought of Bradford it was impossible to tell; if he did so, the memory did not in the least interfere with his brisk cheerfulness of demeanor. A terrier may be brimful of love, but he is never sentimental.

But do not let it be understood that Rowena spent much time in yielding to sentiment in these days. She had too many other occupations. By Allestree's advice she did not touch her brushes and paints. But she began a struggle with the French language, and as this struggle was begun and carried on alone during those quickly-flying weeks of summer, it was bewildering to an extent that terrified her. She had heard some French words spoken by Miss Phillipps; they had rolled so glibly off that lady's facile tongue that Rowena had been pleased with them.

As the girl had a quick mind and an enviable share of resolution, she soon acquired a good idea of the forms of verbs and genders when she saw the words written down. But afterwards she hardly knew if this arduous effort was of much benefit.

It became noised through Middle Village, and even beyond the Corners, that Hiram Tuttle's daughter was not only going to some outlandish place about that painting notion of hers, but that she was actually trying to learn to talk in some outlandish tongue; "just as if our own talk wa'n't good enough for her!"

"Be you really learnin' to talk foreign?" inquired Georgie Warner with some awe one evening when the two girls were walking arm in arm on the road between their two homes. Georgie had entirely recovered from the illness caused by her lover's disposition to yield to the blandishments of Mary Jane Jewett. She was now in the full tide of the production of marvellous wedding bedquilts. She rarely conversed upon any topic not connected with her "things," or with the goodness of Jim Townshend.

This question concerning Rowena's studies was put as a concession to Georgie's interest in one who was not even engaged, and who was only going to Paris. Georgie felt that her friend was getting very odd, but her love for her did not abate. She always made it a point to "stand up" loyally for Rowena if any one spoke the slightest derogatory word. She had even gone so far as to refuse to have Marthy S. "put a single stitch into a single one of her things." The result of this decision was that the story of Jim Townshend's infatuation with Miss Jewett was disseminated over a frightful extent of country, and many people were led to believe that this infatuation was even now at its height, and that the Warner girl insisted upon holding on to Mr. Townshend, notwithstanding that gentleman's pronounced desire not to be held on to.

In answer to Georgie's question, Rowena replied that she had begun to try to learn French, but she found she could not do much without a teacher.

Georgie had about the same horror of French as a language that she felt towards champagne as a wine. They both expressed to her the height of dissolute wickedness.

She could not help shuddering somewhat at her friend's reply. Then it was true.

"I hope you know best," she remarked. And she began to describe the pattern of some "crochet edgin'" which was to be the crowning glory of a white morning-dress.

Rowena did not know what became of the days. As the summer advanced, the girl's feeling of shrinking and of regret became stronger and stronger. It seemed to her that she sat for whole hours looking at her mother as she went back and forth in the house about her work. She helped in the work with an eager desire to do all she could.

She now was continually thinking of that moment when she should put her arms around her mother's neck for the last time before she began the journey. She almost came to believe that that last moment would kill her. But she did not think of retreating. She must go. It was her destiny, her life-work. She must go where she could learn what she so longed to know.

Mrs. Tuttle felt her child's gaze like a knife in her heart. She could not meet it, or only momentarily. She was afraid that, if she looked full in those young, stainless eyes, she should break down and beg the girl not to go so far from her. And she wanted her to go. It was Rowena's chance. She must not throw it away. It was not a matter of much surprise to the mother that Rowena should have such an opportunity, Rowena being what she was.

The two carefully avoided any talk on the subject. Their conversation was what one might almost have called deliriously cheerful. Mr. Tuttle, when he came into the porch for a drink of water, would sometimes hear them laughing loudly. As he drew the back of his brown hand across his dripping lips after his draught, he would mutter that women were the strangest beings the Lord ever created. He did not laugh. It was only by a distinct effort that he could smile in those days. He supposed it was a great thing for his daughter to be able to go to Paris, but he could not help wishing that she did not want to go, that she was more like some other girls. Still, if she were more like them he would not be so proud of her. He used to wonder what had become of that Bradford fellow. And what had Rowena thought of him? He knew of no way of finding out. There was no way of finding out much of anything about women.

Immersed in these gloomy thoughts, he was walking slowly along through his potato field one August day, with meditations concerning potato-bugs mingled with everything else in his mind, when he saw some one coming quickly across the pasture beyond.

In a moment more he recognized Philip Barrett. That young man strode along as if possessed by a very strong propelling idea. He paused suddenly when he saw Mr. Tuttle.

"Is Roweny to home?" he asked, in that aggressive tone which a definite resolution will sometimes give to one's voice.

"I guess she is. I heard she 'n' her mother laughin' jest now when I was to the house for a drink."

That they should laugh struck Philip in much the same way as the fact had affected Mr. Tuttle.

Philip continued his walk for a few rods. Then he returned quickly. His face had been tanned the color of bronze, and his honest eyes looked out from it with a strange intentness that revealed his excitement.

He struck his hand on top of a post.

"I ain't thought of nothin' else," he said. "Mr. Tuttle, why don't you stop her goin'? Why don't you put your foot down? It's for her good."

Mr. Tuttle shuffled uneasily. He picked off a potato-bug and carefully ground it under his heel.

"I know 'tain't my business," went on the young man. "But I've loved her all my life—I can't stop lovin' her."

He paused and clinched his hand on top of the post.

After a silence he asked, "Don't you know what Paris is, Mr. Tuttle? Ain't you never heard? I've ben readin' a lot about it sence I knew Roweny was goin'."

XXIII.

CONCLUSION.

HIRAM TUTTLE looked anxiously at the man the other side of the fence.

"I s'pose it's jest like other big places," he said. "Of course there's a good deal of wickedness there, but Roweny won't be in that part of it."

"She can't help it," returned young Barrett. "You don't seem to realize; you—" He stopped from inability to find words powerful enough. He could not endure this feeling of helplessness. He was sure that there were words that would express what he wanted to say if he could only find them.

From the first he had had that vague, but strong, distrust of all outlandish things, particularly of French things, which is ingrained in the ignorant and suspicious countryman. But he had a desire to be just. A few weeks before he had ridden ten miles to a town where there was a book-store. He had asked the clerk for a "book about Paris." He could not tell what he wanted clearer than that the volume should be concerning that city. The store was not very large and its stock was mostly of a certain kind. The clerk suggested *The Mysteries of Paris* as being about what his customer desired. Philip bought the book, and since then he had been slowly poring over Sue's lurid pages. His worst apprehensions were more than confirmed. He was driven over to the Tuttle homestead by a terror for Rowena's future. What were they thinking? Rowena! Philip Barrett was frantic. And when a slow, somewhat phlegmatic nature is wrought up to this stage the result is pitiable.

He gazed at Mr. Tuttle, who looked back at him and then picked another potato-beetle and destroyed it, this time with two stones.

Philip actually gasped. Could not he make even the girl's own father know what a place Paris was? He had not the power of gesticulation, and he had not the power of words. He thrust his hands deep into his pockets and shut them furiously there.

"D—— it!" he cried out. Then he walked quickly down towards the house, leaving Mr. Tuttle strongly impressed by words which he had never before heard the young man use.

Philip saw Rowena standing on a ladder, which was placed against a tree of late cherries at the back of the house. She had a two-quart "rind" tied to her waist, and was putting cherries into it. Marmaduke was leisurely nosing every cherry that fell to the ground. He looked up and barked when he was aware of Philip's approach.

Rowena quickly descended and advanced to meet her visitor. She had hoped to see him before she left home. But she paused and almost shrank when she noticed his face.

"Is anything the matter?" she asked.

Philip seized her by the arm.

"You can't go," he said. "It's a horrible place —a Sodom. I've ben readin' all about it. I— Oh, you can't go!"

He had hoped he should be given some words. It was all so clear to him; why could not he make it clear to those who ought to understand?

"I don't know what you mean," said the girl, slowly.

"I mean Paris. You can't go."

"Please don't talk like that," said Rowena, "because I shall go if I live. I am to learn all about painting there."

The man felt his strength leaving him. He was powerless then. He had not seen Rowena for many months; now to stand near her and hear her voice, to be indefinitely and hopelessly aware that to him she was more charming than ever, and to know that he could not prevent her from going to Paris—how was he to endure all this? And he could not possibly find words to tell all he knew about Paris. He was sure if he could only tell he should be able to convince even Rowena.

Neither of them noticed that a carriage had driven quickly up to the front of the house. Neither noticed that Marmaduke had dashed round and was now barking a welcome. The terrier immediately returned, conducting a lady, whose glance directly saw the group under the cherry-tree.

She paused slightly in her walk. The two by the tree were very much in earnest; they did not yet know of her approach.

It was Rowena who turned and uttered a quick exclamation of relief and joy.

Barrett also turned, and he immediately knew the stranger as the woman whom he had seen at the play in Boston, Rowena's friend.

He stepped forward and reached Miss Phillipps with one long stride, as it seemed. He did not wait for any greetings from anybody, but the lady silently put forth her hand, with its exquisite gray glove, and took the girl's cherry-stained fingers closely.

"You are the one that can stop it," said Barrett, with heavy emphasis. "If you don't know about that place, and that 'tain't fit for a girl to go to, I c'n tell you. I've read a whole book about it. It's worse 'n Sodom."

The young man paused. The pale, high face and incisive glance were not affected by his words, save that the glance softened in a kind of pity, touched with contempt.

"Do you mean Paris?" asked Miss Phillipps.

"Yes." Philip raised his voice, "I tell you it's worse 'n'—"

"But I shall be with her," interrupted Miss Phillipps, calmly, "and I know my Sodom very well." She turned to Rowena, now ignoring Barrett completely. "I came for you, dear. It is better to go sooner. We will take a Cunard from Boston to-morrow."

Barrett did not know what a Cunard was, but he knew Rowena would go to-morrow. His head sunk. He did not try to speak. Of what use was it trying to speak?

With his head still down he walked towards the road. At the gate a slight figure came to his side. Two hands caught his hand, which hung inertly.

"Good-bye, dear Philip," said Rowena. "Don't worry. Paris shall not hurt me. Good-bye."

Sitting with the Tuttle family that evening, Miss Phillipps explained how some friends of hers had given up going on the next steamer, and that she and Rowena could have their rooms, changing boats with them; it was a better boat;

it was every way better than the one in which they had expected to go, and it was only two weeks earlier.

Mrs. Tuttle was somewhat bewildered by this stranger. She could not think of disputing what was wished. She only said, with a quiver in her voice, not daring to look at her daughter,

"We could have had her two weeks longer."

Miss Phillipps leaned towards the mother in that way Rowena knew so well.

"I know," she said, with penetrating gentleness, "but I will take care of her."

Mrs. Tuttle breathed heavily. Her toughened hands gripped together tightly as they lay on the faded gingham apron. But she said nothing more.

And so Rowena went early the next morning. Her father could only tell her, as he had told her when she had gone to Boston for the first time, that she must "keep straight. The Tuttles always had kept straight."

During the journey to the city Miss Phillipps hardly spoke. She sat back in her seat, glancing sometimes from under half-closed lids at her companion, who did not lean back, but who sat rigid.

When the train had reached its destination, Rowena roused and asked if there were time for her to see Mr. Allestree. She seemed greatly disappointed to learn that her master was out of town.

"I wanted to ask him before I start if he knew who gave the fund."

"He told me he did not know," replied Miss Phillipps. "I hope you are not fighting against good-fortune."

"No, no. But if it were not just as he says, it would be wrong for me to incur such a debt," the girl answered, in a troubled tone.

Miss Phillipps smiled.

"I advise you to believe him," she said. "And let me tell you that good-fortune sometimes comes to one as well as evil."

The steamer sailed out of the harbor. Rowena stood on deck looking rather blindly back at the receding city. She kept asking herself when she would stop dreaming and become herself again. She was aware of her friend standing near, and it seemed to her that this consciousness was what enabled her to maintain any degree of self-control.

She was fully roused when the harbor had been left behind by the approach of Miss Phillipps's maid, who had been arranging their belongings in their rooms.

This person came to inform them that Marmaduke absolutely refused to stay in his basket another instant.

"He is so furious that he'll rouse the whole ship. And the steward says he'll have to go where the dogs belong."

"He sha'n't."

As Rowena made this declaration, she felt that she had come to realities again. She looked at her new friend.

"I don't know where dogs belong on a ship," she said, "but I belong with Marmaduke."

The maid had retreated immediately. As the two followed her and neared their rooms, they heard a muffled sound, and they found the terrier struggling beneath the folds of a shawl in the maid's arms.

"He's just like a tiger," exclaimed the woman.

The individual who was just like a tiger now succeeded in making a rent in the shawl and in putting his ferocious head through the aperture thus made. He trembled with delight at sight of his mistress, who immediately sat down with him held up to her face.

Miss Phillipps assured the girl that a judicious placing of fees would modify laws regarding individuals like Marmaduke. And she proved to be right. Marmaduke made the voyage without being entirely banished from his friends. But he was glad when the travelling was over and he was settled, though in very small quarters, in Paris.

He immediately began to take walks with his mistress, and was soon as knowing as any "dog of the boulevards" of them all. He accompanied her to the studio of the great master, and as she sat at her easel, he reposed himself on a fold of her skirt. Both calmly ignored the edict that young girls should not go out alone.

It was enough, Rowena felt, that this teacher also told her, as Allestree had done, that "she had the touch."

And how was Miss Phillipps employing herself? Was it that she was too absorbed, or that Rowena was too absorbed? Certain it was that, after some months, the two saw less of each other than Rowena had expected. But if anything were occupying Miss Phillipps's mind, she never relaxed her care and oversight over the girl. She was never less than kind. It could not be helped that, because she was not more than kind, Rowena should suffer. But she was too proud to show by the slightest sign that she suffered. Many times as she sat alone with brush in hand she recalled with a keen bitterness some of her old fears and thoughts of her friend. She remembered the face she had painted. But she could complain of nothing. Could she ask for the glance and the touch she missed?

More and more she realized the blessing of work. She applied herself with a sustained and healthy energy. Youth quickly adapted itself. Rowena felt for her work, not a fancy, but a saturating love. Nothing, she believed, could come into her life that could make her give that up.

She was thinking of this one day, of how her master had praised her drawing that morning; of how it was almost a week since she had seen Miss Phillipps; of how quickly a year was nearly gone, and that she could really see her progress, when Marmaduke, who was sedately walking at her heels across the park they frequented, suddenly darted forward, apparently for the purpose of effusive greeting.

Rowena saw a man stoop and pick up the terrier, who was wriggling and barking. The next moment she was shaking hands with Keats Bradford.

I wish this were a love-story, and this were the beginning of it. In that case, I should have the privilege of describing all the interviews which followed between these two—I beg Marmaduke's pardon—between these three, during the next few months.

Bradford had known for a long while that he was in earnest. It may have been previously stated in these chronicles that when he was in earnest he behaved precisely like a young man who did not wear a monocle, who could pronounce the letter *r*, and who did not belong to "the very best set in Borston."

As, however, this is not a love-story, I cannot tell of all which led up to the utterance of the following remarks, to which a small but extremely intelligent dog was a listener.

"Allestree says, everybody says, that a woman virtually gives up her work if she marries. Now, I will never give up my work."

It was Rowena who spoke, apparently in reply to something not here set down.

"I would not ask it; I would not wish it," was the fervent response from Bradford. "Besides, there are always exceptions. Only think of the Brownings. Do you believe they loved their art any less because they loved each other?"

"They are, indeed, exceptions," said Rowena.

"And so might we be," said Bradford, ardently.

Rowena looked up at him for an instant.

"It is too dangerous an experiment to try," she answered, with a touch of asperity. "I am going right on with my study," with an air of finality. "I seem now to have got a hold, to have really begun. I am even contemplating the Salon—in the future," blushing now with a beautiful warmth.

"You shall go right on with your study just the same, if you will only—"

The young man almost paused there in the public park where the three were walking. Some passers-by glanced at them and smiled.

"If you will only give me the opportunity to try to persuade you—"

Again Rowena looked up at him.

It is possible that it was something in her eyes which made Bradford's heart give that sudden, delightful leap. He was quite content to believe her eyes rather than her words.

Nevertheless, the girl had spoken truth when she had spoken of a dangerous experiment.

THE END.